"M"   15.95

Elkins, Aaron

Twenty Blue Devils

TWENTY BLUE DEVILS

AARON
TWENTY BLUE DEVILS
ELKINS

THE MYSTERIOUS PRESS

Published by Warner Books

A Time Warner Company

Mysterious Press books are published by Warner Books, Inc.,
1271 Avenue of the Americas, New York, NY 10020.

 A Time Warner Company

The Mysterious Press name and logo are registered trademarks of Warner Books, Inc.

Printed in the United States of America
ISBN 0-89296-467-7

Acknowledgments

As usual, Gideon Oliver needed plenty of help getting into and out of trouble.

Marcus Walkinshaw, M.D., Élan Plastic Surgery Center, Seattle, Mardie Lane, Supervisory Park Ranger, Hawaii Volcanoes National Park, and Steve E. Studhalter, Special Agent, Department of the Treasury, Internal Revenue Service, Criminal Investigation Division, were all very generous in sharing their expertise.

On the forensic side, Professor Charles F. Merbs of Arizona State University dipped into his case file to come up with some intriguing tidbits about the human *capitulum fibulae*, and Dr. Arthur Washburn, adjunct faculty, Temple University and the University of Delaware, was invaluable in helping me get rid of the body (so to speak).

On-site research on various French matters was conducted by my friend Astri Baillargeon.

And finally, my thanks to Peter Larsen, Master Roaster, Seattle's Best Coffee, and Misha Sperka, Farmer-Owner, Old Hawaii Coffee Farm, Kailua-Kona, Hawaii, for inviting me behind the scenes of the fragrant and fascinating world of coffee-growing and production.

A cup of coffee—real coffee—home-browned, home-ground, home-made, that comes to you dark as a hazel-eye, but changes to a golden bronze as you temper it with cream that never cheated, but was real cream from its birth, thick, tenderly yellow, perfectly sweet, neither lumpy nor frothing on the Java: such a cup of coffee is a match for twenty blue devils, and will exorcise them all.

Henry Ward Beecher

TWENTY BLUE DEVILS

Chapter I

Dear Madame Pele,

Last year I and my husband visited Hawai for our 20th anniversary and stayed overnight at Volcanoe House. Well, the next morning, we took one of the busrides around the park and when we had a stop we picked up these pieces of lavarock even though the driver told us we better not because of the Curse. But we couldnt imagine that a little rock could bring us so much BAD LUCK!

BOY, WERE WE WRONG!!!!! The curse started comeing true before we even got home! Our lugage got sent to Hong Kong (instead of Chicago) and it took a month to get our things back. Since then, things have went from bad to worst. We have had illness, death, and financial destruction one right after the other. Nobody can beleive so many terrible things could happen to one family. Just in the last few months our cat got runover, our porch develped dry rot which cost $2,500 to repaire, and my husbands 88 year old father fell off a roof which he should never have been standing on in the first place and died of a rupture.

Then the other day I was going through some things and ran across this lavarock from our trip and I suddenly realized that the legend must be true!

PLEASE PLEASE PLEASE make sure it gets back to the volcanoe!!! We're sorry and we apoligize for not beliveing. We hope now that Madame Pele and us and our family can find the peace we all so desprately need! I beg you to grant this request and send me a note in the enclosed envelop that it has been done.

> *Sincerely yours,*
> *(Mrs.) Doris Root*
> *408 Howard Avenue*
> *Winnetka, Il 60093*

With a shake of her head and a long-suffering expression on her broad, amiable face, park ranger Brenda Ho put the flowered note card down. Honestly, she thought, you didn't know whether to laugh or to cry. Every day the mailroom table was piled with these pathetic bundles of misery; sometimes only five or six, often as many as twenty. Patiently wrapped with yards of tape, or trussed up with knotted string, or bound with metal straps, all of them bulging with chunks, lumps, strands, and crumbs of lava.

And every one of them making amends to Pele, Goddess of Fire, daughter of Haumea the Earth Mother and Wakea the Sky Father, who lived deep beneath the uneasy floor of Halemaumau Crater in what was now Hawaii Volcanoes National Park. Pele, so the legend said, was a selfish and vindictive goddess who inflicted Job-like calamity on anyone who took even a handful of lava from her domain. The only way to lift the curse was to return to its source that which had been stolen and hope for mercy. And so they came pouring back into park headquarters, these humble objects of atonement, as if what this ceaselessly erupting wasteland needed was more lava.

And what the park rangers needed was more work.

Brenda rooted briefly through Mrs. Root's box. There were some irregular stones about the size of tennis balls, a mass of windblown lava strands that had cooled into the curious formations called Pele's hair, a few cupfuls of black sand, and a shell lei apparently offered as further propitiation. Everything had been sealed in a heavy plastic sack, then embedded in a sea of foam peanuts and finally packaged in a sturdy carton that was wrapped in enough layers of duct tape to survive the next world war. It had taken Brenda several minutes' work with a utility knife to get it all open. And it had cost Mrs. Root $23.20 in postage.

"Pathetic," Brenda murmured.

Across the table, Ruby Laney, the park's part-time administrative assistant, looked up over her half-spectacles.

"Another tearjerker?" With Brenda, she was going through the accumulation of packages, something they saved for four o'clock in the afternoon on Wednesdays and Fridays.

"Aren't they all?" Brenda said. She handed across the letter and the stamped, neatly addressed envelope. "She wants an answer."

Mrs. Laney nodded and added them to the stack on a corner of the table. The responses would go out the next day. They would all say the same thing:

Dear Mr./Ms._____:

Thank you for your letter and the enclosed materials. As you requested, the materials have been deposited within the park.

Sincerely,
Brenda Ho
Supervisory Park Ranger and
Interpretive Specialist

"Deposited within the park" was, to put it mildly, a euphemism. As always, all the detritus on the table would be carted less than a hundred feet, out to the "rock graveyard" in back of the administrative carport and left there. Brenda wondered sometimes what the scientists were going to make of that ample mound of globe-trotting volcanic junk a hundred years from now.

Dumping behind the carport wasn't what Mrs. Root had in mind, but what she didn't know wouldn't hurt her, and neither Brenda nor anyone else had the inclination to lug the stuff out to the rim of the crater and solemnly drop it over the edge. In the first place, that was the kind of thing the rangers were there to prevent, not to perpetrate. You didn't take anything from a national park, and you didn't leave anything either. In the second place, and this was what made all the extra work so aggravating, the curse wasn't even genuine; there was no basis for it in Hawaiian mythology. No, Pele wasn't the kind of deity you'd want to go out of your way to irritate, but she didn't spend her time wreaking catastrophe on souvenir hunters either.

All the same, about fifteen years earlier the packaged lava had started to trickle back, infrequently at first, and now a steady, ever-growing flood. No one knew what had started it. The most likely theory was that the tour bus drivers, tired of cleaning up the volcanic debris left behind in their buses, had invented the story and energetically spread it. Or maybe the rangers themselves had, hoping to keep the tourists from walking off with the park.

However it had begun, it was now a sizable pain in the neck, time-consuming and depressing to boot. And as always, the incredible way people were able to delude themselves got Brenda down. Anything, it seemed, was better than accepting responsibility for a string of misfortunes, or even chalking them up to a simple run of bad luck. No, there had to be some grand celestial plan behind it. But who was it who had let the cat out on the road in the first place? Who had failed to check the porch for dry rot all these years? What *was* Grandpa Root doing out on the damn roof anyway?

Well, the faster she worked, the sooner she'd be done. She reached for another packet, one of the slimmer ones this time, and opened it. Two gleaming pellets, black and tapering, fell onto the table; "Pele's tears," droplets of lava that had solidified while still airborne. The letter with it was on textured, cream-colored stationery, thick and expensive, and written with a fountain pen, not a ballpoint. The handwriting was feminine, as regular and unaffected as a child's penmanship exercise.

Dear Mother Pele,

   I am writing this letter to ask your forgiveness. Recently my father's farm has suffered many disasters. Now I wonder if I am to blame. My husband and I went to your beautiful island on our honeymoon several years ago. While we were there we took the enclosed small stones. Please believe me, we didn't mean to offend you. We just didn't know any better. Now I understand that it was the cause of all the awful things that have happened.

There it was, that pitiful longing to find a *reason* for their troubles. They happen to glance into a drawer one day and see a few shining black pebbles. "Aha," they say, "so that explains it," and somehow it relieves them. There's a meaning to it all: Pele is angry, Pele is wrathful.

   Last year we had the wettest March and April ever, everyone said so, more than 20 inches. And of course it was at the worst possible time, just when the buds were setting, so the crop was a terrible loss.

Oh, sure, that made a lot of sense. Pele's miffed because this sweet young thing made off with an ounce and a half of lava, so she dumps two feet of rain on her *father's* cabbages and rutaba-gas, and on everybody else's rutabagas too.

We didn't realize it then, but that was only the start of our troubles. At harvest time, the pulper broke down and one of the workers got his hand caught in the gears while he was trying to fix it, and he had to be rushed to the hospital in Papeete but he . . .

Brenda frowned. *Pulper? Papeete?* She turned abruptly to the last page of the letter, to the signature.

"I don't believe it," she said aloud. "Thérèse."

Mrs. Laney glanced up from the triple-taped container she had been trying unsuccessfully to breach.

Brenda raised the letter. "Unbelievable. This is from my cousin."

Mrs. Laney's plucked eyebrows rose. Her half-moon glasses slid further down her nose. "Really? Your own personal cousin?"

Yes her own personal cousin. Thérèse, whose mother was Aunt Céline, Brenda's mother's older sister. Thérèse, whose father, the bigger-than-life, transplanted American Nick Druett, owned not a cabbage farm but a thriving Tahitian coffee planta-tion, two thousand prosperous acres carved out of the jungly flanks of Mt. Iviroa, twenty-five miles south of Papeete and three thousand miles southeast of Hawaii Volcanoes National Park.

Brenda bent to the letter again.

. . . but he lost two fingers anyway and had to be made a supervisor. Next, the new drying furnace started a fire and ruined 75 bags of beans that we were processing for the other farmers, and we had to pay them thousands of dollars as a result. Then the brand-new sorting ma-chine broke down three times this year alone, and even though there was

a warranty it took at least two weeks to get it fixed every time, which meant we had to hire a whole lot of extra people to do the work. And I can't tell you how many times the computers have acted funny. My husband says it's like there's a ghost in the system.

Most scary of all, my husband (his name is Brian Scott) has almost been killed two times. Once, the wall of the new drying shed blew down in a windstorm and the roof fell in right where he had just been standing, but luckily it missed him. Another time, the jeep he was riding in went off a steep road and my husband broke his arm in two places and the man who was riding with him lost two teeth, but they could just as easily have been killed because the jeep turned over when it went down the mountainside.

Please, mother Pele, we meant no harm. Please forgive our ignorance. I am returning these stones so that they can be placed in the volcano where they belong, and our lives can return to normal.

Sincerely,
Thérèse Druett Scott

Cripes. Brenda sat back with pursed lips and let out a thoughtful breath. Thérèse, whose gifts lay more in the direction of a sweet-tempered disposition than an abundance of brains, might have things a little scrambled, but she was apparently right about one thing: something was amiss at the Paradise Coffee plantation.

She rose thoughtfully and headed for the door.

Mrs. Laney, who had been eagerly awaiting more information, was indignant. "And that's all you're going to tell me? That it's from your cousin?"

"What?" Brenda was already in the hallway, re-reading the letter as she walked. "Oh . . . I need to make a phone call, Ruby . . ."

* * *

"I don't understand," Thérèse said in that soft, appealingly hesitant voice of hers. "How do you know about my letter?"

"It came right to me," Brenda said. "I'm the one who opens them."

"But—aren't you in California, at Kings Canyon?"

"Not anymore, Thérèse, I'm here at Hawaii Volcanoes. I've been trying to get back here for years. I've been here since March."

"Oh," Thérèse said. "Nobody told me."

There was nothing surprising about that. The two branches of the family were not in frequent contact. Brenda was a Lau by birth, her father a native Hawaiian, her mother a Tahitian-born Chinese who had moved to Hilo in 1950 to marry Brenda's father. Thérèse was a Druett, half-Chinese, half-American. Her mother—Brenda's aunt Céline—had been a famous beauty who had been swept off her feet by Nick Druett, the swashbuckling young American newly come to the South Seas to make his fortune, which he very soon did. They had had a daughter, Maggie, not long after they married (well, before they married, but nobody talked about that); then, ten years later, as something of a surprise, along had come the beautiful Thérèse, now twenty-eight.

Living as they did in two different hemispheres, the Laus and the Druetts didn't see each other often, but there was affection between them, and Brenda was particularly fond of Thérèse, eight years her junior. Thérèse had never quite taken up life in the real world, but she was warmhearted and without guile. What you saw on the surface was all there was underneath.

"Thérèse, I had no idea these things were going on at the plantation."

"No, well, you know my father. He doesn't like to advertise things. Brenda—will those stones really go back into the volcano? I mean, I know you think it's silly but . . ."

Brenda opened her hand to look at the two glassy pebbles, black and shining on her palm. "Yes, honey, I'll see to it personally." She would too. On tomorrow morning's routine drive around the caldera she'd stop at the rim of Halemaumau Crater, Pele's private volcano, and drop them over the edge. And hope her boss wasn't anywhere around to see.

"It's not that I really believe in the curse," Thérèse said unconvincingly, "but I just didn't know what else to do. I mean, I know that it's just a myth, but I didn't think it could hurt."

"Of course not," Brenda said gently. "Thérèse, what does Brian think about all this?" Brian, Thérèse's husband, was the plantation's operations manager.

"He just shrugs it off. You know how he is. He says these things just happen on their own sometimes."

"Well, they do," Brenda said. They did too, but this time she thought there might be more to it. "Um, is Brian around? It'd be nice to say hello."

"No, he's off communing with nature on Raiatea," Thérèse said with no sign of irony, then added a small tinkling laugh: "I would have gone too, but of course I had to stay home with Claudine and Claudette."

Every year Brian spent a week or ten days roughing it at a favorite camping spot on the mountainous, barely populated island of Raiatea, a hundred miles from Tahiti, possibly the only man in history who considered Tahiti a place to get *away* from. He'd convinced Thérèse to come with him once—her first camping experience—and the much-pampered young woman had been appalled at the lack of comfort, hygiene, and amenities that went along with it. She'd also been bored stiff, not that she'd admit any of it to her adored Brian. So when the twins came along later she'd used them as a heaven-sent excuse to stay at home while he continued to make his annual pilgrimage alone. She hated being apart from him, she'd told Brenda once, but anything was better than going ten days without a hot shower and doing your business in a hole in the ground.

"I almost forgot," Brenda said. "Congratulations. I didn't know that you and Brian had gotten married."

"Married?" Thérèse said vaguely. "No, we're not married, we're—well, the same as ever. You know."

"But your letter said he was your husband. You signed it Thérèse Scott."

"Oh." There was a moment's hesitation, and Brenda would have bet she was blushing. "I just thought Pele would think of me as a more sincere person if I was married."

*　　*　　*

"This is nothing to concern you, Brenda," Nelson Lau said. "We can take care of it here in Tahiti, thank you."

Brenda turned her head from the receiver and sighed. Her brother was not one of the world's great telephone personalities. The Stanford-educated Nelson was the only one of the Laus who had gone back to Tahiti from Hawaii, accepting Uncle Nick's job offer of the company's comptrollership fifteen years ago, almost the minute he'd gotten his MBA. And there he'd been ever since, very likely the most straitlaced man in French Polynesia and getting more so every year. Nelson actually wore a suit to work. In Tahiti.

"Nelson, how can I help being concerned? People have been hurt. Brian's almost been killed, and Thérèse—"

Muffled noises of exasperation came from the telephone. "Oh, for heaven's sake, you're making a mountain out of a molehill. Thérèse has always had a way of blowing things up out of proportion. You know what an extraordinarily suggestible—"

"Nelson, I want to know: Do all these accidents have anything to do with that awful gangland business?"

"Does *what* have anything to do with that awful gangland business? You mean all that rain last April?"

"Don't be funny, it doesn't suit you. Tell me honestly: Is this some kind of sabotage? Revenge? Are they getting back at Nick?"

"Now, really, how would I possibly know that?"

"What do you *think?*"

"I think . . . Brenda, I simply don't want to discuss it."

"Fine, but what are you doing about it?" As always, talking to Nelson brought out the bossiness in her in self-defense.

"Doing about it?" Nelson laughed, a sharp, incredulous whinny. "What would you suggest?"

"I think we should get John's advice."

Pregnant pause. "Thank you, no."

"Nelson, be reasonable. John's an FBI agent. Surely—"

"Brenda, the FBI is absolutely the last thing we need."

"I don't mean officially. He wouldn't have any jurisdiction in Tahiti anyway. But he'd know about this sort of thing; it's his job."

"Absolutely not. Out of the question."

Brenda sighed again, which she did frequently when speaking with her older brother. Nelson had a way about him that made it next to impossible to have a simple difference of opinion with him. All you could do was have a fight with him. Either that, or give in.

"Nelson, John's part of the family too. For God's sake, he's our brother. He's *your* brother. He has a right—"

"Brenda, *no.* There's nothing John can do. He wasn't involved before, and nothing's going to be served by getting him involved now. That's the crux of it."

No, that wasn't the crux. The crux was that the FBI agent in the family was Baby Brother; a baby brother who, like Brenda, took more after the Hawaiian side of the family than the Chinese. Consequently, John was five inches taller and sixty muscular pounds heavier than Nelson, with umpteen light years more—well, presence. When John was in a room you noticed him. Nelson could swing from the light fixtures by his teeth and have a hard time getting anyone to notice.

As a child, being four years older, Nelson had been the more dominant one, and if he hadn't been exactly despotic, he had been pretty damned high-handed; with Brenda too, for that matter. Then John had hit puberty and things had turned around, and Nelson had never gotten over it. To ask John for help was for Nelson an unnatural act. And he was never going to change.

"All right, Nelson," she said, "all right."

"Brenda, I mean it! Now I want you to promise me. No John."

"All *right*, Nelson."

"I want a promise."

"I promise, Nelson."

"You promise what?"

Sheesh. "I promise I won't call John."

Nelson sniffed. "All right, then."

Chapter 2

"John, this is Brenda. There's some funny stuff going on in Tahiti."

She had waited until the weekend to call, not out of deference to Nelson, but because she wanted to think things over. *Was* she making a mountain out of a molehill? After brunch, when Gus and the kids, stir-crazy from the week's incessant rain, left for a Disney matinee in Hilo, she made herself a pot of tea, put her feet up, and pondered. The longer she thought about it, the less it looked like a molehill, and finally she had placed the call to Seattle and laid it all out for John.

To her annoyance he didn't agree with her. "Look, sis, all I can say is, if the Mob was out to get Nick, they'd get him. They wouldn't be piddling around with sorting machines. Besides, it's ancient history. Why would they wait all this time to come after him?"

"Well, how do you account for it, then? I mean everything put together. And don't tell me Pele."

"How about coincidence? Businesses have bad luck. That's why they're always going under."

Looked at honestly, it was what she would have said herself—if it had involved somebody else's family, somebody else's business, but of course it didn't. "You're probably right," she said meekly. "I'm sure you are. I—I guess I'm being silly, but I can't help worrying and I didn't know who else to turn to but you."

John let out a long exhalation. He was resigning himself, she thought complacently. She'd always been good at getting around John.

"Oh boy," he breathed, and then, after a moment: All right, what do you want me to do, Brenda?"

She laughed. "That sounds more like my kid brother. One thing you could do is check your FBI files, or the Justice Department files, or whatever, on the whole Gasparone case and see what you can find."

"What is there to find? It's ten years old."

"Twelve. But maybe somebody who's been in jail all this time just got out. Couldn't that be why these things just started happening?"

"Well, yeah," he said grudgingly. "But I still don't think those guys would be fooling around with stuff like this if they really had it in for Nick."

"But you'll check?"

"Yes, sis, I'll check."

She plowed ahead. "And I think you ought to talk to Uncle Nick and the others about it. It just occurred to me—they'll be coming into Seattle soon, won't they? Aren't they due for a visit to the roastery?"

This, John thought, was nothing but soft soap on her part. Since it was the end of October, she knew as well as he did that they would shortly be making their fall trip to Seattle. There would be three of them: their brother, Nelson, in his role as comptroller; their cousin Maggie—Nick's daughter and Thérèse's older sister—who was the plantation's personnel manager; and, of course, Nick Druett himself, the founder, the owner, and the force behind it all. They would be coming for their quarterly business conference with Rudy Druett, another nephew of Nick's, but from his own side of the family. Rudy, the son of Nick's long-dead brother, was manager and roast-master at the Caffè Paradiso plant on Whidbey Island, where the company's beans were roasted and its American business strategies plotted.

"Yeah, I'll bet it just occurred to you," grumbled John, who wanted it understood that while he might be malleable enough, he wasn't any dunce.

"And don't they usually come to your house for dinner after the cupping?"

"They *always* come," John said. "We're having them out next Thursday. I'll be picking them up at the roastery."

"Great, that'll give you a chance to bring it up with them."

"I don't know, sis. Nick's not the kind of guy who's going to appreciate my butting in. If he wants to talk about it he'll bring it up on his own."

"John, you know that Uncle Nick is never in a million years going to admit there's something he can't handle. You're going to have to do it."

"Yeah, but I don't like—"

"I'm relying on you, John."

Silence.

"John?"

"Jeez," he exclaimed, "you know something, Brenda?"

"What?"

"Sometimes you can be every damn bit as bad as Nelson."

"Heaven forfend," Brenda said.

Chapter 3

Brian sat bolt-upright in the unzipped sleeping bag, not sure what had brought him awake with his heart pounding. A sound, a light, a movement in the bushes?

"Anybody there?" he called into the darkness, still muddled with sleep.

There was no answer, of course, and after a few seconds, as consciousness flooded back, his pulses stopped their hammering and he quieted down. What animal was there on Raiatea that would harm a man? And there was probably no other human being within ten miles. Silly to react like that, but he had had such a strong, sudden sense of . . . of *presence*. It had been a dream, naturally—what else?—although it seemed to him that he had been dreaming about Thérèse. He had surprised her with some silly gift she'd wanted and she had laughed . . .

He lay back and resettled himself in the bag. Around him the night was silent and soft, the southern constellations as brilliant as diamonds. An exquisite little breeze, heavy with the fragrance of orange blossom and gardenia, flowed over his face. Hibiscus trees, silhouetted against the star-flecked sky, drowsed at the edge of the clearing. From far away, near the lagoon, came the weird, repetitive cry of some seabird, a hollow, echoing *wuh . . . wuh . . . wuh . . .*

His eyelids drifted slowly down. Relaxed, tranquil, he slid again into his dreams.

It was a long time before the bushes moved again, and when they did Brian only stirred, but did not waken.

Chapter 4

Shhl-l-l-l-p.

The coffee was sucked from the silverplated tablespoon, rolled over, under, and around the tongue, then held at the back of Rudy Druett's mouth for a few seconds. He chewed, he gargled, he tipped his head back. His eyes closed, his eyes opened. Finally he leaned to one side and delicately dipped his chin.

Blupp.

Into the waist-high funnel of the spittoon it went. *"Well now,"* he said, his long, doleful face pensive. "It's . . . in my opinion it's . . . let me see . . ."

He moved his tongue over the inside of his mouth, chewed his cheek, hunched his narrow shoulders, muttered nasally to himself. While he thus marshaled his evaluative powers the others took their own spoons from bowls of water and dipped them one at a time into the sample of coffee under consideration. Four *shl-l-l-l-ps*, four *blupps*.

The tasting session had been under way for an hour. There

were four of them in the room besides Rudy. Three were officers of the Paradise Coffee plantation: Nick Druett, easygoing,
comfortably in charge, and carrying his sixty-nine years lightly;
his nephew and comptroller Nelson Lau—John's older
brother—looking like a Hong Kong businessman, pompous
and serious in a conservative, pin-striped business suit; and
Nick's older daughter, Maggie, casually and colorfully dressed
in a bright Tahitian flowered skirt, but as blunt and outspoken
as ever.

Although Maggie generally attended the tasting sessions,
Nick had never managed to instill in her much interest in the
business of growing and selling coffee. What Maggie was interested in was improving the lot of the world's laboring masses,
particularly the Tahitian laboring masses, and, on a more general level, in saving the earth from the depredations of its human
inhabitants. True to her convictions, she belonged to a number
of native-culture groups and had herself founded the Island
Culture Club, chiefly dedicated to the reintroduction of the native Tahitian musical tradition; in particular the *pahu*, a drum
made from a hollowed-out tree trunk, and the *vivo*, a bamboo
flute played with the nostrils. The society met monthly, had
grown to eleven like-minded individuals over the years, and had
high hopes of someday acquiring a native member.

Taking advantage of her natural inclinations and abilities,
Nick had made her the plantation's personnel manager, responsible for the productivity, morale, and welfare of the workforce,
which varied from twenty to seventy, depending on the season.
He had never been sorry, either, even if she got under his skin
once in a while and sometimes made him wonder whose side
she was on when it came to labor-management relations.

The fourth member of the group was John Lau, who had
twice thus far tried to raise the subject of the accidents and

had twice been brushed aside like a fly buzzing around a sacred altar.

The altar in this case was the rotating, octagonal table around which they stood. In the center of it was an old laboratory beam-balance scale set at 7.5 grams—the precise amount required for a perfect portion of coffee, according to Rudy, who was fussy about such things (about most things, if the truth be told). Sixteen such portions, two of each of the eight coffees to be tasted, had been tumbled in the Probat sample roaster, ground fine, and placed in sixteen squat, thick glasses lined up in pairs around the table's rim.

The glasses had then been filled with water from an electric kettle set at exactly 190 degrees Fahrenheit (191 degrees would scorch the oils and turn it bitter, Rudy insisted with apparent seriousness; 189 degrees wouldn't extract the flavors properly). Without being stirred, the resulting brew was then allowed to cool and form a crust. Rudy would break one of the crusts with a tap from the back of his spoon, as if cracking an egg, then quickly dip his nose almost into the liquid to catch the initial burst of aroma, and then slurp up a spoonful. The others would follow suit. There would be murmurs and gurgles. They would scrutinize, smell, bite, and pinch the sample of beans that lay in a small tray beside each pair of glasses, and they would render their opinions, with Rudy usually leading off, befitting his position as roastmaster.

Thus far, they'd accepted beans from Ethiopia, Kenya, and Sumatra as worthy of purchase and rejected samples from Venezuela, Costa Rica, and New Guinea. Under consideration at the moment was a Colombian Excelso.

Rudy was ready with his judgment at last. "In my opinion, this is . . ." He paused, brows knit in concentration, mouth still puckered to extract the last remnants of taste. Abruptly his face cleared. ". . . *coffee!* Yes, I'm sure of it! Don't you agree?"

John burst out laughing. Rudy often went through one version or another of this routine when he was in a playful mood, always managing to make it funny and surprising, at least to John. But then John hadn't sat in on as many tastings with him as the others had.

"Very amusing," said Nelson, on whom playfulness, Rudy's or anyone else's, tended to be lost. "Now, if you don't mind, can we get back to business?"

"Certainly not," Rudy said indignantly. "Are you seriously suggesting that I permit my dedication to amusement to be diverted by *work?*"

Nelson sighed, or rather hissed, exhaling a stream of air between clamped teeth, and turned to the others, pointedly ignoring Rudy. "I would say," he said through jaws that were even now only barely separated, "that this coffee has decent body, with medium-high acid." He stroked his thin, perfectly symmetrical mustache with the pinky of his left hand. "Also, it's reasonably piquant."

John grimaced. Nelson was his brother and he loved him dearly—well, he loved him—but, Jesus Christ, *piquant?*

"But," Nelson continued darkly, raising his spoon for emphasis, "I detect overtones of earth. There's a definite groundy undertaste here."

"I agree," Maggie said, something of a rarity for her where Nelson was concerned. "It's groundy. Earthy."

"Dear Cousin Maggie and Cousin Nelson—" began Rudy with a sigh of sweet condescension.

"I'm not your cousin," Nelson said. "Thank God."

"—I yield to no one in my admiration for your many virtues, but I feel compelled to say that neither of you would recognize a good cup of coffee if you fell into it from a fourth-story window. No offense."

"Rudy . . ." Maggie glowered at him, her head lowered like

an irritated bull's. Painted, hand-carved wooden earrings shaped like tiny tropical fish swung against plump cheeks. ". . . I know you think you're the be-all and end-all of anything that has to do with coffee, but—"

"I?" Rudy said. "*Au contraire.* I have an absolute and unequivocal lack of belief in my own judgment. Thereby," he added without losing a beat, "confirming the perspicacity of my opinions."

And there was Rudy in a nutshell: droll, biting, double-edged—but ultimately even-handed in his barbs, digging them into Maggie, or Nelson, or himself with equal relish. John had been on the receiving end for his share too. Even Nick had. And other than Nelson, they all laughed now—except for Rudy himself, whose dry, dour expression rarely changed very much.

"Come on, Rudy," Nick said, "what about the Excelso?"

Rudy decided to be serious. "I don't taste any groundiness," he said. "There is a little woodiness, but it has a nice, nutty, buttery finish. Definitely not for one of our premiums, but I was thinking it would be all right for the Weekend Blend."

"That's what I think too." It was rare that Nick didn't go along with his roastmaster's judgment. "*If* you can get it for under a buck-five. You say something, John?"

John shook his head, wiping his chin with the back of a finger; he didn't quite have the others' knack with the spittoon. He had joined in the tasting—the cupping, as they called it—as much to be sociable as anything else, but what was there to say to this bunch once they got going on coffee? Like them, he had tasted seven different coffees from seven different countries. Unlike them, he had liked them all. (He had swallowed down the first few until a scandalized Nelson had noticed and made him comply with international cupping conventions.) But if you had told him that all seven samples were exactly the same coffee, he would have accepted it without reservation.

It wasn't that he didn't like coffee; he liked it as well as the next guy. Two cups with breakfast to get the kinks out, and then one, maybe two lattes during the day, from the SBC coffee bar across the street from the federal building on Fourth Street. Great stuff, got the juices going. But *buttery*, for God's sake? *Earthy?* What were they talking about, coffee or baked potatoes?

He would have had a hard time taking them seriously, except that he knew how well they were doing. Rudy, in particular, had built Caffè Paradiso, Nick's American retail outlet, from a sleepy storefront business with an ancient, secondhand, one-bag roaster in the basement into the number-three coffee-seller in the Pacific Northwest, and he'd done it largely with his nose and his taste buds.

He certainly hadn't done it with force of personality. Dyspeptic, notoriously caustic, with a sharp tongue that was too quick for its own good, his all-too-ready wit had made him more enemies than friends. Once, for example, he had had a celebrated verbal skirmish with a *Seattle Times* food critic at a cocktail party for the opening of a new restaurant. That was bad enough, but when questioned about it later that evening on live television, he had said, with mock wonderment: "But I don't understand why she's so upset. I certainly didn't mean to say anything unkind about her. I merely mentioned that she was dim-witted, undiscerning, fatuous, and uninformed. All perfectly verifiable."

His hangdog appearance didn't help either. Balding, stoopshouldered, and naturally woebegone-looking, with dark, droopy bags under his eyes, he was nobody's idea of the driving force behind a burgeoning and aggressive coffee empire. The fact was, amazingly enough, that he didn't even like coffee and wouldn't have been able to drink it if he did because the acidity gave him gas, or so he claimed.

Rudy's father—Nick's much-loved, long-dead kid brother,

Jack—had been a vintner in California, and Rudy had grown up at his father's small winery in the Simi Valley. From the beginning, wine had been his passion, or the closest thing to a passion that he'd ever had. He had majored in enology at the University of California's Davis campus and returned to manage the winery's production process, expecting to take over the business eventually. But his father, drowning in debt, had sold out to one of the conglomerates that were then gobbling up the vineyards of the Pacific coast.

Shattered, Rudy had fled California for Tahiti, seeking a job with his uncle. The always-generous Nick had come through, putting him to work on the plantation (and, by the by, bailing his father out of his not inconsiderable remaining debts). Hardworking and intelligent, Rudy had learned the coffee business and had eventually taken over management of day-to-day operations. Later, when Brian Scott had arrived on the scene with a sackful of ideas for improvement and expansion and a knack for implementing them, Nick had asked Rudy to return to the States to see if he could turn the struggling Caffè Paradiso enterprise into something worthwhile. And here he had been ever since, successful beyond Nick's dreams, let alone his own, but in his heart of hearts never ceasing to regard coffee as a poor substitute for his beloved wines.

But no one had ever said he didn't know everything there was to know about the coffee business.

His office was still here in this eighty-year-old white frame building, a onetime feed store near Coupeville on rural Whidbey Island, two hours from Seattle by car and ferry. Now, however, there was a spanking-new twenty-thousand-square-foot warehouse and processing plant a few hundred feet up the highway, with eighteen employees and a big, shiny, three-bag roaster that held 335 pounds of beans and was fired up and roasting eight hours a day, five days a week.

In short, things were going like gangbusters. From what they'd told John earlier, they were now selling more than half a million pounds a year. There were sales to gourmet shops and restaurants, there was a thriving mail-order business, and now there were two Caffè Paradiso coffee bars in downtown Seattle department stores, one at the airport, and another two about to open in Portland, every one of them upscale and pricey. Only twenty percent of the beans that went into their numerous varieties came from the plantation in Tahiti these days; the rest were bought from other coffee growers around the world, mostly on Rudy's say-so. It was Rudy too who supervised the roasting, created the blends, and ran what Nick approvingly referred to as a highly innovative marketing program.

It seemed pretty innovative to John too. Who would have thought you could make money with slogans like "Paradiso—The World's Most Expensive Coffees" and "Pure Tahitian Blue Devil, the Highest-Priced Coffee in the World . . . Bar None." But make money they did. Blue Devil, not a blend but solely their own plantation's product, was Paradiso's chief claim to fame.

They were always leaving a few pounds of it with John and Marti when they came. It wasn't bad, John thought, but at $38 a pound? At $4.50 a cup in the coffee bars? You'd have to be out of your mind. Which showed how much he knew about it.

"Look, people," he said, "about these accidents—"

"Johnny, will you shut up?" Nick said amiably. "What else is there, Rudy?"

"One more, from the Celebes. This is a first issue from a Rantepao plantation that was revived four or five years ago."

"I vote no," Maggie said.

Nick laughed. "We haven't tasted it yet."

"We don't have to taste it. If it comes from the Celebes, it was processed with slave labor."

"Oh, for God's sake, Maggie, they don't have slave labor in the Celebes," Nelson said disgustedly.

"Well, they don't pay them a living wage. It's the same thing."

"It's *not* the same thing."

"And what's more, they don't go in for organic processing on the Rantepao plantations. They use chemical nitrogen replacement."

"So? So do we. What do you suggest, bee pollination?" Nelson screwed up his face in case she couldn't tell he was being sarcastic.

Maggie screwed her face right back at him. "Yes, as a matter of fact. Bee pollination—"

"People?" Nick said with a sigh. It was enough to quiet them down. "What do you say we just taste the stuff, okay?"

"The master speaks," said Rudy.

Happily, it didn't take long. The coffee was variously dismissed as "musty," "grassy," and "hidy." The grower, Nelson suggested indignantly, was trying to palm off last year's crop. The others agreed. No sale.

John had thought it was just fine.

"Well, that's that, then," Nick said. "Good job, gang."

"About these accidents," John said.

Nick clapped him on the shoulder. "We can talk on the way to your place." He smacked his lips. "Hey, Rudy, pour us a cup of Blue Devil for the road."

Chapter 5

Nick ran his hand over the pebble-grained dashboard. "So what's this, a Honda?" At half an inch less than John's six feet two inches, but with longer, looser arms and legs, Nick had had to scrunch himself up a bit to get into the front passenger seat. Maggie and Nelson sat behind, with Rudy between them.

"Right," John said as they moved out of the little parking lot and south onto Highway 525, which ran down the center of Whidbey's long, snaky length. He flicked on the wipers against the half-mist, half-rain that was standard November weather. " 'Eighty-nine Civic."

"I'll tell you what you ought to get next. An Infiniti J30."

"Why's that, Unc?"

"Why? Because it's got the best coffee-holder in the civilized world. Out of sight until you push a button, and then it rolls out of the console right where you can reach it. That's what I drive, an Infiniti. Holds two big cups."

That was Nick for you. When you bought a new car you didn't kick the tires, you checked out the coffee-holder. He really loved the stuff, you had to say that for him. "What's the price tag?"

"In the States? Around forty thousand, I think. A lot more than that in Tahiti, I can tell you."

John laughed. "I think I'll just buy one of those stick-to-the-dashboard things for two-ninety-five and keep the Honda for a couple more years. I work for the government, remember, not Paradise Coffee."

Nick smiled and squeezed his arm. "Just say the word, kid. There's always a place for another one of Pearl's boys."

He meant it too, John thought. Nick was a genuinely nice guy, easygoing and good-natured. John had always liked him; respected him too. Nick had convictions, decent ones, and when the chips were down he put his money where his mouth was. That was what had gotten him in trouble with the West Coast Mafia to begin with. It had been a dozen years ago, before John had joined the FBI; he had just started with the Honolulu PD then and what he knew about organized crime had come mostly from the newspapers.

At that time, Nick had been in the coffee business for about five years, but on a much smaller scale. He had managed to break into the American market, which was just beginning to show signs of life, but there were no Caffè Paradiso coffee bars yet, no whopping mail-order sales. And the Whidbey Island roastery wasn't even a gleam in his eye. Like other Pacific growers who shipped to this part of the country, Nick sold his green coffee beans through a small group of West Coast coffee brokers who dealt with restaurants, grocery stores, and the big commercial roasters. Things had gone well for a while. Paradise beans were building enough of a reputation to let Nick charge the higher prices that the sky-high Tahitian wages required, and his sales had been going up for four years in a row.

And then events on the East Coast intervened. Not long before, there had been a successful crimebusting campaign in Massachusetts and Rhode Island. Mafia and Mafia-connected rings that had controlled everything from booze to bagels to knife-grinding were run out of business. A few gangsters from the Gasparone crime family went to prison. Others just dropped out of the limelight, laid low for a while, and then started showing up in other places and businesses around the country.

One of the places was the Northwest, and one of the businesses was coffee-wholesaling. Suddenly, the coffee brokers were whispering to the growers that things had changed, that if they expected the chain grocery stores and big roasters to handle their beans they'd better be prepared to deliver kickbacks. These illegal payments, running anywhere from two percent to ten percent of the price of the beans, were made directly to the brokers themselves, who then (supposedly) passed them on to the roasters and retailers. Without them, the brokers were now saying, they couldn't promise that they'd have much success in moving anybody's coffee. They were sorry about it, it wasn't their doing, it was just too bad, but their hands were tied and that's the way it was.

Whether it was actually kickback money or protection money was hard to say, because if you didn't pay it you didn't merely suffer from disappointing sales; bad things happened to you. Caffè Paradiso, operating on a tiny profit margin as it was, was one of the companies that dug in its heels and resisted, and three months after their second refusal to pay ten percent they found out that two hundred bags—ten tons—of choice Blue Devil had "accidentally" been sitting in a Portland warehouse for four weeks in half a foot of filthy water from a broken drainpipe. It had had to be written off because the insurance wouldn't cover negligence. A little later, a truck with another ton was highjacked fifteen minutes after leaving the Tacoma docks. The robbers were never identified, but the trucker got a friendly warning to the effect that he'd be better off not doing business with Paradise in the future. A friendly warning and two broken hands.

Nick went to the police but nobody was able to do anything about the new racket until one of the creeps in the thick of it, a shyster-accountant named Tony "Klingo" Bozzuto, suddenly changed his spots, working with the FBI for months to gather evidence (which wasn't difficult to come by inasmuch as Bozzuto handled the gang's books) and then testifying against his cronies in court. At that time, two dozen coffee growers were asked by federal prosecutors to submit depositions about the kickbacks and to appear in court if necessary. Only three had the nerve to do it, and one of them was Nick. He'd prepared an eight-page affidavit and shown up in court in Seattle, ready and willing to testify. In the end, the prosecution hadn't had to call him, although his deposition figured strongly. Guilty verdicts came in, the racket was smashed, and a fair number of the men involved went to prison.

All of this John had known before and still he hadn't gone along with Brenda's notion that gangland retaliation was behind the incidents in Tahiti. But the computer search he'd done at her insistence had made him rest less easily. What Brenda had suggested was true: while most of the convicted mobsters had gotten out of jail a long time ago, three of the big ones—"the three G-Men," Tony "Zorro" Gasparone, Dominick "Nutso" Guardo, and Nate "The Schlepper" Grossman—had made the mistake of appealing their convictions on technical grounds. They had won a retrial a few years later, only to wind up with stiffer sentences than they'd started with. The three of them had been released in the last couple of years and were supposed to be living in Los Angeles, Queens, and Orlando and keeping clean, but who knew?

And there was something else John hadn't known.

"Nick, I was looking through some old newspaper reports. When they hauled off Tony Gasparone at the end of the trial he turned around and pointed at you. You and some others." John demonstrated, pointing with his right hand at Nick's temple, forefinger extended, thumb cocked.

"Did he? I don't remember."

"Yes, he did."

Nick shrugged and waved a dismissive hand. "Aaahh, what can you do? The guy was a big talker, that's all."

"Nick—"

But they had pulled up to the ferry-loading dock in Clinton and were waved by the crew aboard one of the old, green-and-white ferries for the brief trip to Mukilteo and the mainland. As the engines started up and the ship slid smoothly over the ruffled gray expanse of Puget Sound, Nick looked placidly at his nephew.

"John, I know what you're driving at, and I appreciate your concern. But forget about Gasparone; the guy was showing off. Look, sometimes we go for years up at the farm without any accidents, and other times they gang up on us. Okay, we've had a string of problems lately. It's just things averaging out, that's all. Believe me, there's no vendetta going on. Even if there was, Tony Gasparone's got bigger fish to fry than me, take my word for it."

That's what John thought too, but he wasn't quite as confident of it as he'd been before he'd seen the files, and it made him feel better to hear Nick say it.

"Well, I'm not so sure," Nelson proclaimed from the back

seat. "I told you twelve years ago that it was a mistake to get involved, and I still say so. You can't go around filing depositions
when you're dealing with human scum like—"

Nick laughed. "Nelson, give it a rest, will you? If I thought
there was anything to it, I'd be the first one to ask for some help
from J. Edgar Hoover over here, believe me."

"Yeah, like hell you would," John said.

Nick laughed again, which was meant to close the subject,
but Nelson, warmed up now, wasn't about to comply.

"Nick, sometimes I don't understand you at all. You're just
sticking your head in the sand. Now, we all know that John has
been talking to Brenda about this. Are you going to deny that,
John?"

John glanced at him in the rearview mirror. "Not me."

"I wouldn't think so. Well, I was against bringing John into
this in the first place, you all know that, but now that he *is* in, I
think we should get his help."

"Oh, hell," Nick grumbled and slouched down into his seat
with his arms folded.

"John?" Nelson said in the peremptory tone that had been
raising the hair on the back of John's neck for over thirty years,
since he had been eight and Nelson had been twelve anyway,
and probably before then.

"Nelson?" he replied mildly.

"Now, then. I want you to find out how we can get in touch
with this Gasparone person. With the others too."

That caught John by surprise. "Get in touch with them?"

"Exactly. I think it's time to lay things on the table with
them. They may be gangsters but they're also businessmen.
They may have something in mind, some sort of . . . remunera-
tion. We're in a sound financial position now. We can afford to
negotiate, to work things out."

"Forget it," Nick muttered without turning around.

"It's not a good idea, Nelson," John said firmly. All the same, in one respect Nelson did have a point. When sleazebags like Gasparone got even with people for doing them wrong, they went out and blew their heads off, or maybe just their kneecaps if the original offense wasn't too bad. The point was to make it clear to others that it wouldn't be a good idea to do the same thing. But when they started in on piddly little things like a minor injury or accident here or there—such as the happenings on the plantation—you had to assume that they were after something; some kind of cooperation, or compliance, or kickback.

That is, if they were involved at all.

"Nick," he said, "they haven't been in touch with *you*, have they?"

Nick looked sulkily at him. "Are you kidding me?"

"What about anybody else that might be speaking for them? Somebody in the coffee business that could be backed by them? Anybody, well, suggesting that—I don't know, that you ought to give them special terms, or—"

"In *touch* with me? No, give me a break."

Nelson took up the attack again. "Just because they haven't approached us doesn't mean we can't approach them. I'm only saying that if they feel they have a grievance, the sensible thing—"

"Lord, don't you love it!" Maggie cried with a laugh. "Nelson the Ethical. God forbid that we file a deposition against these lousy creeps back then when it counted, and now he can't wait to sit down and negotiate with them."

"I'm only saying—" Nelson began.

Nick cut him off. "Nelson, will you use your head for once? If these cruds wanted to get back at me for what happened in

Seattle, why go all the way to Tahiti to do it? And do *what*, when it comes down to it? Bribe our employees to lose a few records . . . to jam the pulper? Hell, no, if they had a score to settle with us, they'd just burn down the building right here on Whidbey Island. It'd be a whole lot easier. That shack would go up like kindling."

Rudy, who had been minding his own business, sat up with a jerk. "Oh, thank you very much. That'll help me sleep nights."

"Or blow it up, or something," Maggie suggested. "That's what I'd do."

"Wonderful, even better," said Rudy.

"Well, how do all of *you* explain it then?" Nelson said hotly. "How do—"

"Hey!" Nick sat up in the front seat and twisted around as the ferry settled squishily against the Mukilteo pilings and John turned on the car's ignition. "Can I just say something? Enough, already. Now, we're going to be at John's place in forty minutes. I haven't seen Marti in a long time, and it'd be nice to talk about something else besides all this warmed-over crap. Okay?"

"Suits me," said Maggie.

Rudy held up his hands, palms forward. "Hallelujah and amen to that."

Nelson stared out the window and grumped an inaudible response.

Nick eyed John. "You too? Can we talk about something else for a while?"

John threw in the towel. "Okay. As long as it's not coffee."

"Fair enough." Nick settled comfortably back. "Ah, I always look forward to seeing that lovely bride of yours. You really lucked out there, old son."

"I'm not gonna argue with that," John said.

Nick laughed fondly. "It's always a treat seeing what she

comes up with for dinner. What's it going to be this time, do you think—boiled tofu, maybe?"

"Don't laugh," John said grimly.

"Oh, come on, you guys," Maggie said generously, "it's not going to be as bad as all that."

Chapter 6

That depended on who was asked. Dinner was rice cakes topped with pecan-garbanzo paste, grilled-eggplant-and-feta-cheese salad, and spicy squash-and-orzo stew, all of it perfectly cooked and beautifully served, but still, from John's point of view, rice cakes, eggplant, and squash.

Rudy uncomplainingly if inattentively consumed whatever was put before him, as he usually did. John sometimes wondered if all that coffee-tasting had burned out his taste buds and immunized them against anything else. Excepting wine, of course. Nelson, whose French-born wife had taught him to like creamed dishes and elegant sauces, picked at his food and filled up on mango-pumpkin bread and apple-fig chutney. Only Maggie ate with any enthusiasm, but then John had once, with his own ears, heard her say that the happiest she got when it came to food was when she sat down to a steaming plate of organic brown rice and poached carrots.

Nick, like John, ate moderately and with an occasional polite murmur of appreciation, but John knew his secret. Whenever

Nick knew he was coming to dinner at the Laus' he first forti-
fied himself with a four-course restaurant lunch, usually of
prime rib and butter-drenched baked potato. (On company-
dinner nights, John did exactly the same, except that he usually
made it T-bone steak and butter-drenched baked potato.)

One of Marti's missions in life was to stamp out what she
thought of as junk food (which included nearly everything John
loved), and most of her menus, John swore, came from TV
cooking shows hosted by onetime gourmet chefs who had suffered heart attacks, seen the light, and were now fanatical
preachers of low-fat, sodium-free living. Fortunately for the
happy state of their marriage, Marti's job as a nutritionist kept
her at the Virginia Mason Clinic until late in the afternoon,
zestfully dishing up fatless, saltless recipes to hapless patients
unable to defend themselves, and Marti and John themselves
had to eat out most evenings.

But once a week or so, there was an unavoidable meal like
this, which John, grateful for Marti's many other virtues, considered a small price to pay. The fact that wine, not on her list
of forbidden matter, flowed freely made it all the easier. This
evening's had been brought by Rudy, three different California
Cabernets, to be drunk (naturally) in a meticulously prescribed
order.

By the time the third bottle was opened, Nick, the natural
and uncontested focus of family gatherings, was in high gear
with reminiscences of his days as a young soldier in the South
Pacific—he had illegally joined up at sixteen—during World
War II.

"Then there was this miserable, no-name island in the
Solomons," he was saying expansively, hands clasped behind his
neck, "all of about half a mile square, but, God, did the Japanese
put up a fight." He shook his head, remembering, and after a
moment went off on a slightly different tack.

"We used to do a lot of gambling, you know? Poker, craps . . . I mean, what else was there to spend your money on? And I had this natural talent I didn't even know I had. I don't have it anymore, but I had it then. Well, a lot of money used to change hands and a few people won big, including me. I had over ten thousand bucks at one point. Well, with everything going on, you'd have to be crazy to carry all that money on you in one place. So we used to split it up and give it to 'carriers'—these would-be buddies who'd keep it on them for you for fifty bucks a day. So—"

His blue eyes swung around the table. "Did I ever tell you this story?"

Maggie laughed affectionately. "Once or twice."

"You never let that stop you before," John said, pouring him some more wine. Everybody enjoyed hearing Nick tell his stories. Even Nelson was wearing his pinched smile.

"Well, *I* haven't heard it," Marti said.

Which was all the convincing Nick needed. "So. This one morning I've got maybe three thousand dollars on me, and another seven thousand split between two carriers, and my unit's out on patrol, and suddenly everything around us is splintering with machine gun bullets. We all jump into the trees and most of us make it, but I see one guy hit in the leg and pinned down behind this tree trunk. Well, I panicked because this is the guy with four thousand dollars of my money. So I make a run for it under fire, I get to him, and I actually make it back with him with my heart in my mouth, and the first thing he says is: 'You gotta go back. They got Julio too.' What are you laughing at, John?"

"I'm out ahead of you, that's all."

Marti was grinning too. "So am I, I think. Go ahead, Uncle Nick."

"Okay, you're right: Julio is the *other* sonofabitch with my winnings. Isn't that something? Two guys get hit, and they're both carrying my money. I practically had a heart attack. Anyway, back I go—by now I have some covering fire—and somehow I get *him* out of there too. Both of them."

"Holy moley," Marti said.

"Wait for the punch line," John instructed her.

"And not only that," said Nick, who was too good a storyteller to let anyone throw his rhythm off, "but the lieutenant, who didn't know his ass—well, he didn't have a clue, period— he couldn't believe it. He said it was the bravest thing he ever saw. He put me up for the Distinguished Service Cross, and damned if I didn't get it!"

The telephone chirped just as he got the last words out, and with Marti sitting there laughing helplessly John got up and went to the wall phone in the kitchen.

"Hel—"

"John, it's Brenda."

Her tone snuffed out the last of his own chuckle. "What's wrong?"

"I just got off the phone with Thérèse. It's Brian. He's dead."

✳   ✳   ✳

His body had been found three days earlier on the mountainous, barely populated island of Raiatea, where he'd gone for his annual camping trip. A pair of backpacking New Zealanders had smelled something unpleasant and had discovered him in a thicket at the foot of a rugged, two-hundred-foot bluff near the base of Mt. Tefatua. According to the police, some of his camping gear had been found on the plateau atop the bluff. Apparently, the police said, he had gotten too near the edge, something that inexperienced hikers were likely to do in the loose, rocky volcanic soil. And, like others before him over the years, he had unfortunately fallen to his death.

"But Brian wasn't an inexperienced hiker," John murmured.
"No. John, I don't believe this was an accident. If you put
everything together—sixteen months ago he almost gets killed
when the shed blows down; a few months after that he almost
gets killed when the jeep turns over. And now he *does* finally get
killed—because he doesn't know you weren't supposed to get
near the edge of a cliff? It's just too much. I mean, forget the
computer breaking down and the beans burning up and all that
stuff. Just think about what's been happening to Brian. Growing
coffee isn't that dangerous. Nick hasn't been having any accidents, Maggie hasn't been having any accidents, Nelson hasn't
been having any accidents . . . I think someone's been trying to
kill Brian, and now they finally did."

John heard her out, his head lowered. Behind him in the dining room Nick was on another story. John could hear Marti's
unrestrained chortling, Maggie's bluff horse laugh, Nelson's dry
whinny. Warm sounds, family sounds.

"John? Say something."

"I admit," he said slowly. "It makes you think."

"What should we do?"

"Do you know if there's been an autopsy? Has a competent
pathologist been over the body?"

An arid laugh came from the receiver. "What, on Raiatea?"

"All right, on Tahiti. Isn't that where the government offices
are? There must be somebody—"

"No, it's too late. For one thing, his body was out there for a
week or more and . . . well, you can imagine . . ."

"Oh, Christ. Brenda, how is Thérèse taking this?"

Thérèse, as heartbreakingly lovely as she was, had neverthe-
less been unhappy as a girl, insecure and bumbling—until Brian
Scott had come into her life. Then she'd bloomed like some
fantastic tropical flower. John had seen them together when she
brought him to Hawaii to meet the contingent of the family

that lived there, and to say that she had stars in her eyes when she looked at him would have been putting it mildly. And Brian, the protective John had been pleased to see, had been just as moonstruck with her.

That had been five years ago, and the periodic reports that he got from Nick and the others suggested that little had changed.

"She just sounded numb," Brenda said. "Hollow. And listen, she's already had him buried, up in the old plantation cemetery. I don't think she'd go along with having him dug up, if that's what you're thinking; not Thérèse."

"He's already buried? Why so fast?"

"Why wouldn't she bury him right away? You know, it's summertime there now; it's getting pretty warm. There must have been a pretty strong . . . well, smell."

Abruptly, something went out of him. He slumped heavily onto a stool at the kitchen counter, bent his head, and passed his hand wearily over his eyes.

Brian Galen Scott, thirty-eight, boyish and bright and handsome and happy, father of a pair of picture-book-perfect four-year-old twins, warmly accepted son-in-law of Nick Druett, fast-rising operations manager and all-around whiz kid at the Paradise Coffee plantation.

Brian, the man with everything to live for.

"Yeah," he said gruffly, "but you'd think she'd have some kind of service so the rest of the family——"

"She's going to have a memorial service after everybody gets back. You don't need the body to have a service."

"No, I suppose you don't. Brenda, what took her so long to call? You said they found him three days ago."

"Yes, the poor kid's just been sitting on this by herself all this time. She just couldn't face telling anybody, especially Nick. Or Aunt Céline for that matter." Céline was Thérèse's—and Maggie's—mother, Nick's wife. "She's not home either.

She's on a shopping trip in Sydney. I promised to call her myself right after I hang up with you. As for telling Nick, I'm
afraid that's going to be your job, little brother. And I think he's
going to take it hard."

When John replaced the receiver he looked over his shoulder
into the dining room. Nick was well into another familiar es-
capade, this one about the time he'd been sailing in coastal island waters on a pitch-black night (why, he never explained)
and had run sharply aground on something. When he tried to
pole himself off it, he couldn't reach anything under the boat to
push off against. But the boat stayed stuck. Bewildered, he
waited for daylight, and when morning came he found that he'd
unwittingly sailed sixty feet into a cave and was caught, not by
anything in the water, but by the cave's *roof*. He was, as he was
about to conclude,

". . . the only sailor in the history of the world who ever got
grounded by the top of his mast."

John, smiling in spite of himself—these would be the
evening's last smiles—waited for Nick to finish the story,
waited for the explosion of laughter, and walked slowly back
into the dining room.

Chapter 7

Nick took it hard, all right. One of his aching disappointments in life had been his failure to father a son. There were Maggie and Thérèse, of course, and indeed he loved them fiercely—especially Thérèse—but girls weren't boys, and Nick was simply the kind of man who needed a son. When Thérèse was a little girl Céline had delivered two stillborn babies, both boys, about a year apart, and after that they hadn't had the heart to try again.

And then, a little more than twenty years later, along had come Brian Galen Scott, MBA, operations whiz, and all-around wholesome young man. Thérèse had brought him to dinner one night, explaining that she had met him during two otherwise ill-fated years as a business major at Bennington College in Vermont, where Nick had sent her mainly because both his sister and Maggie had gone there too. Brian had been a thirty-year-old teaching assistant, and they had gone out once or twice, but it had never come to anything at the time. But two years later, now the business manager of a computer firm in Michigan, Brian had come to the South Seas on a three-week vacation package, had looked up Thérèse, and well, there he was.

And there he stayed. During that first dinner, Nick had naturally enough talked about the problems of coffee-growing, and Brian, nervous and anxious to please, had prattled on, man-to-man, about the principles of work flow and systems engineering; maybe a little *too* man-to-man from Nick's point of view, especially coming from a silver-spoon-in-the-mouth kid who made no bones about not knowing a coffee bean from a garbanzo bean.

But Nick, a fair-minded man on most subjects, mulled over Brian's ideas for a day or two and then invited him to spend an afternoon seeing the farm and discussing the specifics of coffee-processing. This time he liked what he heard, and before Brian's three weeks were up he had offered him a job, at fifty percent over his current salary, as the operations manager—a position that hadn't even been in existence before. Brian had taken him up on it on the spot.

From Nick's point of view it had worked out wonderfully. Brian had caught on with astonishing speed. And he had fallen in love not only with Thérèse but with Tahiti and the coffee business as well. His ideas on automation, computerization, and "organizational reengineering," although they got some opposition—in particular from Maggie—had put the plantation firmly on its feet. It was Brian who had come up with the ideas that had made the Seattle-area roastery a viable operation. From there, as Nick enjoyed saying, it was history.

There was another angle too. Nick got to keep Thérèse, on whom he doted, nearby. He had seen the handwriting on the wall that first night and had known it wasn't going to be long before he lost her. This way, his baby girl stayed within reach—his "wedding" present would be a house in Papara, two miles from his own—and he got himself a fire-breathing production genius to boot. That Brian turned out to be a loving, protective husband to Thérèse and a responsible parent to the twins who came along later was frosting on the cake.

Almost like having a son.

And now it was all ended, done. *"No!"* he whispered when John broke the news. Then his face went grayish yellow, his big body seemed to fall in on itself, and he sat, staring at nothing, like a witless hulk, while John gave them what details he had.

"And that's it," John said. "That's all I know."

It was Marti who broke the queasy silence by pushing back her chair. "I'll put up some coffee," she said quietly and went to the kitchen.

"Tea for me," Rudy called automatically after her, then looked embarrassed.

"We'll have to arrange the funeral," Nick said thickly after another long interval. He cleared his throat and visibly gathered himself together. "Nelson, will you see about getting us on a plane in the morning?"

"He's already been buried," John told them. "In the plantation cemetery."

Maggie—tough, brassy Maggie—suddenly turned brick-red and sobbed like a man, an explosive, gasping, painful yawp that caught everyone by surprise; Maggie too, from the looks of it.

Now everybody was embarrassed. "Oh, hell," she said roughly, scrubbing at her eyes with a napkin while she got herself under control again. "It's only . . . he was so keen on being buried in that stupid old cemetery. I mean, we used to joke about it, didn't we? And now . . . now . . . Oh, God, Thérèse must be . . ." She trailed off as the tears welled up again, and dabbed at her nose with a tissue she'd found somewhere.

Marti came back with the coffee and tea and handed them around. In silence they sipped mechanically or simply stared at their cups.

After a while John spoke, looking down at his hands. "I want to be frank. After everything else that's been happening out there, I think we have to consider, well, that it may not have been an accident."

Nick looked up dully, angrily, as if he didn't comprehend.

Rudy, more nonplussed than John had ever seen him before, opened his mouth so suddenly that his lips popped. "Not an— you don't mean . . . they wouldn't really—they wouldn't—"

"Rudy, don't be dumb," Nick said with uncharacteristic harshness. "What the hell would the Mob have against *Brian?* He wasn't even around back then."

"Yes, but didn't John just say—"

"I don't care what John said. If they have a beef with any-body, it's me—not Brian."

"Now let's wait just a minute here," Nelson said. "Rudy may very well have a valid point."

"How the hell—" Nick began.

"Who prepared the new affidavit?" Nelson asked. "Would someone care to tell me that? Who did all the work?"

"Ah, that's ridiculous," Nick said.

"What do you mean, *new* affidavit?" John asked. "Now what are you talking about?"

But Nelson backed off. "Well, I'm not really suggesting that it had anything to do with—"

"What new affidavit?" John repeated.

It was Maggie who explained. When the gangsters' retrial had come up four years before, Nick had been asked by the U.S. attorney's office to make a new deposition to include some ele-ments that hadn't been in the first one. Nick was eager to com-ply (over Nelson's objections), but was having a hard time finding the data he needed. People had died, firms had gone out of business, old records were impossible to locate. After three frustrating weeks of letters and telephone calls, he still didn't have the vital pieces. That was when Brian, who had been trying to introduce things like computers, modems, and e-mail to his still-reluctant father-in-law, had put together the needed information as a demonstration of what the new online technology could do. It had taken him two and a half hours.

Nick had been bowled over, converted on the spot. The Paradise plantation's changeover to the new technology had begun the next week. And the preparation of the affidavit had been turned over to Brian, lock, stock, and barrel. Nick hadn't done much more than sign it when it was finished. And it had been that affidavit more than anything else, so they understood, that had sunk the notorious three G-men all over again.

"Yeah, but if Nick was the one who signed it," John pointed out, "how would they even know Brian had anything to do with it?"

"I'm not arguing the point, John," Nelson said. "I just thought it ought to be mentioned. You're the one who said you think there's something fishy."

Another leaden silence dropped onto them. Cups clicked in saucers. Chairs creaked.

"I'll tell you what I think," John said at last. "I think we ought to have his body exhumed and then get it examined by somebody who knows what he's doing. Then let's see where we are."

"Oh, my Lord, that's horrible!" said Maggie. "It'd just about kill Thérèse."

"It wouldn't kill her," John said patiently. "If somebody murdered Brian, she'd want to know."

"So would we all," Nick said; his first words in a long time. "But if he was out there in the heat for a week, there's not going to be much left, John. Some bones, maybe."

"I know. It'd take a forensic anthropologist."

Nelson snorted. "Of which there are dozens in Papeete."

"I was thinking of bringing somebody in from the States."

"You know somebody?" Nick asked.

"Yeah, I do. The best there is."

Nick took a while to reply. He sat rotating his cup in its saucer and staring down at its untouched contents: Tahitian Blue Devil, the highest-priced coffee in the world, bar none. At last he looked up and spoke.

"Do it," he said softly.

Chapter 8

High in the ink-black sky over the South Pacific, sprawled at his ease in a roomy Air New Zealand first-class seat, with a first-class meal of duckling with orange sauce comfortably inside him and a stemmed crystal glass of Courvoisier at his elbow, Gideon Oliver was having second thoughts.

He didn't like exhumations. And not merely on aesthetic grounds; that went without saying. More important, exhumations were traumatic experiences for family and friends; especially for family. Digging a corpse out of its grave for a belated postmortem was a sure way to rip open the wounds that had begun to heal when the body was laid down in the first place. And that never failed to make him uncomfortable.

Besides, he had a hard-to-shake conviction that it was all going to be in aid of nothing. The string of accidents Brian Scott had gotten caught in might make one wonder, but accidents did frequently happen. In strings. And what credible reason was there to think they weren't accidents? Would anyone in his right mind try to murder someone by knocking down a shed in a windstorm?

On top of that, John's faith in Gideon's ability to find signs of murder, if murder there was, was flattering but overblown. There were a lot of things that could kill you without leaving a road map on the skeleton. Most things, actually. The chances were good he would come away from the analysis shaking his head, with nothing to say one way or the other about the cause of death. Or let's say that there were indications that it had been due to a fall, which seemed the most likely thing he would find; a fractured skull or pelvis or some crushed vertebrae. Fine, but what would that prove about murder or the absence of it?

And on top of *that* he and John were on their way to a foreign country with the sole and express purpose of second-guessing its official law enforcement authorities. This, he had learned long ago, was unlikely to be a rewarding experience.

And finally, on top of everything else—or maybe underlying everything else—he was going to be away from Julie for almost a week and already he missed her.

John, untroubled by morbid doubts, was stretched out in the seat next to him, headphones on, contentedly watching the end of the new James Bond movie on the screen. As the closing credits began to roll, he took off the headphones and smiled at Gideon. "Good show. You should have watched."

"I've been thinking."

"Worrying," John said. "Okay, what's bothering you now?"

"A lot. How did you talk me into this anyhow?"

But they both knew the answer to that. John had called and asked him on the previous Wednesday, the day after the news about Brian's death had come. Gideon had promptly ticked off his reservations and John had listened patiently.

When Gideon had finished, John had finally spoken.

"I'm asking you as a favor, Doc," he'd said simply. "This is my family."

That had been enough; he and John were old, good friends. They had worked on a lot of cases together and had been in some difficult situations together. They had saved each other's lives.

"I can't get away till the end of next week," Gideon had grumbled for form's sake. "I have a seminar I can't palm off on anybody else."

"Is that gonna hurt the bones? A week or two one way or the other?"

No, Gideon had admitted, it wasn't likely to hurt the bones. Speaking personally, the older the better, as far as he was concerned. He would have preferred them about ten thousand years older, in fact, brown and dry and clean. Still, the air of Oceania was notoriously warm and humid, and a week or ten days out-of-doors there might already have done a pretty good job of getting down to the bare bones of things, so to speak. And the additional time in the ground wouldn't hurt either. Or so he hoped.

Well, then, there wasn't any problem, John had pointed out. Moreover, Nick Druett had offered to pay Gideon's top consulting fees (Gideon had refused) and to fly them out first-class, put them up at the Shangri-La, a nearby beach resort, and pick up all expenses (Gideon had accepted).

The flight attendant came down the darkened aisle with the cognac bottle, paused attentively beside them, and at their nods topped off the glasses. The flight had left Los Angeles forty-five minutes late and the attendant, apparently taking personal responsibility for the delay, had been extraordinarily solicitous of the few first-class passengers ever since.

"Ahh." John resettled himself luxuriously, sipped from the

brandy glass, and smacked his lips. "Does this beat the hell out of government travel, or what? Listen, I've been doing a little digging. I found out some interesting stuff."

Gideon turned toward him.

"Remember I told you Nick wasn't the only guy to file a deposition with the U.S. attorney at that first kickback trial? Two other growers had the guts to do it too?"

Gideon nodded.

"Well, one was from Java, the other one was from the Kona Coast. And they're both out of business now. The Hawaiian guy died falling mysteriously out of a hotel window in Honolulu and what used to be his coffee farm is now the King Kamehameha Shopping Village. The Javanese guy just threw in the towel after three fires on his farm. The place is up for sale." He raised his eyebrows.

"And you think the Mob's behind it all?" Gideon asked.

The question made him feel faintly ridiculous. Most of the six or seven forensic cases he took on in a typical year were everyday, garden-variety murders, sordid and simple: the prostitute's body dragged out into the woods and hurriedly covered with leaves and dirt; the drug dealer cut down in some deserted, filthy house and left where he fell; the victim of revenge or jealousy or domestic rage tossed into the dumpster in a black plastic garbage bag—or in three or four plastic bags. Only once had he been involved with organized crime, and then from a distance. "The Mob" was something melodramatic and unreal, a million miles away from his everyday professorly concerns with Pleistocene Man and hominid locomotion.

Besides, could anyone be expected to take seriously three guys named Nutso, Zorro, and Nate the Schlepper?

John shrugged. "I just think it's interesting. Something to be considered."

"All right, tell me this: Here was Brian on this ten-day camping trip on a remote island in the middle of the Pacific. How would Nutso and the boys know where to find him? How would *anybody* know where to find him?"

"Good question," John said amiably as he finished his brandy.

The attendant, as sensitive to every movement of his charges as an auctioneer watching for bidding signals, was back with the cognac bottle. Gideon shook his head; John accepted a refill.

"You know," Gideon said after a few minutes of near-dozing, "now that I think about it, I think I remember reading about that kickback case. Didn't one of their goons turn state's evidence? Bingo . . . Bongo . . ."

"Klingo Bozzuto," John said, laughing. "They called him that because one of the bosses thought he looked like a Klingon." Reflectively, he rolled some brandy around his mouth. "He did too, sort of. But he wasn't a goon, exactly, he was a Mob accountant. Way handier for state's evidence than some gorilla who could barely write his name."

"Are you serious? An accountant named Klingo Bozzuto?"

"Yeah, it'd look great on a business card, wouldn't it? *Klingo Bozzuto, CPA: a name you can trust.*"

"Well, tell me this. What happened to old Klingo? Did the bad guys go after him? Because if they didn't bother with the guy who broke the case—their own stooge—I don't see them hunting down your cousin."

"No, they didn't go after him," John said.

"All right, then—"

"They didn't go after him because they couldn't. The Bureau got him into a witness protection program. That was part of the deal. Changed his name, resettled him in the Midwest somewhere, and found him some kind of job with the railroads. As far as I know, he's still at it."

"Mm," Gideon said.

"Listen, Doc," John said earnestly, "I'm not saying the Mob had anything to do with this. How would I know? I just don't want to rule anything out. Right now, all I want is for you to look at what there is. After you see Brian's body we'll worry about who did what to who."

And that was another thing that was bothering Gideon. "If *is* Brian," he said, knowing it would set John off.

It did. John's eyes rolled toward the ceiling. "Doc, he had his wallet on him. His watch was lying a few feet away, busted. His wife identified it. Only about six people live on the goddamn island, who else could it be?"

They had been through this more than once, and Gideon was no more convinced than he'd been before. "But his wife didn't identify *him*," he pointed out.

"Well, how could she? He was laying out in the sun for a week. They shipped him back to Tahiti in a body bag inside a box. Thérèse wouldn't even open it."

Gideon shuddered with real empathy. "Who would? But it still means he's never been positively identified."

"So who's arguing with you, but who else could it be?" he demanded again. "It's common sense, that's all. Brian went there and he never came back, right? They found his body right under the, what do you call it, the plateau where he was camping, right?" John's arms had begun to flail dangerously near his brandy glass. "The local police say nobody else is missing, right?"

"Right, don't get so excited. It probably *is* Brian. But 'probably' and 'definitely' are qualitative distinctions—"

"Doc, Doc, don't do this to me. You know what Charlie says about you?"

Charlie was Charlie Applewhite, John's boss, and Gideon knew exactly what the special agent in charge of the FBI's Seattle office said about him. Applewhite had said it to his face not long ago after reading a report that Gideon had turned in.

"Dr. Oliver," he had said matter-of-factly, his small, square hands folded on the gleaming surface of his desk, "I have often wondered why it is that whenever we call you in on what gives every indication of being a simple and straightforward case, it always seems to end up being such a wondrously, stupendously, mind-bogglingly, screwed-up mess."

It had pricked Gideon's temper. If the FBI wanted a cursory analysis from him the next time, he had replied, one in which he accepted things on their surface and told them what they wanted to hear, just let him know and he would oblige. He would even adjust his fees downward.

"Look, John," he said now, "the only way I can work is to start with what I *know* and go from there. I'm not going to accept something as a given because it's common sense. You ought to know that. What do you want me to do, base my findings on what people think?"

"Hell, I don't know what I want," John said, yawning. "I just want you to find out what there is to find out, okay? I'm sorry I said anything. Whatever you come up with is fine with me."

"Fine. That's what I want too."

"Fine. Great." He tipped his seat all the way back and settled down, then cocked one eye open. "Just keep it simple, will you?"

And with that he was asleep, not a man to give a second thought a second thought. Gideon sighed, turned off the overhead light, kicked off his shoes and lay back for a couple of hours of sleep too.

"Good news, everybody," he was informed by the pilot's folksy voice as he began to drift off. "We seem to have picked up a tailwind, so it looks as if we might be arriving in Papeete at a pretty reasonable hour after all."

Chapter 9

But there is no such thing as a reasonable hour at which to arrive in Papeete. By balsa raft, maybe, but not if you're coming by scheduled airline service. International flights over the South Pacific are overnight affairs, geared to arrive on the far side of the ocean—in Auckland, or Los Angeles, or Santiago—at a decent hour of the morning, which means they touch down in Tahiti at midnight if you're lucky, or 3 A.M. if you're not.

John and Gideon weren't. They arrived at Papeete's Faaa Airport at 2:45 A.M. Gideon was not at his best. When he traveled he generally tried to follow the rules laid down by his old professor, Abe Goldstein, in his field anthropology course. Rule One was: never arrive in a strange place at night on an empty stomach. "In the dark and with a low blood sugar level," Abe had warned with somber emphasis, "new places don't look so hot."

Well, there was nothing wrong with his blood sugar level. The breakfast of eggs Benedict served just before landing had been wonderful, and he had amazed himself by eating all of it a bare three hours after dinner, but with less than two hours of sleep in between he was queasy and unsettled. And that second cognac, which had seemed like a good idea at the time, didn't seem like one now. In addition, there was the surreal jet-age shock that came from having stepped into an upholstered canister in funky, familiar L.A., relaxing for the duration of a couple of good meals, and then stepping out of it into a place where everything was abruptly exotic: the snatches of conversation in liquid French and soft, rhythmic Tahitian, the smells, the noises, the way people walked and gestured, the moist, tropical air as thick as cream.

They walked through the marble-walled, open-air lobby, past groups consisting mostly of excited, handsome, bronze-skinned Tahitians, many of the women with flowers in their hair and flower leis in their hands, waiting to greet returnees. At the curbside in front, where Nick had promised to have someone on hand to pick them up, hotel and travel agency vans were lined up with open doors. Beside them, staff members, mostly French or American, were marking off their clipboard checklists in the light of the street lamps, greeting their travel-dazed charges with only slightly forced smiles, and loading them efficiently into the vans, docile and subdued, each with a lei now draped over his or her slumping shoulders.

John looked on with narrowed eyes. "If anybody tries to put a lei around my neck," he told Gideon, "they're dead meat. I'm telling you." John had had three cognacs after dinner, not two, and he was clearly regretting it.

"It looks as if you don't have anything to worry about," Gideon said, scanning the names on the vans. *Tahiti Nui Travel, Sofitel Maeva Beach, Tahitian Odyssey Adventure, Ia Orana Tours, Aroma Travel* . . . "There's nothing here from the Shangri-La."

"There's gotta be. If Nick said he arranged—"

"Johnny! Over here!"

Shambling toward them from the lobby was a large, loose-limbed man in his sixties, wearing shorts, tank top, and thongs. Even from forty feet away, Gideon could see the fuzzy mat of light hair that covered his shoulders and arms.

John brightened. "Nick! What are you doing here? It's the middle of the night."

"Well, hell, I thought I'd take one more crack at convincing you to bunk at my place. There's all kinds of room. You too, Dr. Oliver." He stuck out his hand. "Nick Druett. Nick."

Gideon shook the offered hand. "Gideon."

"What do you say, John?"

John shook his head. "Wouldn't work, Unc. I already explained why."

"Explain it again, would you? I didn't quite get it the first time."

"Because," John said, "when you're coming to look into a fishy death in the family, the last place you want to stay is the family homestead. It cramps your style."

"But why? We wouldn't get in your way, you know that."

"That's not the point, Nick," John said patiently.

"Well, what is the point?" Angrily, Nick pushed shaggy, thinning hair somewhere between blond and white from his forehead. "You can't actually think that anyone in the family had anything to do with it, can you?"

John looked uncomfortable. "It's been known to happen."

Gideon was surprised. Not once had John mentioned the possibility of his family's involvement in Brian's death. That was like him, though; he would have felt disloyal bringing up family suspicions to an outsider, even to Gideon. But he was a good cop too; he wouldn't have discounted them either.

Nick made a grumbling noise. "Well, that's a hell of a note, is all I can say. Tell me, who do you suspect? Céline? Thérèse?" He stuck out his chin. "The twins, maybe?"

"Come on, Nick," John said. "I'm just trying to do it right."
He appealed to Gideon. "Am I right, Doc?"

"Yeah," Nick demanded, "is he right, Doc?"

Gideon hunted for the right words. He wasn't happy about
being in the middle of a family dispute before he even got out
of the airport. "Well, it's not so much a question of suspecting
any particular person, Nick," he said carefully, "it's just that,
um, the investigative process can be compromised if it's not carried out in an environment of strict impartiality and disinter-
est."

John vigorously nodded his agreement. "That's what I said."

Nick's laugh was much like John's, a sudden, sunny burble
that lit up his face. "You *wish* that was what you said." His smile
took in Gideon too. "I always did like professors."

He reached over and ruffled John's hair, something Gideon
had never seen the big FBI agent submit to before, and placed
his other hand easily on Gideon's shoulder. "Okay, you win.
Come on, guys, I'll drive you over to the Shangri-La."

On the way to the car, he said: "So, should I be calling you
'Doc'? Is that what people call you?"

"Only one," Gideon said with a nod in John's direction. "In
all the known world."

John shrugged. "Hey, can I help it? To me he looks like a
'Doc.'"

"He sure talks like one," Nick said.

* * *

"What kind of car do you drive, Gideon?" Nick asked as
they pulled away from the airport onto Highway 5, which like
Highways 1, 2, 3, and 4 was something of a euphemism. There
was only one "highway" in Tahiti, the coastal road that almost
but not quite encircled the island, simply (and inexplicably)
changing its name every now and then. The Shangri-La was fif-

teen miles south of the airport along this road, about a half-mile before Nick's house at Papara.

"Not an Infiniti," John answered for Gideon. "He works for the government too. Did they exhume Brian's body yet, Nick?"

"Uh, no, not exactly," Nick said.

John's and Gideon's eyes met briefly in the rearview mirror. Not *exactly?* How did you not exactly exhume a body?

"When, then?" John asked.

"Oh, there are some details," Nick said airily. "Not to worry. I'll get it all straightened out."

Gideon leaned forward from the back seat. "I only have a few days, Nick."

"Right, don't worry about it. I'm taking care of it." He gestured out the window at the darkened streets. "Sorry it's so late or I'd point out the sights to you, Gideon. It's a pretty interesting place."

"I know," Gideon said. "I was here on vacation with my wife three or four years ago."

"Like it?" Nick asked.

"Very much. Well, I did, anyway. Julie's a native Washingtonian. Three days in a row without rain and she gets restless."

"Is that *right?*" Nick said as if it was the most fascinating thing he'd heard all week. He was certainly working overtime to avoid any talk about the purpose of their coming.

John too had picked up his reluctance. "Something wrong, Nick? Is there a problem with the exhumation?"

"Problem? No, what kind of problem? I filed the papers as soon as I got back. It just takes time to process them, that's all. We have red tape in Tahiti too, you know. But don't get exercised, there's plenty of time. Hell, the memorial service isn't until next week."

"I'll need to be back home before next week," Gideon said.

"Fine, no sweat. Look, I'll fill you in tomorrow—I'll fill you both in. But first I want you guys to sleep in as long as you feel like in the morning, have a swim, lay around in the sun, and then come on over whenever you want to in the afternoon. I'll give you the grand tour of the plantation—"

"I've had the grand tour, Unc," John said. "Twice."

"Well, what about your buddy? Don't you want to see a real, live coffee plantation, Gideon? We'll even throw in a free tasting."

"Sure," Gideon said.

"Good, and then you're both coming to dinner—I have the whole clan over every Monday, you know, and they're all looking forward to—" He threw a narrowed glance at John. "Now you better not start giving me a hard time about this too, pal." The glance flicked around to take in Gideon as well. "The investigative process isn't going to get compromised because you guys sit down for a friendly meal with the family, is it?"

Gideon smiled. "I guess we can take a chance."

"Good, I'm glad to hear it. I'm putting on a real Polynesian feast. Wait'll you see the Twin Terrors, John. Do you realize you haven't seen those little monsters since they were two?"

"I guess that's right, isn't it? How old are they now, four? Can you tell 'em apart yet?"

The two of them lapsed into family talk while Gideon lay back against the soft leather, not sure if something was really off-tone in the atmosphere, or if it was just the early-morning eggs Benedict catching up somewhere in his system with those late-night brandies.

* * *

"This is Dean Parks," Nick said, introducing the scraggy, elderly man in Western shirt, jeans, and silver-buckled belt behind the Shangri-La's reception desk. "The Texas Kid. He owns the place."

"The whole shebang," Parks agreed in what was indeed a measured, mournful, East Texas twang. "Mortgage and all."

"Don't let him kid you," Nick said, "this guy's richer than I am." He looked at him fondly. "Dino and I go back a long way."

"Unfortunately, I go back longer," Parks said. "Not, of course, that you'd know it to look at us."

He was wrong about that. His tanned face was as seamed and dried out as a discarded boot, his throat puckered, his shoulders narrowed with the years, his thin belly sunken. Only his hair was youthful; lank, long, and ferociously black.

"It's clean living as does it," he explained to Gideon and John.

"That and spending half his disposable income on Grecian Formula," Nick said.

Parks grinned. "Don't you believe a word of it. Well, welcome to Tahiti, gents. "Or as we say here, *Ia ora na.*"

Nick laughed. "Yeah," he said, "ask him how many other words he knows."

"More than you, anyway," Parks said. "That's for dang sure."

"You're probably right at that," Nick said agreeably.

The two of them had been friends a long time, he had explained in the car. Private First-Class Nick Druett and Corporal Dean Parks had met during the war, when both of them were in the same platoon, first in the Solomons and then on Bora Bora. Afterward, they had returned individually to French Polynesia to seek their fortunes and had run into each other again. They had talked about going into the hotel business together, but decided to try their luck on their own instead and had enjoyed a friendly competition of sorts ever since.

Nick had put all his money into a large copra plantation on Tahiti. ("The truth is, I didn't even know what the damn stuff was. I didn't know if you farmed it, or grew it on trees, or raised it on the hoof.") He'd done well with it too, but sold off most of the land a few years later and used the money to buy property on the outer islands, where he'd eventually opened a chain of four small hotels that he still owned. The remainder of the old copra plantation was now the Paradise Coffee farm, and although Nick still talked longingly about building more hotels—in particular a huge golf course resort on Bora Bora—his energies had gone increasingly into the coffee business.

Dean, more single-minded, had gone about it differently, sticking to his first project for almost fifty years now. He'd bought a decrepit old hotel on a near-worthless strip of beach between Papara and Paea, torn it down, put up a sprawling collection of ocean-front bungalows—he'd hammered nails right alongside the Tahitian carpenters—and christened the place the Shangri-La. Luck had been on his side. When the new international airport at Faaa eventually opened, turning Tahiti from a remote beachcomber's haven to a jet-set destination, there was only one decent American-style hotel on the island, and the Shangri-La was it.

According to Nick, that's the way it had remained for almost five years, and Parks had raked in the cash. More recently, the hotel chains—the giant Sofitel, the twelve-story Hyatt built into a mountainside—had siphoned off the more lucrative of the American tour groups, but the Shangri-La still had arrangements with several foreign airlines and was holding its own with a steady flow of groups from Chile and Hong Kong. And Dean was a great guy who took care of them in style. Not to worry.

"I'm going to take off now," Nick said. He smiled at his old friend. "I really appreciate your waiting up for them, Dean."

"No problem. At what I'm charging you, I can afford to give personal service. Shoot, their keys are in the office. I'll be right back."

Nick waited for him to leave. "Um, by the way," he said,

looking just a little sheepish, Gideon thought, "tomorrow, at dinner? Could we not say anything about—well, you know." He mimed digging with a shovel. "I haven't gotten around to telling them why you're here yet."

Gideon and John looked at each other. There was something funny in the air, all right.

"Nick," John said, "that doesn't make any sense. They already know why we're here. They were right there when we talked about it at my house, remember? Nelson, Rudy, Maggie—"

"Yes, but they don't necessarily know that's why you're here *now*. They think you're just coming for the memorial service."

"And me?" Gideon said.

"So? John brought a friend along."

Gideon shook his head. "But I'll be gone by then. Besides, I don't like to—"

"Look, guys, could we do it my way, please? Can't we at least have a nice, friendly family get-together first, without spoiling it with . . . Look, I promise I'll straighten everything out the next morning. I just hate . . . ah, what the hell." His face sagged with exhaustion; the exchange, along with the hour, had taken the starch out of him. For the first time he looked his years. His tired eyes appealed to them. "Just humor me, okay? Just trust me." He smiled crookedly. "Hell, I guess you must think I'm being pretty funny about this."

Yes, Gideon thought he was being pretty funny, but Parks returned before he could say anything, and Nick made his goodbyes.

"See you next week, Dean?" He dealt imaginary cards. "Old Geezers' Monthly?"

"Seems like a reasonable assumption," Parks said, "seeing as how I haven't missed but one game in twenty-two years now and that was when I had my gallbladder out."

"Good, I'm planning to get some of my money back."

"Whup your ass," Parks replied.

Nick laughed. "And keep it quiet around here in the morning, will you? See that these two get a good night's sleep. Oh, and book 'em a rental car. On my account. A *good* Renault." And with that he was gone.

Parks rang for a husky, sleep-puffed Tahitian porter in a lavalava to take their bags, then led them back himself through the dimly lit reception lobby, moving on lean, long, stiff-jointed legs. The Western look made it only down to his calves. No boots. He was wearing jogging shoes, the kind meant for comfort, not jogging; old men's shoes, purple and gray and stubby, with Velcro straps instead of laces.

"Kind of quiet here right now," he told them. "You should see it when those crazy Chileans come here. You talk about party animals."

The lobby was built Polynesian-style, without outer walls or doors, more a large breezeway than a room, with rattan chairs and tables arranged in casual groupings on a dully gleaming tiled floor. They went past the empty bar and restaurant, the darkened gift shop, and the travel agent's desk, and finally out to the slate terrace in back, where Parks switched on a flashlight. Then across a lawn of close-cropped grass and onto the moonlit beach. Teacup-sized, pale gray land crabs scuttled sideways out of their path and disappeared into the scores of holes they'd bored in the sand.

Parks stopped at the first of a row of thatch-roofed, bamboo-walled cottages that lined the rear of the narrow beach and handed them keys. "This place's yours, Gideon. You're next door, John. Either of you boys stayed in a thatch-roofed place before?"

Gideon shook his head.

"Not since I was a kid," John said.

"Well, let me show you the way you best go in at night. First you put a light on." He climbed the three wooden steps to the door and flicked a switch. A light came on somewhere inside, but the main room stayed dark. "Now you wait," he said. "Give it a minute or so to let the mosquitoes and things go into the bathroom, where the light's at. Then you run in real quick and spray in there—there's a can right near the front door. *Then* you put on the rest of the lights, see?"

"What do you mean, mosquitoes and *things?*" John asked. "What else you got in there?"

Parks laughed. "Oh, that's about it. Actually, they shouldn't be much of a problem. Been a dry year. But nobody's used these cottages for a couple weeks, so you never know. Oh, yeah, one more thing: when you spray, always spray down. Don't never aim it at the ceiling."

John glowered suspiciously at him. "Why not?"

"Because whatever's up there living in the thatch, you'd best just leave it alone, that's for dang sure."

After a brief pause John spoke. "Say, Dean, you wouldn't have any rooms with regular walls, would you? And a regular ceiling? I mean, this is real nice and everything—"

"Hell, don't worry about it. It's nothing but lizards. The worst they do is fall off, kerplunk, once in a while, but they just pick theirselves up and scoot back up the walls. Besides, they eat the bugs."

"Oh, lizards," John said, relieved. "We had lizards in Hilo when I was a kid. Lizards I can live with."

Gideon wasn't so sure *he* could, but there didn't seem to be much choice, and he was too tired to worry about it. There was only an hour or two left until daylight and he was aching to lie down. If he didn't sleep on his back with his mouth open, which he usually didn't, how much of a problem could falling lizards be?

"Nighty-night, then," Parks said. "I'll see you fellas tomorrow."

They waited until he was out of earshot. John spoke first. "What's this about Nick's not getting around to telling them what we're doing here?"

"What's this about Nick's not getting around to getting the body exhumed yet?" Gideon answered. "I should have been able to get going tomorrow, John. The body could have been back in the ground long before the memorial service. You'd think he'd want that, wouldn't you?"

John nodded. "Something weird's going on, don't you think?"

Gideon slowly climbed the steps, turning around before he opened the door.

"That's for dang sure," he said.

Chapter 10

As Parks had promised, there was an aerosol spray can on a little shelf beside the door. Gideon read the label in the light from the bathroom. *Timor—Protection Contre Insectes Rampants* was the alarming legend, on a background depicting a particularly large and depraved-looking cockroach.

The bathroom was full of flowers and potted plants. He fancied he could hear a contented buzzing coming from it. Above his head, in the bedroom, a tiny movement caught his eye, and when he spotted a three-inch gray lizard, lit by the light from the bathroom, on one of the slanting roof struts, it seemed to run shyly from his sight, burrowing into the thatch. He felt very much the intruder, barging in on creatures that had been living there together for weeks, maybe months, symbiotically if not always peacefully.

He returned the can to the shelf, pulled back the bedcovers, and started getting out of his clothes.

The hell with it, he thought. Live and let live.

*   *   *

Once, in the short time he slept, he was awakened by a little *plop* on the wood-plank floor, followed by a silence during which he fancied a small, surprised animal was collecting its dignity, and then a patter of tiny, scurrying feet making for the far wall. He turned over under the sheet and was asleep again in seconds. But with the first gray smudges of daylight, the tremendous, froglike-cricketlike-crowlike racket from the mynah birds roosting in the trees behind the cottages woke him up for good after not much more than an hour's sleep. He was grumpy and tired, but at least he had established a successful *quid pro quo* with the mosquitoes. Not a bite on him.

Even after he'd showered, using the ubiquitous coconut-scented soap of French Polynesia, and sleepily gotten dressed in a pair of lightweight L.L. Bean pants and a short-sleeved shirt, the sun had yet to come up. Tropical sunsets were famously sudden, but sunrises took their time, as they did anyplace else. The sky was barely streaked with mauve and purple, the land dark, the sea the color of pewter. It was 5:00. Well, he was an early riser at home too, if not quite this early. You could get a lot done getting up early.

A solitary dawn walk along the beach would be a fine way to start the day, he thought. He had some ideas about Nick's odd behavior and he wanted to think them through. With the two-hour time difference it would be 7:30 in Port Angeles by the time he got back. He could give Julie a call before she went off to her job—like John's sister, Brenda, she was a supervising park ranger—at the administrative center of the Olympic National Park, a convenient five minutes from home. After that he would have a few cups of good Tahitian coffee in the dining room and put in some prep time for the upcoming symposium on Bronze Age congenital abnormalities at the winter paleopathological

meetings—for which, with commendable foresight, he'd
brought his notes.

And all this, he thought with something uncharitably close to
smugness, he would do while John, a notoriously late riser at the
best of times, snoozed the morning away. He got a pair of beach
sandals from the closet and sat down on the bed to slip them
on. Still a little drowsy, he stretched and yawned, then lay back
against the headboard and closed his eyes for a moment.

When he awakened the sun was streaming hotly through the
windows and John was pounding at the door. "Come on, Doc,
wake up already! It's nine o'clock! You gonna sleep all day, or
what?"

*　　*　　*

Beneath the outrigger canoe suspended from the ceiling in
the Shangri-La's dining room they breakfasted on guava juice,
croissants, crullers, and fragrant slices of pineapple, papaya, and
the lime green grapefruit of the South Pacific.

Afterward, over coffee, they sat in the breeze of an open
French window, gazing contentedly at a reef-rimmed lagoon as
blue and brilliant as a swimming pool, at fork-tailed seabirds
floating above the cliffs on the warm wind, at the fantastically
shaped, impossibly green mountains of Moorea twelve miles
away over the water.

Aside from the soft plash of the ocean, the only sounds were
the slap-slap of thong sandals from the waitress, a broad-
beamed middle-aged Tahitian matron with a pair of harlequin
glasses on a lanyard around her neck, a gardenia in her black
hair, and her stocky body swathed in a flowered *pareu*, the all-
purpose, wraparound Tahitian garment somewhere between a
sarong and a muumuu.

There were only a few other people breakfasting in the big
room: a crabby French couple having their morning squabble

and two Japanese men who gazed about them in discourage-
ment, as if convinced that they were in the wrong hotel.

The Shangri-La, romantic the night before, looked a bit
grubby in the bright morning light, a little timeworn, the arms
of the rattan furniture greasy with use, the cushions on them
sunken and stained, the straw mats on the floor ground-down
and shabby. Despite the benefits of exclusive arrangements with
the party-loving tour groups of Chile, it seemed clear that the
Shangri-La had seen better days.

"What I think," John said, disposing of yet another crois-
sant, "is that we ought to drop in on the local police this morning."

Gideon looked at him. "We?"

"Maybe Nick's not giving us a runaround about exhuming
Brian, maybe it's just red tape like he says. Maybe we can help
clear it up."

"Maybe," Gideon said without conviction.

"Besides, wouldn't you like to have a look at the police report
on Brian before you get started? I mean, we're not doing anything anyway, we're just waiting around."

"I suppose so, but what are we supposed to do, walk in and
ask?"

"Sure, why not?"

"Why not? Because we're a couple of nosy foreigners who are
here to do some Monday-morning quarterbacking on a case
that's closed as far as they're concerned, and cops can get a little
funny about that, if you haven't noticed. We're here at Nick's
request, and he's the one who should be dealing with the police,
John. Or Thérèse. But not us; we don't have any status here."

"Yeah, that's true," John said. He went to the buffet table,
came back with a sugar-encrusted cruller, tore off a third of it,
shoved it into his mouth, and gestured with the remainder. "But
what the hell, I'm an FBI agent, aren't I? I'm visiting a foreign

country, aren't I? Why shouldn't I pay a courtesy call on my fellow law enforcement officers?"

"No reason at all. Fine, you have my blessing. I'll see you when you get back."

John laughed. "No dice, these guys speak French. I need a translator."

Gideon drank the last of his coffee and sighed. "All right, let's go." He stood up reluctantly. "But I'm not going to like this."

John got out of his chair, finishing the last of the cruller and licking sugar from his fingers. "You're gonna love it. Trust me."

Chapter 11

"Good day," Gideon began in his slow, careful French. "We are Americans. My friend is a special agent of the Federal Bureau of Investigation—"

"And does your friend possess identification?" asked the civilian clerk without discernible interest.

Gideon translated the request for John, who slid his card over the marble counter. The clerk, less than awestruck, nodded magisterially at Gideon to continue.

"My friend would like to examine a death report concerning an accident on Raiatea a few weeks ago—"

The clerk frowned. "There has been no notification from the FBI concerning this."

"No, my friend is here in a personal capacity, about a family matter, you see. He hopes that—"

The clerk's expression had hardened. "Such files are open only to official inspection. I am sorry." He began to turn away.

"I understand, but in this case an exhumation request has already been filed, and we thought—"

"For that you must see the department of health, not the police."

"I understand," Gideon said again, "but my friend has reason to think that a murder may have been committed. We assumed the police would be interested."

The clerk was finally impressed. "I think you had better talk to the commandant," he said stiffly. "Wait here, please." He went to a telephone at the back of the room.

"What'd he say?" John asked.

"He said we'd better talk to the commandant."

"Fine." John turned an accusing eye on him. "Hey, what was all that *"mon ami, mon ami"* stuff? You're not taking any responsibility for this, are you? You're putting everything on my shoulders, aren't you?"

Gideon laughed. "You better believe it."

They had arrived a few minutes earlier at the gleaming white headquarters of the Gendarmerie Nationale de Polynésie-Française, commandingly situated at the head of the avenue Bruat, Papeete's most beautiful, most Frenchified boulevard. A broad (by Tahitian standards) thoroughfare, it was lined with one- and two-story government offices and screened by leafy, arching trees that had already been mature when Gauguin had sipped absinthe in their shade before wearing out his welcome in the better French social circles of Papeete.

The *gendarmerie* itself was the largest of the buildings, a handsome, two-story structure conspicuously flying the French tricolor, surrounded by its own tropically landscaped grounds, and encircled by a wall of iron grillwork and white stone. Notwithstanding its corrugated tin roof, it made an imposing presence.

Inside as well as outside. The lobby was immaculate and austere, with nothing on the walls but a simple, marble plaque inscribed in gold:

Hommage aux gendarmes
Victimes du devoir

"What's *devoir?*" John asked.

"Duty," Gideon said as the clerk returned to the counter.

John nodded approvingly at the plaque.

"The commandant can see you now," the clerk told them.

He pressed a buzzer to let them through a gate in the counter, then motioned them to precede him through a door labeled *Brigade des Recherches.*

John's brow wrinkled. "Research? Who needs research?"

"It means *investigations,*" Gideon told him.

Once beyond public scrutiny, the *gendarmerie* was notably less grand. The upper floor was a warren of cramped offices, most of them shared, and a small, untidy common room—an expanded passageway, really—with a couple of chipped plastic tables and an enormous, illuminated Coke machine that took up half the space. They had to weave their way through four or five sprawling, blue-uniformed gendarmes taking a break at the tables, smoking, drinking coffee, and gossiping.

The decor was basic police station, with battered, shabby furniture and floors covered with linoleum that had been nothing much to begin with and that had now seen more than its allotted span of years. The dull-green walls were almost hidden by charts, posters, and curling scraps of paper stuck on with pushpins, and were scuffed and blackened where shoes or hands or oily heads or the backs of chairs had come into repeated contact with them.

Other than the posted messages in French, the only feature that would tell an observer that this was not a police station in New York or London was an abundance of fresh, fragrant flowers—jasmine, frangipani, gardenia—that lay on desks and file cabinets. While the smells of police stations in London and New York were frequently memorable, they were unlikely to include frangipani.

Like those of the other offices, the commandant's door was open, revealing a room only a little larger than the rest, about twelve feet by twelve, but comprising a small enclave of refinement. There were no posters, charts, or tacked-up notes. Two antique lengths of brown-and-red tapa cloth and a pair of richly carved, wooden canoe paddles hung on the unmarred, peach-colored walls. A bank of four tall windows looked down the tree-canopied length of avenue Bruat to the bustling harbor five blocks away. The heavy desk was oiled teak, with nothing on the sheet of glass that covered it but a single letter, a marble pen-holder, a small gold pendulum clock protected by a bell jar, and, in one corner, a mass of hibiscus and gardenia arranged on a banana-leaf base. In all, it was the office of a man of taste, serene and inviting.

Its occupant was a small, dapper man in his fifties who was going rapidly over the letter with his forefinger. He nodded to himself, signed with three or four elegant, looping strokes, placed the sheet in a tray on the credenza behind him, and removed his reading glasses to examine the two newcomers with eyes of a startlingly clear blue, penetrating and intelligent. His hair, thick and gray, was brushed softly back in a way that made the most of the distinguished-looking wings of white at his temples.

"I am Colonel Bertaud," he said in French-accented English. "Sit."

John and Gideon sat.

He extended a forefinger and leveled it at the clerk. "Go, Salvat."

Salvat went.

"Your names?" His voice was surprisingly beautiful, as mellow and vibrant as a plucked guitar string, with a hint of irony in the inflection, or perhaps it was in his expression or even his posture.

They gave him their names.

"Now, then. What is this about a murder?"

"Well, of course we don't know that there's been one," Gideon said, treading carefully. Bertaud was being pleasant enough, but there was something about him that suggested that kid gloves were a good idea.

John, being John, had no such compunctions. "It's about a man named Brian Scott, Colonel, an American—"

"Yes, I know who Brian Scott was, Mr. Lau. I am familiar with the investigation into his death. I am also familiar with the finding: not homicide, but an accidental death due to a fall."

"Yeah, I know that. But who did the investigation? Some guy out on Raiatea, right? Let's face it—"

The skin around Colonel Bertaud's eyes twitched once. He rose from his desk, walked to the window, and stood looking down on the boulevard, his hands clasped behind him. He was shorter than he had appeared in his chair; no more than five feet six inches tall, and somewhat hippy and short-legged when seen from behind. His uniform, like that of the other gendarmes, consisted of a pale blue shirt and dark blue pants. Unlike the others, however, he wore a perfectly knotted tie rather than leaving his shirt sensibly open at the throat, his pants were full-length trousers, not the rather skimpy shorts that were standard issue, and he had on a dark blue jacket, well cut to make the least of his absence of waist, and fitted out with a gleaming Sam Browne belt.

Either he was something of a martinet, thought Gideon, or he was well aware that his was not the type of build that would be at its best in a pair of short shorts. Gideon was betting on some of both.

The colonel turned from the window to look coldly at John. *"Brigadier-chef* Didier on Raiatea is extremely competent. I have full confidence in him." He paused, then said in that suave, sardonic voice: *"And* I approved the report personally."

Even this was lost on John, who plowed ahead. "Well, yeah, I'm not criticizing him, but there are certain things you don't know . . ."

Bertaud listened without expression while John told him about his suspicions, about the accidents on the plantation, about the old gangland associations. To Gideon it sounded freshly outlandish; he could imagine what Bertaud was thinking.

When John was finished, Bertaud turned blandly to Gideon. "Is he really with the FBI?"

John, finally stung, flushed. "Yeah, I'm with the FBI," he said angrily, "and all I need to know from you is *a:* Are you going to let us see the report or not? And *b:* What's going on with the exhumation order?"

"There is no exhumation order, I'm afraid."

John's mouth opened and closed. "There—"

Gideon cut in. "I understand that it would have been filed with the health department. Let's see, that would probably have been—"

"There is no exhumation order with the health department."

"Now look, Colonel," John said, "Nick Druett told me he filed one. Are you telling us—"

"Your uncle did file such a request. Subsequently, he withdrew it."

"Withdrew!" John exclaimed, jumping to his feet and leaning with both hands on Bertaud's desk. *"Why?"*

"I suggest you ask him. Now, gentlemen, as enjoyable as this has been, my time is limited and I must—"

"Let's go, Doc," John said abruptly.

Gideon rose. "Thank you for your help, Colonel."

"One moment more, please, gentlemen," Bertaud said. The transparent blue eyes held them. "I hope you will enjoy your stay in Tahiti, but I remind you that you are on French soil. I will tolerate no interference in island affairs. This is understood?"

John returned his stare. *"Oui, mon colonel!"* he said.

And clicked his heels and saluted.

Chapter 12

"I am really steamed," John said through clenched teeth. "I mean, I am *really* pissed! I mean, I really let that little crud get to me."

"No kidding," Gideon said. "Really?"

He had convinced John to stop for a cool-down beer at a sidewalk cafe a few blocks from the *gendarmerie,* in the heart of Papeete's downtown; a busy place with bright, cherry-colored canvas chairs, bright cherry-colored plastic tables, and a big, bright, cherry-colored canvas awning over everything that filtered the strong sunshine, letting through only a cool, watery, reddish glow that made it seem as if they were sitting on the bottom of a pink-lemonade ocean. Even the dust motes were rosy. *Café Le Retro,* it said on the awning. *Pizzeria—Brasserie—Bar Americain.* And if nothing else, at least the music on the speaker system was American: Elvis Presley crooning "Love Me Tender."

"Eez he ghrreally weez zuh aef-bee-aie?" John mouthed

doing a savage, surprisingly good imitation of Bertaud. "What a prune."

"He was just trying to be funny," Gideon said. "It was a joke."

"Sure." John glowered at him over the table. "Did *you* think it was funny?"

"Of course I didn't," Gideon said promptly, glad now that he'd managed to resist the impulse to laugh at the time. "But remember, you were getting on his nerves a little too."

"Me!" John was flabbergasted. "What did I do?"

"Well, you did imply once or twice that an investigation that he signed off on might have been botched."

John dismissed this with a grunt. "He's short, that's his problem. He's got a chip on his shoulder, and all anybody—what's the joke now?"

"Sorry, I didn't mean to laugh. I just don't remember you letting anybody get under your skin like this." The waiter arrived with their order: two Hinano beers in squat brown bottles with labels that proclaimed them *la Bière de Tahiti* in bold letters above a Polynesian version of the girl on the White Rock bottles.

John swigged directly from his bottle. "You know who he reminds me of? Not in looks, I mean. My brother, Nelson." Then, perhaps mellowed by the beer: "Well, I don't know, maybe not as bad as Nelson." He heaved a sigh and settled down. "Listen, you think he was telling us the truth about the exhumation?"

"The commandant of police?" Gideon poured a half-glass of Hinano that he didn't really want. "Sure, why would he lie?"

"I don't know. But if he's not lying, that means that Nick is. He didn't run into any red tape, he just changed his mind. And that raises some questions."

"Such as, what are we doing here?"

"Such as, what the hell is going on? Why would Nick back down?"

"It happens, John. Digging up relatives makes people squeamish when the time comes. It's not that surprising."

Maybe it wasn't, John told him, but weasel-words from Nick Druett *were*, no matter the circumstances. When Nick committed himself to something he did it; no fencing, no dodging, no humbug about Tahitian red tape.

"Besides," John added, "if he changed his mind, why would he fly us out here, and put us up, and all the rest of it?"

"Beats me. He's your uncle; you ought to do what Bertaud said and ask him."

"Yeah, I'll do just that," said John. "But you know what I'm starting to think? I think Bertaud and Nick are—" he held up two fingers close together "—like that. I think Bertaud's in Nick's pocket. Nick's a powerful guy around here."

Gideon shook his head. "John, I really don't think so."

"Yeah, well allow me to differ." And with that he sank into one of his rare sulks, slumping in his chair, sipping from the bottle, and scowling moodily into the middle distance.

Gideon was sympathetic, but only to a point. It seemed to him that Bertaud had right on his side, that the more they considered the "evidence" for a murder having been committed the flimsier it got, that while Nick's actions were hard to explain, there was no reason to assume that a cover-up was behind them. He was beginning to think that he and John were here on a wild-goose chase, not that he would mind all that much if that's what it came to. He had been ambivalent from the beginning, and if what it amounted to in the end was nothing more than a few days' winter respite in the South Seas, he could live with that.

Besides, deep down he had the feeling that all these people

John included, would be better off if Brian were left in peace. Exhumations were like lawsuits; once begun they rarely turned out as expected, and however they turned out they had a way of leaving in their wake a family that wasn't much of a family anymore.

He sipped his beer, waited for John to come out of his funk, and abstractedly watched the parade of noontime activity just beyond the cafe tables, along the boulevard Pomaré, Papeete's bustling heart. Guidebooks to Tahiti are near-unanimous in their advice on what to do when in Papeete: get out of it as soon as possible and go someplace that is unspoiled. Papeete, they explain, is noisy, dirty, tacky, commercial, and coarse. The bad press is nothing new. Robert Louis Stevenson sourly referred to it as "the dreaded semi-civilization of Papeete." To Zane Grey it was "the eddying point for all the riffraff of the South Seas." Somerset Maugham hated it. Paul Gauguin hated it. Jack London hated it.

Gideon liked it.

Papeete seemed to him a lively, healthy, unpredictable hybrid on the way to becoming who knew what, a cordial if not quite settled mix of East and West—or rather North and South—of Gallic elegance and reserve and island energy, ease, and unflappability. From where he sat he could see copra being loaded onto age-grayed tramp steamers on the nearby docks. He could see sweating tourists with loaded plastic shopping bags; hefty middle-aged Tahitian women in bright muumuus with loaded grocery sacks and with flowers in their hair; even a few grizzled, hollow-eyed European beachcombers in mildewed white clothes, straight out of a Maugham story. Farther out, in the harbor, a traditional Polynesian racing canoe skimmed through the water, propelled by a team of muscular brown youths at its oars.

And all of this South Seas ambience he looked at from a table in an undeniably French brasserie located on a pretty street of restaurants, boutiques, and airline offices. With Elvis on the speakers.

John came awake with a start. "Jeez, what are we doing sitting here? It's eleven-thirty. I've got a lot of questions for Nick and I'm gonna want some answers." He caught a hesitant look in Gideon's eye. "Doc, you'll come with me, won't you? You wouldn't chicken out on me?"

"Well, actually, I was thinking of doing a little shopping while I'm in town, looking for a present for Julie."

"Yeah, but—"

"John, look. I signed on to do my thing with a set of skeletal remains, and I'm still ready to do that. But I'm not going to go argue with Nick about it. I don't know what's right, and I just don't feel as if I have any business interfering in this."

Glumly John swirled the last half-inch of beer in his bottle. "Okay, yeah, you're right, Doc. It's my family, not yours. Lucky me." He finished the beer. "I'll collar Nick and find out what the hell is going on. How'll you get back to the hotel?"

"I'll hop a ride on *le truck*."

John nodded. "All right, you go ahead, do your shopping, have a nice lunch, and go on back and lay around in a hammock all day. *I'll* deal with my screwball family."

Gideon beamed at him. "Now that," he said, "is what I call a first-rate idea."

*　*　*

John left the Renault in the parking area beside Nick's sprawling white house and walked around to the French doors that opened onto the beachside terrace in back, which was the way all but strangers entered. At the edge of the flagstone terace in the feathery shade of a couple of tall, slender mapé trees, his aunt Céline—Nick's wife, the mother of Maggie and Thérèse—was standing at an easel, her back to him, an artist's palette hooked over one thumb, a brush in the other hand, and a second brush between her teeth. She was contemplating the half-finished oil painting in front of her and the immense panorama of sea and sky beyond. Once a famous island beauty who had even had a brief juvenile career in a few Hollywood movies, she was now a chubby, twinkling little woman of sixty with thinning black hair, forever dressed in a capacious, all-concealing, flowered muumuu from which her small, round arms stuck out like a couple of dusky sausages.

When she heard him come up she turned. Her face lit up. "Hello, you!" she cried in the rich Tahitian lilt that she had never lost, although she had spoken little but English and French for decades. Like John's mother, she had been born in Tahiti to Chinese parents who had come to work as laborers on the great Atimaono cotton plantation, and Chinese had never been more than a second language to her. "Hey, why you still so skinny? She don't feed you?"

Daintily, and somewhat absentmindedly, she proffered her cheek to be kissed. He kissed it, smiling. Céline was a good-natured, garrulous woman, but usually a little remote as well; not in an aloof or offensive way, but as if in a reverie of self-absorption, as if there were always something intensely interesting on her mind, only it never happened to be you or what you were talking about at the time.

Her approach to painting had some of the same quality. Céline, who lived three months of the year in Paris and the rest in Papara, unvaryingly painted French pictures when in Tahiti and Tahitian pictures when in France. She claimed it stimulated her creativity.

She took the brush from between her teeth and gestured at the painting. "So tell me, what you think?"

True to form, with a sparkling Polynesian seascape of lagoon, foaming reef, and limpid, cloud-studded blue sky spread out in all its glory before her, she was painting a picture of Notre Dame Cathedral from a dog-eared postcard tacked to an arm of the easel.

"Looks great, Céline. You get better all the time."

"Don't bullshit me," she said, but she beamed. "Hey, you early, boy. Nick said you not coming up till later."

"Well, I wanted to ask him a couple of things. Is he in the house?"

She shook her head. "No," she said, "up at the farm. In the shed, I think. That man in one hell of a mood."

"Well, with poor Brian—"

"No, everybody feel rotten about that. This something else. What you do to him last night?"

"Not a thing, Céline. He probably just missed his beauty sleep, that's all."

"Well, he goddamn mad today," Céline said, her attention returning to the painting. She chewed her lip and scowled at it. "Now where the hell I gonna find vermilion in this dump, you tell me that."

"Nice talking to you, *Makuahine makua*," John said fondly. "Look forward to seeing you later."

"Just gonna have to use lousy cadmium red instead," she said and stuck the brush back between her teeth.

*   *   *

In the half-light of the drying shed, a large, round-bellied Tahitian looked up at John from his knees, where he was rolling a coffee bean in his fingers, having picked it from one of the amber mounds that were being systematically spread by a couple of workers with blunt wooden rakes.

"The boss? Yeah, he down below, by the furnace. You got to go outside and come in again. Hot as hell down there."

"Thanks," John said.

"If you selling something, don't bother, come back another time."

"That seems to be the general opinion." John smiled. "I guess you don't remember me, Tari."

The Tahitian took another look. His neutral expression changed. "Oh, hey, the boss's nephew, right? How you doing, John?"

"Fine, how about yourself? Running the place yet?"

Tari Terui was one of Maggie's "projects." The son of a man who had himself worked on a coffee farm all his life, he had been with the Paradise plantation for fifteen of his thirty years, starting as an unskilled laborer on the loading dock and eventually working himself up to a crew chief, which seemed to be as far as his vocational aims went. But Maggie had seen some spark of intelligence or aptitude in him and had gotten him, against his own judgment, to enroll in the technical college in Papeete. To everyone's surprise but hers he had stuck to it, seen it through, and emerged with a certificate in hotel management and tourism, the closest thing to a management degree that one could get on the island.

Since then he had been her shining example, and she had nursed and groomed him all the way to his present job as production foreman, the highest position that had ever been held at the farm by a native Tahitian. Now, John had heard, she had him in mind for bigger things still. Last week, when Nick had begun to wonder how he was going to replace Brian at the farm, she had argued that he would have a hard time finding a better operations manager than Tari Terui, or one who knew more about the coffee business. Given a little coaching and a month or so to learn the ropes, he would do a wonderful job.

Nick had surprised her by promptly accepting the idea, and Tari had now been the official heir apparent for going on two weeks.

"Oh, be a while before I'm ready to run things," he said, getting to his feet. "Not till Thursday, anyhow." And he laughed, but with a nervous little hiccup that suggested less assurance than the words did.

Despite his accomplishments, Tari had always struck John as a simple soul, a big, likeable islander who had been goaded by Maggie, with all good intentions, to a level he would never have wanted or reached on his own; a man who was in over his head or who thought so at any rate, and dearly wished himself back hefting bags at the loading dock with the other *kanakas*. As a result, under the friendly exterior and the high-pitched giggle there was an edge of uneasiness. If anything, John had seen it grow sharper over time.

Well, what the hell, it was Tari's life. If he didn't like it up there with the big boys, all he had to do was say no thanks. Nobody was forcing him. Still, he couldn't help rooting for the guy.

"Ah, you'll do fine, Tari. You know more about coffee than all the rest of them put together. So Nick's in a bad mood, huh?"

"You said it, brother."

"How bad? On a scale of one to ten."

"Oh, I don't know. Around seven hundred?"

"Thanks for the warning. See you later, Tari."

This was starting to get worrisome, John thought as he walked around the shed to the other entrance. Nick could be just about the most stubborn, contrary man in the world when he felt like it, and John wanted some answers—now, before Nick had time to concoct some kind of elaborate, cockamamie story. Obviously, a little psychology was called for, a little buttering-up.

A little coffee-talk.

Chapter 13

"Hi there, Unc," he said, nephewlike and chipper. "God, don't you love the smell of coffee beans?" He inhaled deeply, swelling his chest. "Nothing like it."

Nick, his matted shoulders running with sweat, was using a scoop to poke through the open lid of a large, slowly revolving drum full of beans, one of four identical drums connected to a thrumming furnace a few feet away. "Coffee beans don't have any smell," he muttered without looking up. "Not till later."

"No?"

"No."

"Must be my imagination, then." He cleared his throat. "Because they *look* so good, you know?"

Nick merely glanced at him. "Christ."

So the preliminary reports on Nick's mood were accurate. John watched the older man sift a few more beans, feel them between his fingers, toss them back through the opening, close the lid, and move silently on to the next drum. The only sounds came from the furnace and from the masses of beans, shifting as the drums turned: *sshhpp . . . sshhpp*, like surf on a sandy beach.

John made another try. "Roasting, huh?" he asked brightly.

Nick closed the lid on the drum, straightened up, and eyed him levelly. "I'm not roasting, I'm a coffee-grower. Growers don't roast. Roasters roast."

"No?"

"No."

The count: no balls, two strikes.

"So what are you doing then?"

"I'm drying. I'm pretty busy here, John."

"I thought you only air-dried—the 'slow, natural Paradise way,'" John said, plucking this happy tidbit from a Caffè Paradiso ad he hadn't known he remembered.

"Paradise beans, yeah," Nick said grudgingly. "But these are for some of our not-so-picky wholesale customers. That was one of Brian's ideas, you know—putting in a drying furnace for people who didn't want to spend for air-drying. And it's earned us a lot of money. Not everybody gives a damn, you know."

"Oh," John said.

"Oh," Nick said. He looked carefully at one of the beans he'd taken from the drum, then bit judiciously into it.

"How's it taste?" John asked.

"I'm not *tasting* it," Nick snapped and spit it out. "I'm testing the moisture content. For Christ's sake, John."

"Moisture content? Really? So—"

"John," Nick said, his voice rising, "is there something I can do for you?"

But John, like his uncle, was not overequipped with patience. "Yeah, there's something you can do for me," he shouted back. "You can tell me why you've been jerking us around."

"What do you mean, jerking you around? Where do you come off—"

"Nick, we were at the police station this morning—"

"Yeah, I know," Nick said sourly.

"—and the colonel there told us— You know? How do you know?"

"I know. Things get around. It's a small place."

"Do you know what he told us?"

"Suppose you tell me."

"That you withdrew the exhumation order, that you don't intend to have Brian's body dug up at all, that you're hiding something but he doesn't know what, that you've been giving us a royal runaround."

Strictly speaking, this was quite a bit more than Bertaud had told them, but from Nick's deep sigh it was clear that all or most of it was on the mark. He took off the fireman-red bandanna that had been loosely tied around his neck and mopped his head and throat with it. "Lord, it's hot. Let's go outside."

Near the platform scales at one end of the open shed Nick pulled a couple of liter cartons of papaya-and-pineapple juice out of a cooler and handed one to John. They went to sit at an ancient, splintery picnic table under a row of eucalyptus trees that bordered one side of the drying shed.

Nick slowly, wearily pulled his carton open, tipped it up, and swallowed a long, gurgling draft, his Adam's apple bobbing. Then another. He looked tired, washed-out.

"I'm sorry I lost my temper, Uncle Nick," John said when he set the carton down.

"I'm the one who should be sorry, Johnny. I guess I owe you an explanation. Your friend too."

He crushed the carton against the table, carefully flattened it out, smoothed down the seams, took his time getting going.

"It was Thérèse," he said, still working over the carton. "I sat down with her and told her we were having him exhumed and why, and she just about came apart. You can understand that, can't you? You know she's kind of . . . delicate. And she took Brian's death hard, John. They really loved each other."

"Yeah, I can understand that. So you called it off?"

"No, not then. I thought she'd come around after a day or two . . ." He shook his head. ". . . but I just couldn't get through to her. She was really . . . so yesterday I finally called the health department and canceled it. You guys were already on your way so I couldn't tell you not to come, and then when you got here I just didn't want to tell you you'd made the trip for nothing in the middle of the night." He finally pushed the mashed carton aside and looked up. "So that's the story. I'm sorry if it screwed you up, but I still think I did the right thing."

John was silent for a moment. "I don't, Nick."

"Hell, it's not as if it was going to amount to anything."

"That's not true, Nick. There are a lot of unresolved questions here."

"I tell you the truth, John, I don't much care. Even if Gasparone's goons really knocked him off, then let that be the end of it. I don't think you understand how shook up she is, and I'm not going to put that girl through hell all over again. For what? I mean, let's say you turn out to be right, which I don't think you are, but just for the sake of argument. So what happens then, a trial? Testifying? Drag it out for two more years? And then what? Have you thought about that?"

John peered at him. "That doesn't sound like you, Nick."

Nick shrugged. "I'm not the man I was, John. I don't do battle with the world anymore. I'm almost seventy, you know. Wait'll you get there; you'll see."

That didn't sound like him either. "Nick, you can't just let this go. This was *Brian.* I want you to change your mind."

"No." But Brian's name had brought a wince. "I can do whatever I damn please, John, and in this case I'm putting Thérèse first." He got up. "I've got to get back to the dryers."

But he stood there a little longer, leaning on his knuckles on the table. "Look, I'm really sorry about your friend Gideon coming out here for nothing. But as long as *you're* here, I know Thérèse would appreciate it if you stayed for the service. Gideon too, if he wants; he's more than welcome. Until then, why don't you loosen up and relax, for Christ's sake? Lay back for a few days, see some of the islands, go over to Bora Bora, eat some good food, get reacquainted with the family. Some people actually like it here, you know."

John replied with a shrug, not unfriendly but meaningless. He walked back with Nick and watched for a while as he scooped, studied, poked, and bit the revolving beans. "You have any objection if I talk to Thérèse about it?" he said after a few minutes.

"Jesus, can't we even have one dinner like a normal family before you start—"

"I don't mean today," John said quickly. "Tomorrow, maybe."

Nick stopped his work and looked at John for a while. "I don't want you browbeating her, Johnny. She's been through enough."

"Hey, Nick." He put his hand on the shaggy forearm and stopped him in mid-scoop. "You really think I'd browbeat Thérèse?"

Nick studied him hard for a moment, then relaxed. "No, I guess not. Sure, talk to her about it if you want. Just take no for an answer, will you?"

"Don't worry," John said. "I've had lots of practice at that." The air between them had almost cleared. "So tell me, how do you tell moisture content from chewing on the beans?"

"Don't start patronizing me. I'm not that decrepit."

"No, I'm really interested. Tell me."

Nick told him. The beans had to be dried to a ten percent

moisture content before being bagged. Dryer than that and they lost flavor. Wetter—with a moisture content of even twelve percent, say—they were likely to mold within a few weeks. But at ten percent they stayed fresh indefinitely.

"You can do it scientifically, of course," Nick said, "but I like the old eyetooth-crunch technique. Here, take one of these. Have a bite."

John bit.

"Sort of gummy," Nick said, "right?"

John nodded.

"That's because the moisture's at twelve or thirteen percent. Now try this one." He handed him another bean, slightly paler, from a drum that he had turned off earlier. "This one's right at ten percent."

John bit again.

"Crisp, isn't it?" Nick said. "Sort of snaps right in two. Feel the difference?"

"I sure do," John said, nodding. "That's really interesting."

Nick's good-humored laugh rolled easily out of him. "You always were a good faker. Can you really tell the difference?"

John grinned back at him. "Not if my life depended on it, Unc."

Chapter 14

There is no rail system on the island of Tahiti, no commuter plane network, no bus service. If you want public transportation you do what the locals do: you climb aboard *le truck,* as everyone refers, individually and collectively, to the ubiquitous and whimsically painted fleet of "cabooses" mounted on individually owned flatbed trucks (which is why they are called *le truck* and not *le bus*).

Gideon waved down a southbound one on rue François Cardella and found an unoccupied section of padded bench. On his left was a smiling old man clad only in shorts, with a wire crate containing two plainly disgruntled white chickens on his lap. On his right was a middle-aged woman wearing a bright *pareu,* with a hibiscus flower in her hair, thong sandals on her feet, and a braided string of gleaming red mullet in one hand. In the other hand was a leather attaché case with a cellular telephone clamped to it.

Across from him a gaggle of high school girls, already Polynesian stunners at fifteen or sixteen, tittered and chattered away in Tahitian, bothered by neither the reggae music blaring from *le truck*'s loudspeaker nor the transistor radios plugged into their ears.

Culture in flux, he thought. At the lively, sprawling market an hour earlier he had bought Julie a handsome black-pearl pendant. The native woman at the stall, shy and smiling, had spoken no English and only a little French. She had struck him as a charming throwback to the unspoiled Tahiti of the eighteenth century. But when he had made his choice she had revealed a minimal knowledge of English after all. "Visa? MasterCard? American Express?" she had inquired in a charming accent and then processed the transaction on a computer screen equipped with Windows.

Le truck made its stop-and-start journey through the outer reaches of Papeete's urban sprawl: a long string of convenience stores, bars, restaurants, shoddy two-story apartment buildings, and metal-roofed shantytowns. But after twenty minutes the smelly, noisy commercial traffic eased off and the shantytowns thinned out and then disappeared entirely, to be replaced by occasional native villages, one much like another: modest, compact assemblages of small stucco houses—some nice, some not so nice—set among astonishing profusions of hibiscus and gardenia, often with old stone churches as centerpieces.

Between the villages the vegetation thickened and became more tropical, and clefts in the coastal mountains opened up to reveal the stupendous hanging green valleys of the interior. When Gideon saw the sign for the Shangri-La coming up, he pressed the old-fashioned doorbell-button above his head and *le truck* pulled up beside the trellised arch over the entryway to the grounds. He walked around to the driver's window, handed over the fare—200 French Pacific francs, about $2—and went to his cottage to get in some work on the Bronze Age symposium.

But he hadn't been at it five minutes when he knew his heart, and more important, his head, weren't in it. He yawned, threw his notes down, and looked at his watch. Not much after one o'clock. Another yawn. Finding a hammock was starting to sound like a pretty good idea, and he was giving serious thought to the possibility of acting on it when he recalled Nick's invitation of the night before: a tour of the coffee farm.

Why not? Considering the thousands of gallons of the stuff he'd downed in the last twenty years, it was about time he visited one. Besides, underneath all that reasonable and healthy skepticism he'd been expressing to John, he had to admit to a certain curiosity about seeing the murderous pulper, the falling-down shed, and the various other inanimate objects that seemed to have it in for Nick Druett and the Paradise Coffee enterprise.

The hammock could wait; Gideon went to find Dean Parks at the front desk.

"Dean, how would I get up to Nick's plantation from here?"

"Easy, I'll have Honu take you up in the van. Whoops, not for a couple of hours, though; he's in town picking up supplies."

"Is it too far to walk?"

" 'Bout eight miles. Uphill every blessed inch."

"Too far," Gideon said.

"I'd say so. His house is less than half a mile down the road, though. Easy walking. If you don't want to wait for the van, somebody there's bound to give you a lift up to the farm."

"I think I'll try that. How do I recognize his house?"

Dean laughed. "Keep your eyeballs peeled for the place that looks like it belongs to the Wazir of Kitchipoo."

* * *

Dean was exaggerating, but not by that much. Nick's house stood in splendid isolation, in walled, parklike grounds that jutted out into the sea on their own private promontory. Like ninety-nine percent of the houses in the South Seas, it was covered with a green, corrugated metal roof. Other than that, it would have been right at home on the French Riviera. Faced with white stucco and polished river rock, embellished with ornate white grillwork on its several balconies and verandas, and fronted with rows of French doors instead of windows, the handsome two-story structure stood on a wide lawn commanding a wonderful view of beach, ocean, and, in the distance, the domed green peninsula of Tahiti Iti.

Gideon walked between the twin stone pillars of the driveway and headed toward the house at an angle across the lawn.

"Can I help you?"

He looked toward a trellised patio on the right to see a pair of women finishing off a meal with mugs of coffee at a round, glass-topped table; one about forty, the other in her sixties, with scant, dark hair that sat on her scalp like a cloud. The older one was Asiatic—Chinese, he guessed—the younger a mixture of Asiatic and Caucasian and a foot taller, but the shape of their jaws, the slope of their shoulders, even the inquisitive tilt of their heads marked them as relatives. Mother and daughter, he thought. Céline and Maggie.

"Hi," he said. "I'm Gideon Oliver. I'm—"

"Oh, you Johnny's friend," said the older woman, her round face crinkling into a smile not all that different from John's. She held up a pitcher. "Want some coffee?"

He shook his head. "Thanks, I had some with lunch. You're Mrs. Druett?"

"You bet. Johnny's Auntie Céline."

"And I'm Maggie. John's cousin," said the younger one, the one who had called out, frankly appraising him with sharp, black, intelligent eyes. "Well, well. The family's heard some pretty strange stories about you over the years."

Likewise, Gideon thought but didn't say. He laughed. "Well, you can't believe everything John says, you know."

Maggie swallowed the last of her coffee and stood up, a solid, thick-bodied woman with a Chinese-style, bolerolike silk jacket decorously buttoned over shoulders left bare by her *pareu*. She leaned over to kiss her mother on the forehead. "See you tomorrow, Mom."

"Okay, honey," Céline said absently, "you be good now. Gideon, you know something? You looking at the only woman alive who work with John Barrymore."

"Really?" said Gideon.

"He gonna be my uncle in *Pippi of the Islands.* Nineteen forty-two. He drop dead right before filming start. Damn picture never got made."

"Really," said Gideon.

"He don't believe me," Céline said.

"It's true," Maggie told him. "More or less. Mom was the Tahitian Shirley Temple for a while. Listen, I'm on my way back up to the plantation. How about a lift? Poppa said you were coming up for a tour."

"Sure," said Gideon. "I was hoping for a ride. Goodbye, Mrs. Druett. Nice meeting you."

"Work with Abbott and Costello too," Céline informed him.

Chapter 15

"The man without a mission," said Maggie as she got into the driver's seat of her gray Peugeot.

"Pardon?"

"Well, you were coming out to do your thing on poor Brian, weren't you? Until Poppa changed his mind?"

Gideon turned to face her more directly as she steered the car onto the highway. "Do you know what made him change it?"

She shrugged. "Nothing *makes* Nick Druett change his mind. He just changed it, that's all. I guess he thought it wasn't such a good idea after all."

"And what do you think?"

Not a good question. Maggie's face hardened. "What I think is that my father usually turns out to be right about most things."

But after a few moments, when she saw he wasn't going to pursue it, she softened. "All the same, I'm a little sorry we're not going through with it. It would have been nice to lay that stupid gangland business to rest once and for all. This way, there'll always be rumors."

"You don't believe them?"

"That they had him killed? Of course not." She paused, then glanced at him, one eyebrow lifted. She was wearing carved wooden earrings shaped like conch shells. "Do *you?*"

Gideon replied with a shrug of his own. "What about those accidents?"

"Such as?"

"I don't remember them all. Didn't his jeep flip over? Didn't the roof of one of the sheds almost come down on him?"

Maggie clucked irritably. "Oh, for God's sake. That jeep was an antique, forty years old, and the 'roads' up there are more like goat tracks. It's amazing it never flipped over before."

"What about the shed?"

"That thing was rickety from the start. I was in there doing a time-management class for the foremen the evening before and after everybody left I stayed there another couple of hours doing some paperwork, but then I had to get out because the wind came up and I thought the place was going to come down on me. I mentioned it to Poppa, and he was going to have it checked, but it collapsed first and Brian just happened to be there when it did. I mean, organized crime might be pretty powerful, but I don't think they can order up a windstorm on demand."

Gideon nodded. There wasn't much to say. He agreed with her.

"We turn there," she said. "At the mini-mall."

And mini-mall it was, the Centre Apatea, plopped down into the brush-jungle beside the highway and looking startlingly like a street-corner mall that had been shipped whole from East Los Angeles, with only the signs changed, to French and Tahitian. There was a pharmacy, a video store, a fast-food place that specialized in sugary crullers and *casses-croûtes*—sandwiches on crusty bread—and a *magasin*, the island's version of a 7-Eleven. And as in L.A., this was where the local kids hung out, brown, lean youngsters in T-shirts, shorts, and turned-around baseball caps, lounging against the cars in the parking lot. As Maggie turned from the highway onto the unmarked gravel road that led toward the interior of the island, he was able to read the legend on one of the boys' shirts: *Hard Rock Cafe, Fiji.*

Just on the other side of the mall a herd of brown-and-white, picture-book-pretty Guernsey cows browsed in the grass in a grove of tall, slender coconut palms, with the woolly green flanks of Mt. Iviroa beyond. To Gideon's eyes, at least, it was an unlikely sight, like some fanciful tropical collage with barnyard cow figures amusingly (and improbably) pasted on.

Once past the last of the palm trees, the car began climbing through relatively open rangeland spotted with neatly terraced fruit and vegetable orchards: mangoes, pineapples, taros, citrus.

"This is all our property," Maggie said. "Two thousand acres. My father leases most of it to local farmers—Chinese, mostly. The coffee farm's only part of it. Here we are," she said as they drove under a peeling stucco arch from the copra-farming days or even earlier, from cotton-picking times. The sign beside it was in both French and English.

Paradise Coffee Plantation
Home of Blue Devil Coffee

A cup of coffee—real coffee—home-browned, home-ground, home-made, that comes to you dark as a hazel-eye, but changes to a golden bronze as you temper it with cream that never cheated, but was real cream from its birth, thick, tenderly yellow, perfectly sweet, neither lumpy nor frothing on the Java: such a cup of coffee is a match for twenty blue devils, and will exorcise them all.

Henry Ward Beecher

"Great quote," Gideon said. "Certainly gets the salivary glands going."

"Haven't you ever seen it before? We put it on every package of Blue Devil, or don't you like Blue Devil?"

"No, I like it a lot." But not enough to be intimately familiar with the package. Not at almost $40 a pound. When Gideon bought a bag of Paradise coffee, it was generally one of the less expensive ones like the House Blend or the Weekend Blend. And even then it was a splurge compared to almost everything else on the market. Paradise coffees didn't come cheap.

They pulled up at a rutted parking area beside a big, barnlike building with Plexiglas walls and a roof made of plates of Plexiglas and corrugated metal. "And this is the famous drying shed itself," Maggie told him.

"It does look a little rickety," Gideon said.

"Well, of course it does."

"Still, it's funny that it should have decided to collapse just when he was there." Fishing. What for, he wasn't sure.

Maggie leaned her elbows on the steering wheel and looked him in the eye. "Gideon . . ." She hesitated, considered her words. "Frankly, those accidents were a bad spell that everyone would like to forget. We don't even like to talk about them anymore. But let me tell you something that I would never say to Nick, or, God help me, to Thérèse. Brian wasn't the *target* of all those damn things that happened, he was . . . well, he was the *cause*, when you come right down to it. I'm sorry to say it, especially right now, but it's true."

Gideon frowned. "How do you mean, the cause?"

"I don't mean directly," she said, backing off a little, "not on purpose, but in a way, yes. Take the jeeps, for example—we actually bought five of them, if you can believe it; four to drive around in and one for spare parts. Old codgers from the

Korean War. It was Brian's idea to get them; part of his 'system-reengineering.' We got them at a ridiculously low price, and he claimed it was the perfect way to get around in country like this. Maybe it was, but the damn things were *old*. Three of them broke down—I mean, they practically decomposed in front of us—inside of the first month, and then Brian happened to be in the last one when it finally gave up the ghost too. He drove it every day, so is there anything so surprising about that?"

"Well, not—"

"Now we use a couple of Toyota four-by-four vans to get around the place and we haven't had any accidents. The money we spent on the jeeps? A total waste. And the new shed? That was one of Brian's ideas too—to build it with these prefabricated roof trusses and floor joists or something. It was going to save all kinds of money. Fine, no problem—as long as the wind didn't blow. But it didn't stand up to the first halfway decent storm we got."

"But it's stood up since."

"Sure, because it's been propped up and strengthened—see that concrete footing? Cost more money than it took to build it in the first place. Some savings. And I still don't trust it."

She was off and running now, chewing the cud of some old sense of grievance, real or imagined. Did Gideon know about some of the other accidents they'd been having? The pulper, had he heard about that?

He nodded. "One of the workers lost a finger."

Two fingers, Maggie told him. And why? Because Brian, Mr. MBA, was bent on automating production at Paradise. So he brought in the very latest, slickest equipment. Only he forgot about the human element. He didn't allow enough time for training. Maggie had demanded a week, but Brian had convinced Nick anyone could learn to operate it in a day.

"Well, Poppa and Brian were both wrong," she said bitterly, "only it's Puarei Marae who has to get along without his thumb and index finger."

It was much the same story with the bean sorter that had broken down several times and the drying furnace in the basement that had burned up $15,000 worth of other people's beans: more "improvements" of Brian's. Lots of attention given to researching the equipment, choosing the right model, drawing workflow charts . . . and zilch given to the *people* who had to make it work.

"The thing is, Gideon, for all his love of Tahiti, Brian never came close to understanding the people, the culture. And workflow charting, let me tell you, isn't part of the Polynesian culture. And I haven't even talked about the computerization. The thing is, you have to work *with* native values, not rely on typical Eurocentric misassumptions. You can't . . ."

She trailed off, apparently feeling that she'd gone on too vigorously and too long, considering the recency of Brian's death, or maybe that she was overstepping her bounds teaching an anthropologist about anthropology. She toyed, scowling, with one of the conch earrings. "Oh, heck, here I am making it sound as if Brian was this awful person, and he was anything but. He was the sweetest . . . my only point is that everybody goes around whispering about all these mysterious accidents, and there's nothing mysterious about them, nothing. Brian had a lot of new ideas, good ideas, and he was hell-bent on putting them into effect, but this is Tahiti, not New York. You can't go around messing with traditional cultural values and expect not to have any problems. People—"

She stopped again and laughed good-naturedly at herself. "There I go again. I guess I don't have to tell you all that."

"No. You're right, of course."

And yet he was oddly unsatisfied. It wasn't that he harbored any conviction that these incidents were prelude to Brian's murder—he still didn't honestly think there had been any murder—but the more the string of accidents was explained away, the more doubtful and uneasy he became about them. And in an unanticipated way, about Maggie. Was everything that had gone wrong truly Brian's doing, or was there a bit of revisionist history under way? The only thing she hadn't blamed on him was the rainy spring. Not yet anyway.

As they got out of the car Nick came from the shed, wiping his hands on a ragged brown towel. Shirtless, shoeless, wearing nothing but a pair of old, stained khaki shorts, he was as furry as a sheepdog.

"Ah, Maggie, you found him! Tour time, Gideon." He looked around as a dusty pickup truck crunched up the graveled road and pulled into the parking area. "Oh hell, here comes Antoine. This won't take any time at all. It's just one of the other growers. I've been doing some processing for him and we're still working out the costs. This'll just take a minute, Gideon."

"*Bonjour, Antoine, comment ça va?*" he boomed, striding toward the newcomer.

"Don't *comment ça va* me, you tight-fisted, money-grubbing sonofabitch!" replied Antoine, stepping down from his truck and slamming the door. He shook a piece of paper, a bill or a receipt, under Nick's nose. "Tell me what the hell you call this?"

"I don't know why," Gideon said to Maggie, "but I have this feeling this is going to take more than a minute."

"You're right," Maggie said. "These two have been known to go at each other for hours. It keeps their blood oxygenated. I think I'd better get Tari to give you the tour."

Through waves and gestures she communicated her intention to Nick, who responded through the screen of Antoine's gesticulations with a helpless shrug.

"I've been wanting you to meet Tari anyway," Maggie said as she took him around the shed to a loading dock at the rear where several men were wrestling hundred-pound burlap bags of coffee beans from the back of a pickup truck, loading them onto the weighing platform, recording the exact weights, and then emptying them into a pneumatic conveyor tube. "He's my prime example of employee development the way it *ought* to be done. The one with the clipboard—that's Tari."

At the sound of his name—Maggie's voice was like a trumpet most of the time—an immense man in a striped tank top shirt and shorts looked over one massive, brown shoulder. "'Lo, Maggie." The thin, piping voice didn't go with the powerful body.

"Hoa, maita'i anei oe?" Maggie said gravely, much the way Joel McCrea or Randolph Scott used to intone "How," when addressing the chief of all the Apaches, in order to show respect for the great Apache nation and the ways of their people.

"Oh, pretty good, Maggie. How you doing yourself?"

Tari looked a little embarrassed, or maybe it was only a reaction to Maggie's Tahitian, which didn't strike Gideon as any too accurate. From up close, Tari was not quite as gigantic as he'd first seemed, but he was built like a sumo wrestler—no, more like a giant baby, with a round, smiling face, fat, lusty arms and legs, and a belly like a beer keg. All told, three hundred amply fleshed, formidable pounds.

"Maita'i roa," replied Maggie solemnly. "Gideon, this is Tari Terui," she said proudly—and a little proprietorially, it seemed to Gideon. "Paradise Coffee's next operations manager. He's been doing an outstanding job of filling Brian's shoes."

"Oh, I don't know 'bout that," the huge man mumbled, shuffling wide, dusty feet in their thong sandals. Gideon got the impression that this was more than mere modesty. Under the naturally genial and placid planes of Tari's flat, broad face there was something worried.

"Nonsense," Maggie said. "What's bothering you?"

Tari looked at his feet. "Lot of things."

"Such as?"

Tari shrugged. "Accounts payable . . ." he mumbled unhappily. ". . . supply-invoice stuff . . ."

"Well, don't you worry about it," Maggie said, "we'll straighten it out at our Friday meeting. And if I can't make any sense out of it, we'll get Nelson or Rudy to explain. Don't worry, Tari, you're doing just fine." She beamed at the big Tahitian. "Tari's the wave of the future," she said to Gideon. "He's a role model for every Tahitian employee we have."

Tari glanced uncomfortably around, and Gideon caught the tail end of a scowl he cast at one of the workers, who had paused in his manhandling of the bags to eavesdrop with undisguised amusement. Obviously, being a role model to his fellow Tahitians was not something to which Tari aspired.

"Gideon is a friend of John's," Maggie told him, "and Poppa wants him to see the farm. Can you take an hour or so and show him around?"

"Sure, you bet," Tari declared, practically rolling his eyes with relief. Rattling around the plantation was clearly more to his liking than talking about accounts payable.

They started with the drying shed itself, a single room about eighty feet by a hundred, a good ten degrees warmer than it was outside, redolent with a pungent smell that Gideon associated more with wineries than with coffee plantations, and suffused with a milky glow from the light coming through the translucent walls and ceiling. The floor was made of wood planking, but except for a couple of cleared aisles down the center from each side, most of it was three or four inches deep in a sea of coffee beans ranging from greenish brown to palest beige and separated into different-colored sections by movable lengths of white plastic pipe. Workers shuffled slowly, sleepily, through them in the heat, spreading and rearranging the shallow heaps with homemade, blunt-toothed wooden rakes.

Tari, now in his element, was an enthusiastic and knowledge-able guide. Gideon learned that the beans varied in color be-cause they lightened as they dried, that drying took ten days to two weeks, depending on the weather, that they had to be raked and turned over three or four times a day to keep them from drying unevenly. He learned that when the coffee berries came in from the field they were loaded into the pulper, a gleaming, stainless-steel contraption of belts, pulleys, gears, conveyors, and tanks that took up one end of the shed, and then, via con-veyor belt, into several large vats, where they fermented for two or three days—that was where the winerylike fragrance came from—before being washed and spread on the floor to dry. And that was it. They were then bagged and shipped to warehouses and roasteries around the world.

"Interesting," murmured Gideon in the sober, receptive tone one uses at such times. "And so this is the pulper. Impressive piece of machinery."

"Plenty bells and whistles," Tari agreed, looking at it fondly.

"Looks as if you must have to be pretty careful around it."

He was fishing again, but Tari wasn't biting. "Oh yeah, you bet," he said amiably. "You sure don't want to get no parts caught in there."

"Mm. Seems to me I remember hearing that one of the men was hurt a while back."

"Yeah, two fingers chopped off, but now we got a training program. Nobody losing parts no more."

"I'm glad to hear it," Gideon said, speaking with a personal stake in the matter. Opening a bag of Weekend Blend some morning and finding somebody's parts in with the beans would be a hell of a way to wake up.

When they left the shed, Tari drove him up the mountain in one of the white Toyota vans, and with Gideon hanging on to the window frame to keep his seat—Maggie proved right about the goat-track roads—they bucked and wobbled over sinkholes, rocks, and streambeds. A fifteen-minute drive took them past neatly tended plots of Chinese vegetables and banana and breadfruit trees and up into the wilder, more spectacular vegetation of the interior: tall, arching acacias with their naked pink trunks wreathed with moss; flame trees alight with brilliant, red-orange flowers; a thousand kinds of ferns growing anywhere there was space. The temperature cooled when they moved underneath the cloud cover that hung about the top of Mt. Iviroa most afternoons. At about the two-thousand-foot level, Tari pulled over at the base of a hillside that had been cleared and re-planted.

He waved an arm. "Coffee trees."

They didn't look like trees to Gideon. Bushes, maybe, and not very impressive ones. Eight or nine feet tall, straggling, droopy, and undernourished-looking, they seemed like poor cousins to most other growing things on the mountainside.

"*These* are coffee trees?" he couldn't help saying.

Tari looked at him with amusement. "Sure, man, you bet. Big, fat trees—lousy berries. Crummy, skinny trees—berries taste great, all the flavor goes into them. This part here, we on the Blue Devil farm. Best damn coffee in whole world," he said reverently, and then a moment later: "Bar none, man."

The trees didn't look like trees and the farm didn't look like a farm; not the farms Gideon was used to (admittedly, not all that many). There were no neatly laid-out rows, no straight lines of furrowed earth. The spindly coffee trees were planted helter-skelter on the hillside, with other plants—banana, papaya, avocado—growing among them, seemingly at random.

But there was a reason for the apparent disorder, Tari was quick to let him know. Coffee trees did not replenish nitrogen in the soil, but banana, papaya, and avocado did. It was all a matter of conservation.

"Ah," said Gideon.

Tari plucked a berry from one of the trees, a little red fruit about the size and color of a small radish.

"Hey, Gideon, how many these buggers you think it take to make one pound coffee?"

"A hundred?" Gideon said, trying to please.

Tari, pleased, threw back his head and laughed. "Guess again, man."

"A thousand?"

"*Two* thousand! And they all got to be hand-picked, no machines, because they don't get ripe all the same time. See?" He showed him two berries growing on the same branch; one a bright red, ready for harvesting, the other as green and hard as a dried pea. "Two thousand, hand-picked!"

"Wow, no wonder it's expensive."

"You bet!" Tari plucked a ripe berry from the tree and squeezed it between thumb and forefinger. The coffee bean itself, a relatively large seed with a white, fibrous covering, burst from the berry into the palm of his other hand.

"You know what always gets me?" he said, studying it with what was surely affection. "This here is from the same kind of tree like cherries, you know, or peaches, I forget the name . . ."

"Drupes," said Gideon.

Tari showed mild surprise. Gideon had risen in his estimation. "Yeah, that's right, drupes. Only with cherries, peaches, you eat the fruit, throw away the pit. Simple, right? But coffee, you throw away the fruit, keep the pit. Then you got to dry it, roast it, grind it, pour hot water over it, and then drink the damn *water*. How you figure they ever think of it?"

Gideon smiled. "It beats the hell out of me, Tari. It was probably the same guy who first looked a lobster in the eye and had the nerve to wonder if there was something good to eat in there."

"Beats the hell out of me too," said Tari.

✳ ✳ ✳

As they bumped back down the mountain road, Gideon noticed something he hadn't spotted on the way up. Lying on its side in a jungly gully fifty feet below the road, half-overgrown with wild ginger and lantana, was the rusting carcass of a U.S. Army jeep, ghostly and forlorn, the white star still dimly visible on its olive-drab side.

"Is that the one that went over the side a few months ago?" Gideon asked.

"Yeah," Tari said. "No fun, man."

Gideon looked at him. "You were in it?"

For an answer Tari hooked a thumb behind his upper front teeth and popped them out: a finely made removable bridge consisting of the two central incisors. "Best you can buy. The boss, he ordered it for me from France." In it went again, with a little click. "And Brian, he bust his arm really bad. Two places, you could see the bones sticking right out. We damn near get ourselves killed. No fun, man," he said again. "I don't even like to talk about it."

For something nobody liked to talk about, Gideon thought, those accidents seemed to crop up a lot in conversation. "You're lucky you weren't killed," he said, hoping it might draw the big Tahitian out a little more.

It did. "You bet," he agreed soberly. "Maggie even luckier.

Brian, he the unlucky one. Didn't have no business riding around Thursday morning."

Thursday morning, it seemed, was when Maggie usually made her weekly personnel tour of the plantation, with Tari at the wheel. They would stop and chat with the workers at the various locations, eliciting gripes and suggestions and holding informal "tailgate sessions." The other four mornings of the week Brian and Tari made their normal production rounds. But on this particular Thursday morning, the Thursday morning that the jeep's rear axle decided to come loose at the worst section of the road, Maggie was scheduled to give a guest lecture on employee relations at the Lycée Technique de Hôtellerie et Tourisme in Papeete. So she and Brian had traded days: Maggie and Tari had made their rounds on Wednesday, and Brian and Tari on Thursday; the fateful Thursday.

The result? A compound fracture for Brian, two dislodged teeth for Tari, and a brush with death for both.

And Maggie? mused Gideon. Maggie had gotten off scot-free. Almost on its own, the thought tucked itself away for future retrieval.

Chapter 16

Gideon's single-minded intention, when Tari delivered him to the Shangri-La, had been to go to his room and buckle down to work on those symposium notes. But at the meeting of lawn and sand in front of his cottage—in front of each of the cottages along the strand—a net hammock was slung invitingly between two sturdy guava trees. As he passed it his resolution wavered, just a little. It was John's fault, really, for bringing up the idea of a hammock in the first place. But the thing was, it looked so comfortable swaying there in the cool, dappled shade, and it had been such a long time—years?—since he'd been in one, that he climbed in to get the feel of it, pushing off with his foot against a nearby lawn chair to start himself swinging. Overhead, the thick green leaves swayed soothingly back and forth against a cobalt sky.

He woke up an hour later, at a little after four, with his foot still hanging over the side, a warm breeze off the lagoon stirring the hair on his arms. He felt rested and loose. The temperature was about 70 degrees, the air like satin on his skin. Stretching away on either side of him, along the curving fringe of the beach, coconut palms nodded on slender, arching trunks. The air was perfumed with wildflowers and the crisp tang of the sea. He remembered the last weather report he'd heard before leaving home a day earlier: snow showers mixed with sleet and changing to freezing rain, but with a slight possibility of late-afternoon "sunbreaks," those rare, brief phenomena offered up almost daily throughout the gray winter by the sadistic weather forecasters of the Pacific Northwest.

Like Julie, he preferred coolness to warmth, fir trees to palms, and misty, pearl-gray skies to flat, hot, sunny ones, but, by God, he had to admit that there was something to be said for the tropics, particularly at this time of year. Assuming that the confusion over the exhumation order was some kind of mix-up that could be straightened out, he had three, maybe four, more days of summer ahead, three days to bake the winter hunch out of his shoulders, three days of tropical flowers, and lush fruits, and no sleet-changing-to-freezing-rain weather forecasts.

One long sunbreak.

"Hey, Doc, what is it with you, sleeping sickness? Come on, wake up, it's almost five o'clock."

"John," Gideon said with his eyes still closed, "I really wish you'd stop doing that. It's extremely annoying."

"What do you want me to do? Every time I need to talk to you, you're flat on your back. It's amazing. We haven't even been here one day and you're already going to seed."

Gideon smiled placidly. "It does seem that way, doesn't it?"

Well, why not? Going to seed was what you were supposed to do in Tahiti. Anyway, what was the hurry? Unless John had accomplished the unexpected with Nick, they still didn't have an exhumation order.

He yawned, stretched enjoyably, and pulled himself to a sitting position in the hammock. "How'd it go with your uncle?"

"Interesting. Come on, let's take a walk on the beach; I'll tell you about it. I mean, if you think you can stand the exertion."

* * *

"There's something I don't understand," Gideon said ten minutes later. "Why is it up to Nick anyway? Why isn't it your cousin Thérèse who's involved in it? It's her husband's body we're talking about, isn't it?"

"Not exactly. Brian and Thérèse never got married, you see—"

"They weren't married? I thought—"

"Well, as far as everybody's concerned, they *are* married—only they're really not. I never heard all the details, but the upshot is that Brian had an ex-wife somewhere, except she isn't exactly 'ex.' Didn't want him, but had some way of blocking him from getting a divorce."

"And Nick knew about that? It didn't bother him?"

John shrugged. "This is the South Seas. Just about everybody who washes up here and stays has something back home he'd just as soon not talk about. Anyway, the point I'm getting at is that Thérèse doesn't have any more say about what happens to Brian's body than anybody else does. And the main thing is, Brian's buried in this little cemetery up in a corner of the coffee plantation; it's private property and guess who it belongs to."

"Nick," Gideon said.

"Nick," John confirmed. "And Nick says no dice."

"Because he doesn't want to upset his daughter."

John didn't answer right away. They continued walking northward along the edge of the lagoon, their soles squeaking against the sand. On the landward side of the narrow beach were groves of coconut palms, and beyond them the land rose toward the hypnotically, impossibly green flanks of the jagged mountains that formed the island's core.

"So he says," John said at last.

Gideon glanced at him. "You don't believe him?"

"No," John said shortly, and then after another brief hesitation: "I'll tell you what I think. I think he got back here and thought things over, and pulled the plug on us because he's afraid somebody in the family killed Brian."

"Not the Mob?" Gideon stopped walking and stared at John. "Somebody in his own family—in your own family? Who?"

"I don't think he has any idea who, Doc. I think he's just worried that it might turn out that way. He never did think too much of the Mob idea. Neither did I, to tell you the truth."

"Neither did I, to tell you the truth. But what *does* he think, then? Why would he assume it's one of your relatives?"

"Well, he didn't tell me this, you understand, but there's been some pretty heavy-duty fighting going on between them for a few years now."

This came as a surprise. "So how come you're always telling me how great everybody gets along?"

"They do get along," John said defensively. "What the hell, we're a family like any other family. We can always find things to argue about."

"Like what?"

John shrugged and started them walking again. "Business," he said testily, his hands thrust into his pockets. "It gets pretty complicated; I never did get everything straight."

The family coffee business, he explained, was very much that: a family business. Nick was the sole owner, but his management team, consisting of Maggie, Nelson, and Rudy, also held shares in it. So had Brian, although in his case, the shares were actually held, and were still held, by Thérèse. This had been at Brian's suggestion; he had felt that the plantation had always been a family affair and was better off continuing that way. The suggestion, needless to say, had been willingly taken up by Nick.

What it all amounted to in practical terms was that instead of being paid salaries for their work, they all received a percentage of the profits. Nick's share was fifty percent, with the remaining fifty percent going to the others in ten or fifteen percent portions, depending on their positions in the organization. John wasn't positive what the amounts came to, but he believed that Nick had been getting over $300,000 a year recently, and the others from $70,000 to $100,000.

"A fair amount of money," Gideon observed.

"Sure, but that isn't what the real hassling's about."

The real hassling had begun about a year earlier, when something called Superstar Resorts International had set its sights on the plantation as the ideal property for its planned South Seas megaresort. They had made Nick a huge offer for the land; in the neighborhood of $5 million, John understood. And that was when the fly had landed in the ointment.

"You see, the way Nick drew up these so-called shares, whatever profit-percentage people have, they're entitled to the same percentage from any sale of the company. You following me?"

Gideon nodded. "So if they'd sold it, even a ten percent share would net half a million dollars. And Nick would come away with two and a half."

"You got it. And Superstar has upped the offer at least twice since then. Nick was right on the verge of selling a couple of times."

"But obviously he didn't."

"Nope. When it came down to it, Brian always talked him out of it."

There was only one boss of the Paradise Coffee plantation, John went on, and that was Nick Druett, founder and president; when big decisions were to be made, Nick made them. But he was open-minded, as autocrats went, and he liked to get the advice of his management team and his immediate family before committing to a major course of action. In this case, as John understood it, most of them had been eager to accept the offer and walk away with the money—but not Brian, who had made a strong, emotional appeal to Nick on the grounds that the plantation was the glue that held the family together; once it was sold, they would scatter to the four winds. And in the end it was this that had carried the day with Nick the Patriarch. Twice.

"And you think," Gideon said, "that Brian might have been killed by one of the others so they'd have a better chance of convincing Nick to sell?"

"Who knows? I think that's what *Nick* thinks. If you ask me, it's pretty far-fetched, but all I want right now is for you to have a look at Brian and tell me what *you* think.

"It's funny when you think about it," he mused after they'd gone a little farther. "I mean, here's Brian, the one guy who's not related to everybody else—he's not even an in-law, officially speaking—and he's the one who's always getting all choked up about family."

They stopped walking, and for a few moments John stared without speaking toward the white, curling ribbon of surf that marked the coral reef half a mile out, dividing the sea into a bright green foreground and a deep blue background. "Well, Brian didn't have any family of his own left, you know, and Nick was like a father to him. It went both ways—Brian was practically like a son to Nick too."

"But if that's so," Gideon said, "why would he call us off? Wouldn't he want to see the killer caught?"

"Would he? How would he feel if it turned out to be—just say—Thérèse? Or Céline? Or—"

"Or Maggie."

"Yeah, or—wait, what do you mean, Maggie? What'd you say it like that for?"

"A couple of things, John." He started them walking again. "Did you know that the day Brian had the accident with the jeep he wouldn't have been in it except for a change of schedule that Maggie arranged? Did you know she'd been in the drying shed for a couple of hours—all by herself—the night before it gave way and nearly killed Brian?"

"So?" John demanded aggressively. "What's that supposed to mean?"

"Probably nothing. But it's also pretty clear she wasn't particularly fond of Brian—"

"Sure, she was. She loved Brian. He was like a, like a—"

Brother to her, Gideon said to himself.

"—like a *brother* to her. Only once in my life did I ever see Maggie break down and bawl, and that was when she heard he was dead." His arms were flailing now, the way they did when he got stirred up. "Where do you come up with these ideas?"

"From talking to her," Gideon said, moving off a step or two to get safely out of range. "For someone who loved him she sure found a lot to criticize about him."

"Oh hell, Doc, that's just Maggie. You should hear her take after me sometimes; or poor old Nelson."

"John, relax. I'm sure you're right. I just thought I ought to mention it, that's all."

"Yeah, well, sure, of course." After a moment he smiled. "Sorry, Doc, I didn't realize I was so touchy. I apologize. Obviously, it's all right for *me* to say one of my family could be a killer—but not *you*. That's not right."

"Human nature, John. Don't worry about it."

"Well, but I do worry about it. We're a team, Doc. The last

thing I want is for you to hold back what you're thinking because you think it might hurt my feelings."

"Not a chance, you know that."

All the same, if a few vague uncertainties about his maternal cousin could bring him to the arm-waving stage, how was John going to feel if the finger of suspicion were to begin to point toward his own brother, Nelson? Gideon pondered that for a few steps, and then brought himself up short. Suspicion of *what?* Was he starting to wonder, against his own considered judgment and in the absence of anything close to plausible evidence, whether murder had been done after all?

The end of Nick's private beach was marked by a falling-down cyclone fence laid out across it, with a sign alongside in three languages. *"Propriété Privée,"* it said. Underneath was "Keep Off, Private Beach, This Means You," and underneath that, *"Tabu."* In the lower corner was a picture of a snarling dog.

"Gee, I wonder what they're trying to tell us," John remarked as they started back.

There was no one snorkeling along the hotel's beach, no one scuba-diving, no one sunning, and only one lumpy body in the long row of hammocks. A mile farther along the shore, in opulent contrast, the grounds of the modernistic Hotel Captain Cook were crammed with sunbathers and snorkelers. If this was a typical day at the Shangri-La, Gideon thought, Dean Parks wasn't doing as well as he claimed in his battle with the big players.

"John, what do you suggest we do now?"

"What do you want to do?"

"Well, you might want to stay on, but I think I ought to pack up and go home," said Gideon. "Regardless of what did or didn't happen to Brian, there's nothing here for me to do. I don't like living on Nick's money for nothing, and he's made it clear that he doesn't want us poking around after all. Neither do the police, so that would seem to be that. There's nothing we can do about it."

John stared at him, open-mouthed. "You just want to go home and forget anybody's been murdered?"

Gideon sighed. "John . . . the thing is, I don't really think anybody *has* been murdered. I've felt that way from the beginning, you know that." Well, more or less.

"You honestly think all those things were accidents?"

He hesitated. "Let's just say I think Thérèse's alternative hypothesis makes as much sense as anything else."

John frowned at him. "What's Thérèse's alternative hypothesis?"

"Pele's Revenge," Gideon said.

"Ah, you're probably right," John said with a smile, "but I just can't let go of it. Look, would you at least take a look at the death report? There are pictures."

"Brian's death report? Sure, I'd love to see it, but I don't think there's much chance of that."

John looked highly pleased with himself. "I've got it in my cottage."

"You—how did you manage that?"

"Easy. I stopped in at Bertaud's office on my way back and got on his case again."

"I bet he loved that."

"That's his problem. Anyway, I bugged him until he finally broke down and let me see it. I made copies of it all."

"He let you make copies? I'm amazed."

"He didn't exactly *let* me make them, he just left me in the records room with the folder, and there was this copier right there . . ." John spread his palms. ". . . and he didn't say I *couldn't*—"

Gideon held up his hand. "Don't tell me any more, John. I don't want to know these things. I'm a law-abiding man."

"Oh, I get it. But as long as I'm the one who does the dirty work and sticks his neck out, you don't mind looking at what I come up with, right? You just don't want to hear about it."

Gideon laughed. "I'd say that about sums it up. Let's see what you have. If there's anything there, I'll go back to Bertaud and wave it under his nose myself, how's that?"

"Spoken like a true skeleton detective."

The clasp-envelope that John brought from his cottage contained two typed sheets and six eight-by-ten-inch, black-and-white photographs of a body on a morgue slab. There were full-length shots from various angles and distances and two gruesome close-ups of the head, all a bit blurry, probably as a result of the photocopying. The corpse was in a relatively late stage of decomposition, beyond what forensic specialists referred to—with good reason—as the "bloated" stage, but not yet to the final or "dry" stage. In other words, while the process of decay was clearly and disagreeably under way, it wasn't far enough along to allow a useful examination of the bones. Add to that the blurriness and it was quickly clear that the pictures weren't going to be of much use.

John watched him expectantly as he leafed through the pictures, but Gideon shook his head. "I'm not going to be able to make anything out of these, John."

"Sure, you will, Doc," John said with simple confidence. "You always do." And then after a moment's reflection: "Almost always."

"Thanks, I think." Gideon dropped into one of the lawn chairs beside the hammock and turned to the printed material.

John wandered restlessly back and forth for a while, his hands in his pockets. "I'm gonna go over to the bar and bring back a beer," he said. "If it's open. God, this place is dead. You want one too?"

"Just something cold. Some juice, maybe."

John nodded. "Be back in a minute." But he paused before leaving. "Doc? Try and stay out of that hammock for a change, will you?"

Chapter 17

The printed sheets had nothing helpful to offer either. On top was the *acte de décès*, the certificate of death, filled out by the examining physician. The body of Brian Scott, a white male (American) age thirty-eight, had been found by two hikers from New Zealand on October 28, in rugged terrain near the Maoroa River, one kilometer east of Tehiupa on the island of Raiatea. The decedent, dressed in a sleeveless shirt, walking shorts, and socks, had been judged by Dr. Claude Masson to have been dead for seven to ten days. The manner of death was listed as *par hasard*—accidental; the cause as multiple internal injuries. These injuries had presumably been the result of a fall of some thirty meters from the path along the edge of the bluff immediately above. The remains had been shipped to Thérèse Druett of Papara, Tahiti, on October 30.

The other sheet was a brief case summary that took less than half the page. The body had been identified from a wallet in the hip pocket of the shorts and from a wristwatch identified by Thérèse Druett, common-law wife of the decedent. Decedent had been hiking and camping in the area since October 17. No autopsy had been deemed necessary. The decedent's remains and possessions, including a pair of walking sandals found near the body, had been crated and shipped to Thérèse Druett at her request. The report was signed by Alphonse Didier, *brigadier-chef*.

Nothing. Nothing unexpected, nothing unusual, nothing suspicious.

Gideon put the papers aside and returned with reluctance to the photographs for a more thorough examination. For a forensic anthropologist, he was downright squeamish, and a dead human body that has been lying outdoors for seven to ten days in warm, humid conditions is not a sight to appeal even to the strong-stomached.

Still he felt that he owed it to John to do what he could. He went back to his cottage to get a magnifying glass from his equipment case, sat down again to the photos, steeled himself, and began.

Corpses left outside in the summertime often lost ninety percent of their weight in a week or less, and Brian was no exception. Withered, much dwindled from what he had been as a living man, he lay on his back in a blood-caked T-shirt and shorts. There was no indication that carnivores had been at work, but that wasn't surprising in Polynesia, where the only native animals aside from birds were bats and rats, and not very many of those, and anyway, the rats had become rather delicate in their appetites, preferring young coconuts to everything else.

But even Polynesia had plenty of insects, and as usual they had concentrated heavily on Brian's face, assuming this *was* Brian. Maggots swarmed in frothy mounds, spilling from mouth, nasal aperture, and ruined eye sockets. The beetles had made their arrival too—scarabs, dermestids, carrion beetles—to feed and rear their young on what remained of the soft tissue and on the maggot masses. They were all there and hard at work, all the merry members of what is called, in the neighborly graveyard language of forensics, the host corpse community.

He shivered suddenly and raised his eyes to take in the healthy green guava leaves and the deep, clean blue of the sky beyond, then returned to the photo. The left arm appeared to be dislocated at the shoulder, and perhaps broken, but that was hardly remarkable in a fall of any distance. No picnic to go through, not that Brian was likely to have noticed, but once again nothing to excite suspicion.

He set the close-ups of the head on the flat arm of the chair and peered at them for some minutes, again learning little more. The hair was light, the teeth that were visible were unbroken and seemingly well-cared-for, and that was all he had to say. He leaned back in the deep chair and shook his head. That was it, then. The file gave them no grounds to press a murder investigation and no grounds to question the handling of the case. Unless John could get his uncle to change his mind about the exhumation, of which there appeared to be no chance whatever, he was simply going to have to accept the situation as it was.

He looked up to see John returning from the bar, drinks in hand.

*   *   *

"No reason to question the handling of the case?" John exploded. "You're out of your mind!" He leaped from his chair to pace furiously back and forth, his big hands chopping at the air again. "You call ten lousy lines a case summary? Why wasn't there an investigation? Why wasn't there an autopsy?"

"John, calm down, will you?" Gideon said, snatching his carton of Orangina out of the way. "There wasn't any reason for an autopsy; not from Didier's point of view. People fall off those trails all the time."

"Yeah, but he was alone, no one saw it happen—"

"That's not reason enough. Autopsies are expensive, you know that. There aren't enough pathologists in the world to autopsy everybody who gets killed without witnesses. You have any idea what percentage of accident and suicide victims get autopsied in the States?"

"No," John said grumpily, flopping into the other chair, "but I've got a hunch you're gonna tell me."

"Twenty percent," Gideon said. "One in five. You don't call for an autopsy unless there's valid reason to presuppose—"

Wearily, John flapped his hand. "Ah, forget it, what difference does it make anyhow? Thanks for your help. I appreciate it. Really." He swigged moodily from his bottle of Hinano and looked out to sea.

Gideon scowled, feeling ill-used. He was accustomed to people asking his professional opinion and then getting annoyed at him when it wasn't the one they wanted, but you'd think John would know better.

"I'm sorry," he said curtly. "I just haven't seen or heard anything from anybody that makes me think Brian's fall wasn't just what it was supposed to be."

John shrugged and took another swig.

There was a touchy silence while Gideon gathered the pictures together, slipped them into the envelope, and handed them across to John.

He got them halfway there and stopped rock-still, his arm out. The image of the picture on top of the stack was still in his mind's eye and one small peculiarity in it that he hadn't even been aware of noticing had just clicked into sharp, meaningful perspective.

"Holy cow," he said.

John looked up. "What?"

"John, I owe you an apology." Gideon tore open the envelope, pulled out the photograph on top, one of the full-body shots, and stared hard at it. "How could I have missed it?"

"What?" John said, his voice rising.

Gideon gave him the photograph. "Look at this." He handed across another one. "Here, you can see it in this one too. Damn, it just didn't register. I wasn't looking for it."

John put his beer down on the lawn and studied the picture. "I'm looking. What am I supposed to be seeing?"

"The hand. Look at the hand. He must have been lying on it, or it was in the shade or something, but for whatever reason, the decay process isn't quite as advanced, and there's still a fair amount of flesh left. If you look at the hand—"

"The hand, the hand . . ." John cut in impatiently. "*Which* hand, goddammit?"

Gideon leaned across to tap the picture. "The *right* hand, goddammit. Don't you see?"

"See *what?*" John cried. "All I see is a bunch of maggots."

"No, you don't. You see a *line* of maggots, not a bunch. Can't you see what that means?"

"No, I can't see what it means," John shot back. "Hell, it took *you* long enough to figure it out and you're a big-time Ph.D. I'm just a poor, dumb cop, remember? I have to have things explained to me."

They had been glowering at each other, almost nose to nose, and without quite knowing why they burst out laughing.

"John, I'm sorry," Gideon said. "I'm a little testy too, but it's because I'm mad at myself, not you. I can't believe I almost didn't pick this up."

He got out of his chair to stand beside John's so that they were both looking at the pictures right side up.

"Now look at this." With his forefinger he traced a column of maggots that ran diagonally from the web of the right thumb, across the palm, and onto the lowest joint of the little finger.

"It's a defense wound," he said.

"Defense wound?" John murmured with interest, peering at the photos.

"It couldn't be anything else. From a blade; a knife, probably. Brian tried to fight somebody off and this is where he caught hold of the blade."

John took Gideon's magnifying glass, leaned over the pictures, and shook his head. "I can't see any wound at all. Just the maggots."

"If there are maggots there, there's an opening underneath," Gideon said. "And an opening in the palm of the hand is a wound."

As he had frequently told John and told him now again, he was no forensic pathologist; the less he had to do with bodily fluids, soft tissues, and nasty secretions, the happier he was. But he had been involved in enough cases by this time to know that the insects that help decomposition along do it in a systematic and predictable manner. Within minutes of death the Calliphoridae—the blowflies—arrive, soon to be followed by their many cousins. These insects head directly for the natural openings—in a clothed body, the eyes, nose, mouth, and ears; in and around these moist, dark recesses they lay their eggs in yellowish white masses easily visible to the naked eye (and looking for all the world like wads of grated Parmesan cheese, as an entomologist had once pointed out to him, thereby permanently changing his attitude toward that formerly relished cheese). Within a day, in warm weather, the eggs have hatched into great, wriggling clumps of the blind, wormlike creatures known as larvae or maggots, which then begin their allotted task of consuming the body's soft tissues.

And if there are open wounds, the same process occurs there.

Eventually the larvae spread out from these initial sites, but for a while they remain busily clumped around the body's orifices, natural and otherwise. Thus the maggots on Brian's face.

Thus too, the diagonal, linear column of maggots on his right palm; they implied a diagonal, linear wound beneath.

"Okay, I can buy all that," John said, "but why defense wounds? Why couldn't he have cut his hand in the fall?"

"Pretty unlikely. First, I can't see any scrapes or bruises anywhere else on his right arm; just this one clear cut on his right hand. And second, it *is* a cut—not an abrasion, not a tear, not a puncture. Look how neatly lined up the maggots are. One long, straight, slicing cut. What but a blade would be likely to do that? Not to mention that it's precisely where you'd expect a defense wound to be."

Gideon didn't expect John to take much convincing, and he didn't.

"Doc, you're *right*," he shouted, clambering up out of his chair. "See, did I tell you or didn't I tell you?" There went the arms again. "Come on, let's go see Bertaud. There's no way he can argue with this."

"John, it's going on six o'clock. He's not going to be in his office."

"Wherever he is, then," John said righteously. "He's the head man. He always supposed to be available."

"Maybe so," Gideon said tactfully, "but do you suppose maybe he's seen enough of us for one day?"

John laughed; the sudden, burbling, babylike explosion that never failed to make Gideon laugh along with him. "Of *me*, you mean. Yeah, you're right about that. Okay, tomorrow morning then. Nick's expecting us up at the house for dinner about now anyway."

They looked at each other, an unspoken question in the warm air.

"I say we don't mention this to Nick right now," John said after a moment. "Let's find out what Bertaud says first. Besides, Nick's the one who didn't want anything about it mentioned at dinner, right?"

"I agree, but you know you're going to wind up in the dog-house with him when he finds out we went to Bertaud behind his back, don't you?"

John shrugged this off. "It won't be the first time. He always gets over it fine. Come on, time to go up and meet the family."

Gideon looked down at the dusty clothes he'd been wearing all day; in Papeete, on *le truck*, and at the plantation. "Give me a minute, I'm a little travel-stained for dining. I ought to change first."

John guffawed. "Forget it, come-as-you-are is the order of the day. Dining at Nick's is like dining at Chucko's All-You-Can-Eat, except the food's better."

Chapter 18

The setting was better too. Dinner was *al fresco*, on a lush, rolling lawn that formed a promontory extending two hundred feet seaward from the house, hanging ten feet above the beach and reminding Gideon of nothing so much as a gigantic seaside golf green. Along one side, a stand of coconut palms and elegant, gray-green mapé trees had been thinned out to make a pleasant, shaded grove, and there, just out of range of falling coconuts, the Polynesian feast that Nick had promised was being prepared by a busy team of Tahitians in tank top shirts, shorts, and baseball caps. Driftwood fires smoldered in two longitudinally split fifty-gallon oil drums set on pipe-metal frameworks, and mahimahi steaks, sliced pork, and huge Taravao Bay prawns were just beginning to sizzle on the grills atop them.

A few feet away, fresh palm fronds had been laid over a twelve-foot-long table to serve as a base for trays of fruit—neatly sliced papaya, watermelon, pineapple, and coconut—and a variety of native foods: *poisson cru,* the lime-marinated tuna salad that was Tahiti's version of sashimi; *fafa,* a dish of taro greens, chopped chicken, and coconut milk that would have passed muster in a soul-food restaurant; and a few other fruit, vegetable, and seafood combinations that Gideon couldn't name. About the only nod in the direction of Europe was the substitution for taro root and breadfruit of thin loaves of crusty, flaky French bread, which the bakers of Papeete had long ago learned to make almost as well as their counterparts in Paris. That and the well-stocked bar.

By the time that Gideon and John arrived, it was plain that the bartender, a coffee-guzzling Tahitian who contributed the sole touch of formality by wearing a waiter's white jacket over his shorts and Bart Simpson T-shirt (*"Don't have a cow, man"*), had been keeping busy. The Druett clan, nibbling *crudités* and sipping their drinks at a large, round table gave every appearance of being well-oiled. The laughter, loud talk, and heated debate were audible from a hundred feet away, and when the two men came into sight they were warmly greeted by Nick—warmly enough for Gideon to feel a few pangs of guilt about not being forthcoming with him—steered to the bar, and then hauled off to be welcomed by, and in Gideon's case introduced to, the others at the table.

There were six of them altogether: the three that Gideon had already met—Céline, Maggie, and Nick himself—along with Nick's other daughter, the beautiful Thérèse; John's older brother, the imperious Nelson Lau; and John's deadpan, ironic cousin, Rudy Druett, the roastmaster at Whidbey Island, who was in Tahiti for the time being, holding down some of Brian's old responsibilities and helping to prepare Tari Terui to shoulder them on his own when the time came.

Playing in the grass in the care of a nanny a few yards away were the Twin Terrors, Claudette and Claudine, Thérèse's daughters, two mumpish, fat-cheeked, un-terrible-looking little girls in pink-and-white frocks who refused outright, despite their grandfather's urging, to address Gideon as Uncle Giddie, which suited Gideon just fine.

He was accepted more readily by the adults, but naturally enough it was John who got most of the attention. Thérèse, every bit as meltingly lovely as John had told him she was, hugged him for a long time, bowing her slender neck to press her face sweetly into his shoulder before she let him go. John, embarrassed but pleased, clumsily stroked her hair and murmured a few words. But the brotherly embrace with Nelson, Gideon couldn't help noticing, was less spontaneous, a mere momentary resting of the fingertips on each other's upper arms, with a good foot and a half of open space between the two men.

Their greeting was equally restrained:

"John," Nelson said, his cool tone rising slightly.

"Nelson," John replied in kind.

When everyone was seated again, with Gideon tucked between Céline and Rudy, there were a lot of questions for John—about his job, about Marti, about when they were going to start having a few little Laus—and from there the conversation turned to general family reminiscences and eventually to stories about Brian. It had been a week now since the news of his death, and enough alcohol had been consumed so far tonight, to make the atmosphere more jolly than mournful, more like a wake than a funeral.

Nick, dressed in the work-stained shorts he had been wearing that afternoon, plus a striped tank top and a faded, curly-brimmed Boston Red Sox baseball cap, basked in his dual role of paterfamilias and number-one storyteller. Gideon, with little to contribute, sat back and sipped his Scotch-and-soda, put the reason that he was in Tahiti more or less out of his mind, and gave himself over to enjoying the anecdotes, the shared affection that flowed around him, and the people themselves. Interesting people, wonderfully different from the quiet, undemonstrative uncles and aunts that had made the Thanksgiving and Christmas dinners of his childhood such excruciating ordeals to a boy of eleven or twelve; he could still remember entire meals, or so it seemed to him now, when the only sounds from a dozen diners had been the steady, private clicking of forks and scraping of knives on the plates.

Not so the Druetts and the Laus, who were animated and spontaneous enough for three families. True, they had their idiosyncracies—maybe Nelson was a little too self-important, and Maggie was a little too brusque, and Rudy a little too vinegarish, and Céline a little too self-absorbed . . . but they were a lively, entertaining bunch—and they all seemed genuinely fond of John (even Nelson, in his own superior way) and for that alone he liked them.

This relaxed and pleasant interlude went on until a private dispute between Maggie and Nelson grew too loud to be ignored. They were arguing about Tari Terua, and Maggie was flushed with anger.

"If you're saying that Tari is—is embezzling, or—or—"

"Oh, spare me," Nelson said. "I'm not accusing him of being a crook, for God's sake—"

"So what are you accusing him of?"

"Of screwing up, if you'll pardon the expression. The man is simply—and I've said this from the beginning, I don't think anyone can deny that—the man is simply not capable of handling figures. In the few weeks that he's had access to them, our books have become an incomprehensible mess. He finds something that doesn't make sense to him in accounts payable, and rather than come and ask someone in a position to know, he 'corrects' the entry, so that naturally it is no longer consistent with either the purchase order or the invoice—"

"You've never given him a fair chance, you've—"

"May I say something?" Rudy interrupted. "Unprecedented though it may be, Nelson is actually making a cogent point. I've been concerned with Tari's—shall we say, whimsical—approach to the finances myself."

"Then why aren't you helping him instead of telling us? You're supposed to be coaching him, not criticizing him behind his back."

"I've been trying, Maggie," Rudy said, "but getting the man to understand is an ordeal approximately on par with a double root canal. No, worse. It's like having to sit through an entire performance of *Cats.*"

"I'm not saying it's his fault," Nelson cut in. "It's a well-known fact that the Tahitian numerical system lacks—"

"Oh, balls," Maggie said disgustedly.

"People," Nick admonished quietly. "We have company."

But Nelson was just warming up. "Let me give you just one example—our account with Java Green Mountain. We owe them for four thousand pounds of beans, duly purchased at $12.45 a pound and due at the end of the month. That's $49,800."

"Nelson . . ." Nick said a little less patiently.

"Only our friend Mr. Terui took it upon himself to 'correct' it for us. I suppose you could say he made only one *teeny* mistake, shifting the decimal point one little place to the left. But what would the result have been if I hadn't caught it? We would have sent Green Mountain a check for $4,980 and not the $49,800 we owe them."

Nick burst out laughing. "Hey, I like the guy's approach. Maybe we should put him in charge of the books."

Predictably, this failed to amuse either Nelson or Maggie.

"You don't *want* him to succeed," Maggie said hotly. "Neither of you, not really. You just—"

Fortunately, one of the workers yelled "Chowtime!" from the cooking area at this point, whereupon everybody headed for the buffet table, most of them making a detour at the bar first. Gideon refreshed his Scotch, then helped himself to rice, string beans, and grilled mahimahi, surprising and perhaps offending the server by declining her offer to dress the fish with coconut milk hand-wrung from a clump of pulverized coconut wrapped in cheesecloth. Coconut milk was the one staple of the sweet, pleasantly bland Polynesian diet that Gideon could do entirely without. No doubt it would look pretty good if you were perishing of thirst on a desert island, but it was hardly something you'd use to spoil a two-inch-thick chunk of nicely seared mahimahi.

"Hey, Gideon," Céline said as she resettled herself beside him with her plate, "why you think my hair's so thin?"

"Oh, it's not really that—"

"Sure, it is. You a scientist. Guess."

"Well, it's hard to say. In a lot of people—"

"Tennis."

Gideon studied his Scotch. "Tennis," he said.

"That's right, tennis. Used to play all the time. Douglas Fairbanks teach me. Junior, not father. You looking at the number-one player, Papeete Racquet Club, 1948, '50, '51."

"But how," Gideon asked, intrigued now, "did tennis affect your hair?"

Céline laughed. She had tiny, rounded teeth, like little pearls. "Not tennis, God love you. Too many showers with lousy shampoo." She shook her head ruefully. "Didn't have no Vidal Sassoon back then. Oh-oh, they at it again."

This last was a reference to Maggie and Nelson, whose arena had now shifted to the French plans to renew nuclear testing, suspended since 1992, at Mururoa atoll, southeast of Tahiti. Nelson was all for them because of the economic benefits that a renewal of testing would bring.

"And what about the radiation?" Maggie wanted to know, having more than recovered her composure since the earlier dispute.

"Poppycock," said Nelson. "Do you seriously think, for one moment, that the French government would put our lives at risk? Don't be ridiculous."

Maggie looked pityingly at him. "Unbelievable," she said through a mouthful of prawn.

Nelson waggled a finger at her. "Can you point, in all honesty, to a single verified illness from all the previous tests?" Nelson demanded. "Has a radioactive cloud ever once passed over Tahiti? Has it? Has it?"

Aside from a faint similarity in the set of their lips, Nelson was about as different from John as one brother could be from another. Where John was big and beefy, Nelson was compact, with small, feminine hands and feet; where John seemed to take up more space than his size strictly demanded, Nelson seemed to fill less; where John was generally easygoing but easy to ignite, Nelson seemed to operate at a constant, irritable simmer. And altogether unlike John, he appeared to be totally devoid of humor.

Add the finicky little mustache—two dainty, symmetrical, upturned commas—to everything else, and John's older brother put Gideon in mind of nothing so much as a pompous fussbudget of a hotel manager in morning coat and striped pants; the little man who postured and sniffed behind the reception desk (and said things like "poppycock" and "don't be ridiculous") in one old Hollywood comedy after another, only to end up being put inevitably in his place by a suave and impeccable Cary Grant, or David Niven, or Katharine Hepburn. Huff and puff as he might, there was simply something about Nelson that made it hard to take him seriously.

Even now, while his finger remained leveled magisterially at the space between Maggie's eyes, she continued to chew away at her prawn, unruffled. "If those tests are so safe . . ." she finally said when she was good and ready, then chewed some more.

"Yes," an impatient Nelson prodded, "if those tests are so safe . . . ?"

". . . then why don't they blow them up over France?"

There was a splutter of laughter from Nick and the others. Nelson merely stared at Maggie. "If you're not going to be serious," he said scornfully, "I don't see the point of discussing it any further."

"Good!" Nick said, whacking the table. "It's about time."

"Besides," Nelson went on, addressing the group at large, "there's something else we need to talk about." He waited for the others to quiet down and listen, which they didn't. "We have a new offer from Superstar."

That got their attention. A near-perceptible current sizzled around the table. Conversations stopped in mid-sentence. Forks were laid on plates. Faces that had been relaxed and open-countenanced a moment before, abruptly looked shifty and cunning. Gideon and John exchanged glances, both thinking the same thing: maybe the connection between Superstar's offers and Brian's death wasn't so far-fetched after all. Half the people around them looked ready to kill over it right now.

"Umm . . . Superstar?" Maggie said off-handedly.

Nelson nodded significantly. "In this afternoon's mail."

"For God's sake," Rudy said, "don't those people ever give up? What do they want to give us now, Rockefeller Center?"

"No," said Nelson, "as a matter of fact—"

"Now, wait." Nick was on his feet and leaning over the table, his long arms propped on sandy-haired knuckles (in a strikingly simian manner, Gideon couldn't help observing). "This is a family dinner, not a corporate business meeting. And we have company—"

"John's not company," a tipsy Maggie said, raising her glass to her cousin.

"Well, Gideon is. There's no reason this can't keep till tomorrow morning."

"I won't be here tomorrow morning," Nelson said. "There's a chamber of commerce meeting in Papeete."

"All right, Wednesday."

"Sorry, I'll be in Hawaii Wednesday," Rudy contributed. "Pacific Growers meeting."

"All right, Th—"

"No can do," said Maggie. "Training sessions morning and afternoon."

"They've asked for an answer by the end of the week," Nelson said.

Nick was starting to show his frustration. "Well, that's too damn bad," he snapped, "they just might have to wait. For Christ's sake, we're having dinner! You think John and Gideon came all the way out here to listen to us hash over company business?"

Good question, Gideon thought; he wouldn't mind the answer to that himself. What *had* they come for?

"Hey, don't worry about us," John said with another sidewise glance at Gideon. "Go ahead and talk about it. It'll probably take less time than arguing about whether you should or shouldn't talk about it."

At that Nick capitulated, taking his seat and throwing up his hands with a sigh. "Go ahead and talk, what do I know?"

Now Nelson stood up. "As I see it, it's a relatively straightforward proposition."

It was. Superstar Resorts International, of Omaha, Nebraska, had upped its offer for the property by a generous ten percent, said amount to be—

"What about the training center?" Maggie interrupted.

"The earlier stipulation still stands. Two acres to be set aside as a training and placement institute for young Tahitians interested in entering the hotel and tourist industry. Adequate funding to be provided."

Maggie jerked her fist with boozy satisfaction. "All *right!*"

"And that's it, really," Nelson said. "Other than the money, the earlier offer holds in its entirety. What's your reaction, Nick?"

Nick inclined his head thoughtfully. "It's a lot of money . . ." Maggie, Rudy, and Nelson started speaking at once, with Nelson carrying the day through sheer tenacity. "Not only is it a lot of money, Nick, but it's the right time to get out of the coffee business. Are you aware—"

"Out of the coffee business and into what?" Nick asked.

"What about Bora Bora?" Maggie said. "What about that destination resort you're always talking about building on the Bora Bora property? With this kind of money, couldn't you just up and do it?"

Nick gave it some thought. "Maybe I could at that," he said quietly, and the look in his eyes made it clear that the idea had its attractions. Nick Druett was an entrepreneur at heart, Gideon realized, not a coffee baron, or a land baron, or any other kind of baron. For men like Nick, the possibility of something new, of something big, of making something from nothing, was what got them out of bed every morning.

"Not me," said Céline flatly. "I'm not going to Bora Bora. No art supplies on Bora Bora. No nothing on Bora Bora. Tahiti is plenty bad enough."

"But you wouldn't have to *live* on Bora Bora, Momma," Maggie said. "You could live anywhere. You could—"

"May I just finish my point?" Nelson cut in. He was still standing at his chair and he spoke directly to Nick. "I think it's time for us to take a good look at market trends. Has anyone besides me given any thought to the fact that coffee consumption, worldwide, has been going *down*, not up? That despite all the talk about a coffee boom, people consume less than half of what they did thirty years ago? That the world market has been stagnant for decades? That with Japanese demand driving up prices and higher wages driving up costs, the profit window for growers shrinks every year? I grant you, Paradise is doing fine for the time being, but all the same—"

"All the same," a mocking drone interrupted, "the reports of coffee's demise are greatly exaggerated."

The comment had come from Rudy, on Gideon's right. One of the three Caucasians at the table—the others were Nick and Gideon—he was the only one there who was from the "other" side of the family, being the son of Nick's dead brother, and the only one who had spent most of his life in the continental United States as opposed to Tahiti or Hawaii. As a result he had contributed little beyond droll, oblique footnotes to the family reminiscences.

He was far from oblique now, however. The only stagnant part of the market was the *robusta* sector, the others were crisply informed; the big industrial roasters, the Folgerses, the Maxwell Houses. The *arabica* sector, the specialty growers and roasters, were doing better than fine, and not just for the time being either. They now had twelve percent of the market, up from less than one percent only a few years ago, and were still climbing with Paradise near the front of the pack. As for coffee prices, when had they *not* been going up and down and up again? Back in the eighteenth century it had been $4.68 a pound for ordinary green beans, four times what it was now—had they known that?

They hadn't. "Even so—" said Nelson.

But Rudy wasn't easy to cut off when he chose not to be. Did they know that the coffee industry employed almost thirty million people in one capacity or another? Would they care to guess what the earth's most-traded commodity just happened to be?

"Coffee?" asked John, being helpful.

"Wrong," said Rudy, "petroleum. Now: Would anyone care to guess the world's second-most-traded commodity?"

"Coffee?" asked John.

"Excellent guess," said Rudy. "Somebody give that man a coconut. Last year, eleven billion pounds were traded at the wholesale level alone."

For all his waspishness, Rudy was amusing in a dry, puckery kind of way. With his balding dome, his pruney, disapproving mouth, and his baggy-eyed sad sack of a face, his sharp, funny thrusts rarely failed to surprise.

"I take it," Nick said, on the dry side himself for the moment, "that you're suggesting that we don't accept their offer?"

Rudy nodded. "As before, *padrone*."

The others started talking again. Nick held up his hand. "Let's save some time. "Maggie, Nelson—you think it's time to sell."

More nods. "A training center would be a fantastic legacy, Poppa," said Maggie, her eyes shining. "A way to pay back all we've plundered from the island."

"Right, plundered. And Céline? You'd still like to sell the farm, of course?"

"You bet, Nicky! Buy a nice villa in Antibes, get out of this dump."

"So everyone feels the same as they did before," Nick said reflectively. "The only thing that's changed is the money." He turned to his right. His voice, his entire manner, became gentler. "Thérèse, do you want to say anything, honey?"

Thérèse looked startled. She too hadn't said much until now, and what little she'd said had left Gideon with the impression that she was very sweet, very solicitous of others—of John, of her parents, of her children—and not very bright. Not very self-assured either. Most of her remarks faded away in mid-sentence, in a soft, not unattractive flurry of confusion and discomposure: oh gosh, she seemed to be saying, there I've gone and put my foot in my mouth again, haven't I?

That said, she was certainly a knockout, with clear, fresh skin somewhere between copper and bronze, features that combined the best of her Chinese and American heritage, and as classically beautiful, heart-shaped, and perfectly symmetrical a face as Gideon had ever seen.

"What a skull she must have under there," Gideon had said to John in quiet admiration shortly after they arrived.

"You be sure and tell her that, Doc," John had said. "I mean, what female wouldn't love to hear that? No wonder you swept Julie off her feet."

Thérèse's reply to Nick's question was, as usual, self-effacing. As far as she was concerned, she would be happy with whatever he decided—but in her heart of hearts she hoped they wouldn't sell, that was all.

Nick prompted her to continue.

Thérèse chewed her lip and went hesitantly forward. Since she had been a little girl, not a day had passed, not a single meal, when coffee hadn't been discussed, and pondered over, and argued about. For as long as she could remember, the growing of coffee had been the focal point of the family. More than that, much more, it was the coffee farm into which Brian had poured so much of his energy and thought and devotion. He had left his stamp on it, and to her—she knew how silly this sounded—it was a kind of monument to him. The idea of abandoning coffee simply because someone offered them money—did they really need more money?—of letting all that work and achievement be bulldozed away for just another tourist hotel . . .

As usual, she trailed off into mumbled fragments. "I'm sorry . . . I just . . . I can't really . . . you know . . ." She hunched her shoulders and looked down at her hands.

Treacly as it was, Thérèse delivered it with such patent, awkward sincerity that Gideon found himself moved. Nick was moved too. Moist-eyed, he put his hand over his daughter's.

Nelson, who was not moved, rapped peevishly on the table. "Pardon me, but may I suggest that this has nothing whatever to do with Brian, for God's sake? We grow *beans* here, not holy relics, and the reason we grow them is so people can make something called coffee out of them. And what is coffee? Coffee is no more than a mixture of burnt hydrocarbons, alkaloids, and mineral salts suspended in an aqueous solution . . ."

That was one way to look at it, Gideon thought.

Next to him, Rudy raised his glass of Médoc in a salute to Nelson. "Here's to a true romantic," he said.

Nelson glared briefly at him. "My point is—"

"Enough," Nick said, his hand still on Thérèse's. "Tell Superstar we're still not interested. We're doing fine right here."

Thérèse, still looking down, said something so softly that Gideon couldn't hear it but read it on her lips. "Thank you, Poppa."

"Anybody have any more comments they just have to make?" Nick asked.

They knew better than to bother. Nelson sulked. Maggie pouted. The others went back to eating.

"That's that, then," Nick said, his spirits visibly lifting. "Dessert time."

He turned in his chair to call over his shoulder.

"Hey, Poema . . . you suppose we could get a cup of coffee around here?"

Chapter 19

"You have reached Julie and Gideon Oliver," Gideon was informed by his own voice, sounding very much like a robot, and a pretty listless robot at that. "We aren't available to take your call, but if you'll leave a message at the tone we'll get back to you."

This was disconcerting. Why *wasn't* Julie home? It was after 10:00 in Tahiti—past midnight in Port Angeles—and she hadn't said anything about going anywhere for the night. He chewed his lip for a few moments before it occurred to him to press the pound button to see if she had left him a message. When he did he was immediately relieved to hear her voice.

"Hi, love," she said, sounding very much like Julie; bright, and sparkling, and pretty. "I hope you remembered to listen for this message, because it's the sort of thing you always forget you can do, and if you call me and I'm not home and you don't know where I am you'll worry, right? But then if you *did* forget, then you're not listening now anyway, and you can't hear this, and if you *didn't* forget, then obviously you *are* listening, so what's the point of my babbling on about it?"

Gideon smiled as she caught her breath.

"Anyway, since you weren't going to be home for a while, I thought I might as well get out in the field for a couple of days and join the winter elk count in the Hoh quadrant; it's better than sitting behind a desk at the admin center, although you probably don't think so."

She was right about that. Two days of moldering in the raini-est river valley in the United States during the wettest, coldest, gloomiest month of the year, never getting quite dry, never get-ting quite warm, was not his idea of a good time. He liked the Northwestern winters all right, but he preferred to look out at them through a double-paned window with a log fire crackling in the fireplace behind him. And he preferred dry beds to wet sleeping bags. For an anthropologist, as she sometimes re-minded him and as he readily admitted, he had an unseemly fondness for the soft life.

"So that's where I am," she went on. "I hope everything's all right in Tahiti and I hope your corpse isn't too terribly messy. I'll talk to you when I get back. Hi to John. Tell him I'm meet-ing Marti for lunch on Wednesday. And that's about it. I miss you, Gideon. I wish you were already back." She paused. Her voice softened and dropped a notch. "I *do* love you."

"I love you too," he said to the recording, then left a message on the machine to that effect.

He leaned back, warmed by the call but feeling oddly vexed too. It didn't take him long to figure out why: he was always a little grumpy when Julie was away from home. The fact that he wasn't there either had nothing to do with the matter. When somebody traveled, he liked it to be *him*. Julie he preferred safe at home where she belonged—not that he would ever admit it to her. It was an attitude he didn't seem to have much control over, probably a genetic residue dating back to *Australopithecus afarensis* and before: man come back to cave from hunt, man want find woman waiting, cooking, loving . . . not out chasing stupid elk.

Well, what the hell, it was dangerous, wasn't it? What if they stampeded or something?

But of course he had to laugh at himself, remembering how extraordinarily capable Julie was; whom did he know that could take care of herself better in the out-of-doors? In fact, hadn't she once found and rescued *him* after he'd gotten himself hopelessly lost, confused, and miserable in the deep woods?

He was still thinking about that when he fell asleep with a smile on his face.

* * *

The following morning at 9 A.M. Gideon and John again appeared at the *gendarmerie* on the avenue Bruat. They were treated in the same supercilious manner by the same supercilious clerk, but this time made to wait half an hour before being admitted to Colonel Bertaud's presence. By the time they were seated in the commandant's office John was already steaming, not a good sign.

Bertaud was not in a good mood either. "And what have we this morning, gentlemen?" was his soft, steely greeting. "A new murder to report?" The folder in front of him remained open, the fountain pen remained between his fingers, poised to write.

"No, the same old one," John said bluntly.

All things considered, Gideon thought, not an auspicious beginning.

"Colonel," he said, "we're sorry to bother you again, but we've come up with something that I think will interest you. I looked at the photographs of Brian Scott's body yesterday, and in my opinion there's pretty good reason to think he was stabbed to death."

Bertaud screwed the cap on his pen. "The photographs?"

"These," John said, and handed him the clasp-envelope across the desk.

Bertaud opened it and slid the contents out. "The top two," Gideon said. "If you look at——"

"You made photocopies without asking for permission?" Bertaud said to John. "No doubt that is the way the FBI conducts itself in America, but——"

"If I asked for permission, would I have gotten it?" John shot back.

"Certainly not," said Bertaud.

Gideon repressed a sigh. It was looking like a long morning. "Colonel," he said, "with your permission I'd like to show you what I found."

"What *you* found," Bertaud said, focusing his attention on him as if he hadn't really been aware of him before. "Forgive me, but you are . . . ?"

"I'm a forensic anthropologist."

"Ah, you're the gentleman who was going to examine the body?"

"Yes," Gideon said, surprised. He'd thought that Bertaud had understood as much.

"He's famous in America," John pointed out as Gideon winced. "They call him the Skeleton Detective. The Bureau uses him all the time for its biggest cases."

This had the effect on Bertaud that Gideon might have predicted. One corner of a sleek gray eyebrow went up a few millimeters, the sharp, knowing eyes narrowed, the mobile lips pursed. "I see. Well, then, I am flattered that the great Skeleton Detective would concern himself in our small affairs. You were saying . . . ?"

Gideon was starting to feel the way John did about Bertaud but where would it have gotten them to show it? The colonel held the cards, all fifty-two of them, and there was no point in antagonizing him any more than he already was. Gideon nodded politely and began to explain his findings. Impatient and preoccupied at first, Bertaud soon seemed to grow genuinely interested. After a few minutes he had the original file brought in, in hopes that the photographs might be sharper, but they were equally blurry. At one point Gideon had the impression that he was on the edge of swaying him, but in the end Bertaud remained unconvinced.

"No, Dr. Oliver," he said with a sigh, "it's all extremely interesting but in the end simply not persuasive. What do we have after all is said and done?" He treated them to a full Gallic shrug—shoulders, mouth, chin, eyebrows, and hands. "A group of maggots that might or might not be—"

"A *line* of maggots," John pointed out.

"A line, then. In any case it's simply not enough. I'm sorry, gentlemen. There will be no police interference. I cannot justify it."

The interview was over but John wouldn't say die. "Not enough for what?" he demanded. "We're not asking you to bring charges, we don't want you to arrest anybody, we just want the body dug up so that Dr. Oliver here can have a look at it. Then you take it from there. Or don't take it, depending on what turns up. We'll be long gone. What do you say?"

Bertaud shook his head. "I'm sorry." He fixed them each in turn with a long, unmistakably cautionary gaze. "And *that*, I trust," he purred, "is the end of it."

* * *

"Well, that was sure a howling success," Gideon said as they left the *gendarmerie*.

John shook his head with frustration. "God, that guy ticks me off. Did I tell you that before?"

"You told me before. But cheer up, you get under his skin too."

"Yeah, that's something, I guess." He took in a deep breath and blew out his cheeks. "Doc, what the hell do we do now?"

"Go get some lunch, would be my suggestion."

John responded with an abstracted nod. Inside his head he was obviously still arguing with Bertaud.

"Any suggestions as to where?" Gideon asked.

"What? No, we always stay out in Papara with Nick when we come over. We eat at his place. I don't know any restaurants. Where'd you eat yesterday?"

"I just grazed the stands at the market, but I remember a place on Pomare that used to be pretty good. Maybe it's still there."

"Fine, whatever," John said listlessly.

The Acajou was still there, much as Gideon remembered it, a pleasant, tile-floored place with a shaded dining veranda separated by a line of potted shrubs from the clamor and bustle of the street. They ordered Hinanos and sat beside the plants. The menu was much the same as it had been three years earlier, and John cheered up as soon as he saw it, as Gideon had hoped he might.

"Hamburger?" John said. "I never knew you could get hamburgers in Tahiti. What do you know about that?"

It was more than he'd said on the entire four-block walk to the restaurant. John was a complex man in some ways, but not so complex that the likelihood of a decent hamburger couldn't be counted on to set him to rights.

The waitress, clad in a flowered *pareu* that highlighted firm silky shoulders, came smiling to take their orders. Like so many Tahitian women she might have stepped out of a Gauguin painting: effortlessly graceful, strikingly handsome, skin like beaten copper, a giant hibiscus blossom in her black hair (was there anyplace but the South Pacific where a huge red flower tucked behind one ear looked perfectly natural?), and exuding a lazy, good-natured sexuality as artlessly as the hibiscus released its heavy scent.

Gideon asked for an *omelette espagnole*.

"Hamburger," said John.

She looked up from her pad, frowning charmingly. *"Pardon?"*

"Hamburger," John said again, *"s'il vous plaît."*

The *s'il vous plaît* didn't help. She shook her head.

Gideon took a hand. "Ahmboorgaire," he explained.

"Ah, ahmboorgaire," she said with a smile. *"Avec le ketchup?"*

"Ketchup!" John exclaimed, brightening even more. "Sure. You bet. *Mais oui!"*

The hamburger came on sliced French bread with an elegant dab of creamy sauce on it—Bernaise, Gideon thought—and with a separate plate of fries. With barely a glance at the sauce, John scraped it off with a knife, poured on ketchup from the Del Monte bottle that the waitress had brought, and got happily to work. Gideon's Spanish omelet was more like a stir-fry mixed into some scrambled eggs, with tomato sauce on top, but there was a French flair to it and it tasted good, and it was a few minutes before the subject that was on both their minds came to the fore again.

"Doc, where do we go from here?" John said.

"Where is there to go? Look, I think Bertaud is wrong. But I could be wrong too."

John peered at him. "Where did this come from? You seemed pretty sure of yourself yesterday."

"I'm pretty sure today too. I think those maggots mean Brian was attacked with a knife. But I wouldn't swear to it, I wouldn't bet my life on it. All we saw were a few fuzzy photographs. We're dealing with probabilities here, John, not absolutes. To me, it seemed as if the probability of foul play was high enough to justify an exhumation; to Bertaud it didn't. I think he's wrong, but I can't really blame him." He speared a piece of cooked celery and popped it in his mouth. "And this being French Polynesia, Bertaud gets the last word. Unless you think Nick could be swung around—"

John shook his head.

"—I don't see that we have any options."

"Mm," John said and thoughtfully munched another couple of ketchup-logged fries. Gideon thought that was the end of it, but a moment later John spoke.

"We could always dig the body up ourselves," he said offhandedly.

Gideon's celery nearly went down the wrong pipe. He managed to get it rerouted without choking, then stared at John. "You couldn't have said what I thought you said."

"I said we could always dig the body up ourselves."

"You can't be serious! What, in the dead of night? With hooded lanterns, and cloaks pulled over our faces? What the hell kind of thing is that to suggest? Christ, from an FBI agent yet!"

"Well, I don't hear anything better coming from you."

Gideon couldn't argue with that.

"Anyway," John said, "it wouldn't be the dead of night." He raised his eyebrows and looked quizzically at Gideon; a why-don't-we-just-talk-about-this-a-little-more kind of look.

Gideon started to say something, then thought better of it and took a slow, steadying sip of the coffee they'd ordered after their meal. The thing to do was simply to stare coldly at John, as he was now doing, making it clear from his stony expression that it was out of the question. To discuss it at all would be to suggest that it was within the realm of possibility, and that would be a mistake. He had done some damnfool things in his life, a rather high percentage of them at John's instigation, and he was sincerely afraid of getting himself talked into another. He more than understood his friend's point of view, after all—somebody had almost certainly murdered Brian Scott and was going to get clean away with it, and that galled Gideon too, who hadn't even known Brian. But, good God, he certainly wasn't going to go around digging up corpses on his own, particularly in the face of Bertaud's repeated warnings to mind their own business. It was crazy even to think about it, let alone talk about it.

He sighed. "What do you mean, not the dead of night?"

John smiled at him. "I mean—"

"And you can wipe that grin off your face. I'm just asking a question. I didn't say I'm going along with this. I'm *not* going along with this."

"Naturally, of course not, we're just talking theoretically," John said, smiling some more, so that the skin around his eyes crinkled up. "What I meant is that the cemetery Brian's buried in is this old native graveyard in a back corner of the plantation. It's just this little place, maybe a quarter of an acre. Nobody goes near it from one year to the next. It's where they used to bury the copra workers in the old days. They don't even use it anymore; I think Brian's the first person to be buried there in ten years. And we can take a back road to it that doesn't go anywhere near the working part of the plantation. I'm telling you, even in the middle of the day there wouldn't be anybody to see us."

"Theoretically speaking," Gideon said.

"Theoretically speaking," agreed John. "So what do you say?"

"I say you're out of your mind. Aside from breaking the law—"

"That's not a problem. Look, we dig up the body, you have a look at it right there, check out that hand, see if it's what you think—"

"What do you mean, right there? At the grave?"

"At the grave, yes. If you don't find anything that means anything, we just cover him back up and leave quietly. But if you do, then we bring the police in on it. Bertaud would have to do something about it then. He wouldn't have any choice. You've got a reputation—"

"Yes, I know," Gideon said. "The Skeleton Detective. I'm real famous in America. I remember how deeply it impressed him last time."

"Look, Doc, Brian's an American citizen; we could make an international incident out of it if they didn't do anything. And, believe me, Bertaud may be a jerk but if we can really convince him it's murder, he'll follow up. And he's not going to make a fuss about us breaking some health department regulation by digging up a grave." He gulped down some coffee. "Theoretically."

"John," Gideon said, "you're not seeing the whole picture. You're imagining we go get a couple of shovels, dig down six feet—"

"Not even six feet, probably."

"—and there he is in a box and all we have to do is pry the lid off. Well, they don't bury people that way anymore, not even here. The plain old hole in the ground went out with 'Alas, poor Yorick.' Those holes are lined with cement nowadays, or maybe cinder block, and they usually have a concrete cap on top. You need heavy equipment to get it off—a crane, a back-hoe—"

John was shaking his head. "Not this grave, Doc. No concrete, no cinder blocks, not even a coffin. Not even a headstone. Brian was kind of a nut about Tahiti. He really fell in love with it, with the history. He always said he wanted to be buried in the old native cemetery, and he wanted his body treated the old native way. And that's just the way Thérèse handled it."

"I doubt that," Gideon murmured, mostly to himself.

"What do you mean, you doubt it? I'm telling you."

"Well, the old Tahitian way was—you don't want to know."

"Sure, I want to know. What do you mean?"

"Well, what they used to do here, and in the Marquesas and the Tuamotus too, was to puncture the skin to let out the fluids, take out the brain, use a hook to remove the viscera by way of the anus, then mummify—"

John looked horrified. "Yikes! No! That's disgusting! I only meant there's no coffin, no concrete. And he's buried in sand, not dirt, just a few feet down. Thérèse hired an old Tahitian priest to do the burial. Nick took me up there yesterday; I saw for myself. It'd be a snap, Doc. Twenty minutes' work."

Gideon shifted uneasily. "John, I'd like to help, you know that, but it just doesn't—"

John leaned earnestly across the table. "Look, I'd do it by myself, you know that, but what would I do with the body when I got it up?" He looked at the tabletop. "I need you. Brian needs you. I know you, Doc, you're like me; you can't just let something like this pass. It's not right."

Gideon sighed deeply and drained his cooling coffee. *Brian needs you.* How was it that Doug Ubelaker, the anthropologist at the Smithsonian put it? *We are the final chance for the voice of the victim to be heard.* The Hippocratic oath of the forensic anthropologist.

He sighed again, even deeper this time, and rose. "I saw a *quincaillerie* on the way over here. On rue La Garde."

John looked at him, puzzled. "A . . . ?"

"Hardware store," Gideon said. "We can pick up a couple of shovels and whatever else we need."

John let loose a sigh of his own, then grinned and flopped

back in his chair. "Whoo, I tell you, you had me worried there for a while."

"Sure, I'll just bet I did," Gideon said with a faint smile. "Come on, let's go. We better get it over with before I return to my right mind."

Chapter 20

With Gideon at the wheel of the Renault and John navigating, they drove south on the coast road half a mile past the Centre Apatea mini-mall, then turned left onto a rutted, one-lane dirt road and began to climb the flanks of Mt. Iviroa, quickly leaving behind the coconut groves and rangeland of the coast and tunneling into the fragrant, gorgeous forest of the interior: frangipani, wild ginger, flame trees, gardenia trees, pandanus, wild orchid, everything prodigiously and brilliantly in bloom. A jungle of flowers. Overhead, the feathery leaves of acacias and eucalyptus filtered the sun; they seemed to be driving through a rolling net of shadows.

"Doc, we're doing the right thing," John said, slouched in the passenger seat, one knee up against the dashboard. "In the great scheme of things."

"I know that, John. I'm not too worried about the great scheme of things."

"I know. You're worried about waking up tomorrow morning in the Papeete jail."

"Yes. Charged with grave-robbing." Not, he admitted to himself, that such a prospect lacked a certain poetic aptness.

John folded his arms and looked soberly out the window. "Me too. You know, Doc, you really should have talked me out of this."

The afternoon mists that clung to the mountain suddenly enveloped them. One second they were in bright sunlight and sharp shadow, the next in a silvery fog that turned everything, even the air, a gauzy, spooky gray-green. The vegetation, profuse to begin with, became even more extravagant. Mosses hanging from the tree branches drooped like great, hairy swaths of drapery. Giant ferns ten feet tall pressed in on every side. And they began to catch glimpses of exotic birds—scarlet, blue, peacock-green—flitting through the foliage, and to hear strange calls.

"Welcome to Jurassic Park," John said. "Don't hit any pterodactyls."

They crested a ridge and swung downward into a broad valley after that, and, as suddenly as they had entered it they were out of the fog and back in the sun. A few minutes later the road, barely a road by this time, ended at an old, tin-roofed, falling-down greenhouse on a square plot of land that had long ago been hacked out of the jungle. Once upon a time it had been landscaped into a semiformal garden but the plants hadn't been cared for in many years. In Tahiti that didn't mean they died, it meant they took over the place. Bougainvillea, poinsettia, and shrub acacia thrived, choking the yard and patio and clutching at windows, awnings, and porches.

"This is where the minister lived in the old days," John said, then pointed directly across the road. "And that's the cemetery."

It was, as he'd said, tiny; a grassy plot perhaps a hundred feet square, with a slowly collapsing white picket fence around it.

Unlike the lot across the road it wasn't totally abandoned, but it wasn't well cared for either. The grass had been mowed sometime in the last few weeks, the fence painted sometime in the last few years. The afternoon sunlight was harsh, the air still and hot—hotter by far than on the coast below—and the immediate scene stark and unwelcoming.

Gideon turned off the ignition and sat, squinting into the glare without moving, listening to the steady rasp of insects from the bush.

John, halfway out his door, glanced at him sharply. "You're not gonna get cold feet on me, are you?"

Gideon shook his head. "How can I? I already have cold feet." But of course this was mostly to make John feel guilty, to let him know that if anything went wrong they both damn well knew whose fault it was.

They put on straw hats they'd gotten at the hardware store, took from the trunk a plastic sack with digging equipment and a couple of liter bottles of Vittel mineral water, and stepped through the cemetery's open, leaning gate. There were about fifteen graves in all, scattered in no particular arrangement. A few were French burials with simple, straightforward headstones ("*Ici repose Pierre Leblanc*"). The rest were in the traditional Polynesian style: rectangular beds of white sand protected by low, lean-to roofs of corrugated metal and rimmed with a border of whitewashed stones. Some of the Tahitian graves had long-dead potted flowers on them, the pots overturned, the dry stems scattered. None had names or headstones.

John led Gideon to a grave along the far fence. "This is him."

"We think."

"Hey. Don't start that again."

Clearly, the grave was new. The lean-to roof had no stains of rust. The flowers were fresh; nine pots filled with gardenia and jasmine were set out in three equally spaced rows. A small, white wooden cross at what Gideon took to be the head distinguished it from the other Tahitian burials.

"Well, I guess we should start," John said with noticeably less than his usual resoluteness.

So, Gideon thought, notwithstanding the ovenlike heat it appeared they had four cold feet between them, not two. He finally took pity on his friend, knelt down decisively, and began to remove the potted plants and set them aside. "Come on, John, we'll see what we see." He took two spade-shaped hand shovels from the sack. "We'll start at the center and work toward the ends. Just take it down about an inch at a time. Skimming motion. I don't think this is going to be very hard."

But it was. Although the sand was easy enough to get through, they had to dig on their knees because of the low roof. And while the layer of metal just above their heads shielded them from the direct rays of the sun, it focused the heat downward and kept it there. In less than five minutes they took off their shirts and then had to remove their sunglasses because the lenses were greasy with perspiration. Sweat ran down the hollows of their backs, gleamed on their forearms, dripped from the ends of their noses.

The sand turned out to be only a top-dressing. At about eighteen inches it gave way to a dark, moist, loamy soil.

"Bad sign," said Gideon, breathing hard.

"No problem," said John, also huffing. "It's easy to dig." He tossed a shovelful onto the growing pile beside the plot.

Gideon sat back on his haunches to unkink his spine and to gulp from one of the blue plastic bottles. "That's not what worries me. When you put an unprotected corpse in ground like this it can bond with the soil as it decomposes. It can take days to get it free."

"That could be a problem," John agreed. He took the bottle from Gideon, drank deeply, worked his shoulders, and picked up his shovel again. They returned to the first-Gideon-then-John-then-Gideon pattern they had fallen naturally into and dug, rhythmically and silently, for twenty minutes. They had gotten down to about two feet below the surface, kneeling face-to-face in a trench about three feet by five, when Gideon spoke abruptly.

"Stop."

John stopped instantly, looking at the lumpy, earth-colored protuberance that the last sweep of his spade had exposed.

"What is it?"

"The left knee, I think. Slightly flexed." With his hands Gideon brushed the dirt away.

They were looking directly down into the open joint. Gideon could see the knucklelike distal end of the femur, the smooth concavities of the tibial condyles into which it fit, the small, pointed eminence of the fibula's styloid process. There were still some shreds of ligament and meniscus—the slippery, round pad of fibrocartilage that kept the bones from grinding on one another—but all in all a relatively clean joint. This was good news; it suggested that the defleshing process had advanced since the time the photos had been taken. The fibrous ligaments and capsular membranes of the knee were among the toughest tissues in the body. If they were gone, then maybe there wouldn't be much left on the bones anywhere else, and that would make his job easier and faster, not to mention a great deal less unpleasant.

Bone, ligament, and cartilage were all the same color: an ivory-brown, somewhat lighter than the surrounding soil, but with the same reddish tinge.

"Here's where we get the trowels out," Gideon said. "We want to more or less scrape the dirt away layer by layer—carefully, a few millimeters at a time. You work up from the knee. I'll work down from the head region."

John studied the bone from several different angles. "Which way's up?"

"Behind you." Gideon tossed him a few wooden tongue depressors from the sack. "When you're anywhere near the body, use these or your fingers. And we just want to uncover it; don't try to dig it out."

Gideon quickly troweled down to the level at which he thought the skull would be, then laid the metal tool aside and worked through the soil with his fingers. Within seconds he touched a hard, curving surface.

"Skull," he said.

John troweled for a few seconds longer, then silently put down the tool and watched.

It took only another few minutes, working with fingers, tongue depressor, and a two-inch-wide paintbrush to expose the area from the crown of the head to the throat.

"Jeez," said John when he got a good look.

Jeez is right, thought Gideon. The head, not as skeletonized as the knee, was horror-movie stuff, with greasy rags and scraps of red-brown tissue clinging to the bone. A few clumps of hair, still blond in places but already fading to a dingy reddish brown, adhered to the sides of the skull. Where the nose and eyes had been were black holes with dried larval casings in them. The throat musculature had congealed into an unrecognizable, liver-colored mass, the mandible gaping and disarticulated from the skull.

John stared at it, obviously shaken. Below his eyes, under the natural bronze of his skin there was a muddy pallor that Gideon had never seen before. "God," he murmured.

They had looked at more than one decomposing body together before, and if anybody was going to get queasy it could always be counted on to be Gideon; by now it was a running joke between them. But John had never before had to look at someone he'd known closely—one of the family—in this condition. Gideon had, and he remembered what it felt like.

"Listen," he said gently, "why don't I just finish up here myself? The hard work's done anyway; you'll just get in the way from here on. Take a walk and come back, oh, in half an hour, and I'll tell you if—"

But John, still staring at the skeleton-face, was shaking his head. "It's my fault for getting us into this. I'll stick around. I owe you that much."

"Oh, hell," Gideon said, "don't start making me feel guilty. If I didn't think it was the right thing to do, all I had to say was no."

"You did say no."

"Well, all I had to do was say it two or three times, then. And I didn't. Because it *is* the right thing to do."

"Thanks, Doc." John smiled wanly.

"He *was* blond, wasn't he?" Gideon asked after a moment.

John nodded.

"What about the diastema? Does that look right?"

"Diastema, what the hell is a diastema?"

Gideon gestured at the skull. "That space between his front teeth."

"Yeah, he did have a space between his—oh, I see what you mean. Look at that." He rubbed his hand back and forth over his eyes. "Look, on second thought maybe I'll go sit under a tree and cool off for a couple of minutes. It's just so . . . I mean, to see him like this . . . you know, he was so . . . ."

"Go, already," Gideon said gruffly. "Here, take some water."

He went back to work. There had been no bonding; the cool soil came away easily in his fingers. And, thank God, there was little stench, no more than an earthy, tomblike odor with only a vague, intermittent edge of rankness. Just your basic, everyday grave smell.

In fifteen minutes John strode back looking his old steadfast self, picked up his tools without a word, and got to work on the lower half of the body. Twenty minutes after that the two of them sat back on their heels to catch their breath and use their wadded shirts to swab perspiration from neck, back, and forehead. The entire upper surface of the body was now exposed, and Gideon took his first long, considered look at it.

Brian was dressed in the T-shirt and shorts that Gideon remembered from the morgue photos. Either he'd been put back into the clothes he'd been wearing when he'd died or he had never been undressed at all. The shirt, stiff with dried blood to begin with, was now black with mold as well, the shorts speckled with blotches of gray-green fungus. Most of the body's soft tissue, as he'd expected, was gone. What was left was rotted to tatters in some places, gummy and shriveled in others. Still, getting down to clean bone for even a cursory examination wasn't the sort of thing that could be accomplished in a few minutes or even a few hours, especially under that roasting pan of a roof. Other things aside, they'd have heat prostration before they were halfway finished.

John heard his sigh. "Doc? What's the matter?"

Gideon jerked his head. "Nothing." All he could do was what he could do. "Let's get down to business. I'm going to start checking him out." He opened and laid out a worn leather packet of dissecting tools that they had stopped to pick up from his cottage; Gideon had had it ever since his student days at the University of Arizona. "May as well start with the right hand. If those really were defense wounds, there's a good chance there'll be some corresponding nicks in the bones. If not . . ."

"If something's there you'll find it," John said with his appealing but slightly irritating confidence.

The hand lay in a natural position at the body's side, still largely articulated, palm uppermost. That is to say, where the palm had been was uppermost. Stuck to the metacarpals was a mass of tarry, unidentifiable tissue, which Gideon examined with care, hoping to find unambiguous signs of the wound, but without success. It would have to be cleaned off, and he used a tongue depressor to rub away at it, a slow, necessarily painstaking process. Both men kneeled over it, absorbed.

"*ARRÊTEZ-VOUS, S'IL VOUS PLAÎT!*"

The *thunk* that followed immediately upon this was the sound of Gideon's and John's near-simultaneous cracking of their skulls against the underside of the metal roof. Clutching their heads, they spun around to see a large, bearded, patently displeased Tahitian policeman looming over them, blocking the sun, his hands on his hips.

It is no easy thing to look intimidating in short blue pants and sky-blue knee socks, but this particular cop, about the size and shape of a UPS delivery van, brought it off with no difficulty.

And standing beside him, not as physically impressive, but no less formidable and every bit as displeased, was the small, globular form of the commandant of the Gendarmerie Nationale de Polynésie-Française, Colonel Leopold Guillaume Bertaud.

"Now why is it," wondered the colonel with his hands clasped behind him, "that I fail to be amazed?" He sounded cheerful, even happy.

"We can explain," John said. His arms and hands were filthy, his face streaked with sweat and dirt.

Bertaud, crisp and dapper, looked down on him from what seemed to be a very great height.

"No doubt," he said.

"Give us one more minute," John said. "One lousy minute, that's all we ask."

"And what will happen in one more minute?"

"Doc'll prove to you we're right."

Gideon winced. Thanks, John.

"By all means, then," Bertaud said, "continue."

*   *   *

It took five minutes, not one, of painstaking scraping and probing, but at the end of that time Gideon picked a last bit of tissue off with his fingernails and looked up from his knees with a sense of satisfaction.

"Now then," he said, shifting instinctively into professorial gear. Bertaud moved in closer and leaned over Gideon and John, his hands on his knees. The big Tahitian cop, on the other hand, appeared to be happier keeping his distance.

"As you see, some of the smaller bones have come loose—" He gestured at four terminal phalanges, heaped together like miniature arrowheads. "—but the dirt and the ligaments have held the rest of the hand together pretty well. These, here, are the metacarpals, the bones that form the body of the hand; the fingers themselves start here."

"We are seeing the palm?" Bertaud asked.

"Yes, the palm. And can you see this little notch near the head of the second metacarpal—this one, the one that leads to the first finger—and then this notch a little more distal on the third metacarpal, and then this groove on the first phalanx of the fifth digit's—"

"No, I see nothing," Bertaud snapped. "Bones have many natural grooves and notches. They all look very much the same. Make your point, please."

"In English," added John.

"Does anybody have a knife?" Gideon asked.

At a nod from Bertaud, the Tahitian took a Swiss Army knife from his pocket and handed it to Gideon, who opened it to its largest blade, about four inches long, and gently laid it, edge down, across the skeletal palm. It fit so perfectly into the line of notches that when he let go of the knife it remained upright, lodged in the bones.

He looked up. "There are no such natural grooves, Colonel. These are defense wounds."

Bertaud peered intently at the knife, eyes keen, lips set. It didn't look as if he was taking this very well. Gideon carefully lifted the knife from the bone, laid it across his own palm in approximately the same position, and closed his fist around the blade. When he opened it fifteen seconds later for Bertaud's inspection there was an indentation in his skin, running from the webbing between his thumb and forefinger, diagonally across the palm, and onto the bottom portion of his little finger.

"Ho!" John exulted, and then, just in case Bertaud failed to comprehend: "That's just where those maggots were, remember?"

"That son of a bitch," was Bertaud's surprising response. He walked a few paces off and stared fretfully into the jungle.

Gideon and John looked at each other and shrugged. It was nice to have the colonel ticked off at somebody else for a change.

Chapter 21

With the help of two more men from Bertaud's office, it took only an hour to get the remains up from the grave. At Gideon's request, Bertaud had gotten a thin, flexible panel of sheet metal from a shop in Papeete, and they used it to slide under the body and lift it all at once. This was done successfully, although it did disarticulate at the pelvis and skull, and a few additional bits and pieces came loose as well. Along with displaced odds and ends—the left patella, a few phalanges—that were located with the aid of a sieve, these were placed in paper bags, and by 4 P.M. all of the existing mortal remains of Brian Scott were lying on a table in the autopsy room located in the basement of the Centre Hospitalier Territorial on Papeete's avenue Georges Clemenceau. There Dr. Viennot, the police physician, had been waiting to perform the autopsy, but after one look at the body he took a thin, black, crooked cigar from his mouth and laughed.

"I hereby certify that this man is dead and has been so for

some considerable time," he said in French. "Beyond that"—this to Gideon—"he's all yours, colleague, and welcome to him."

"When can you have a report ready?" Bertaud asked when the doctor had gone.

I haven't been invited to consult yet, was the answer that sprang to mind, but better to let well enough alone. Bertaud was irritated enough as it was. "What's left of the soft tissue will have to come off first," he said.

"And that will take how long?"

That was the problem. Ordinarily, with chemical help, it took four or five days to deflesh and properly clean a skeleton, but Gideon intended to be on his way home by that time, not working in this bleak, sterile, windowless room. On the other hand, this particular corpse had made substantial headway on its own toward becoming a skeleton, and with a little extra attention the process might be speeded up considerably.

"We're going to have to cook him down some first," he said. "Can I get a vat or something to do that in?"

A look of distaste flitted across Bertaud's features. "I'll see that the hospital makes available to you whatever you need. You need only speak with Mr. Boucher in the director's office."

"Good. Then maybe I'll have a report for you by tomorrow afternoon. The next day at the latest."

"Very good. And if you require additional . . . supplies, Mr. Boucher will—"

"It'll be easier to get what I need in a supermarket," Gideon said.

Bertaud looked at him queerly, possibly to see if this was some curious American joke. "As you wish. There is a large one, English-speaking, nearby on rue des Remparts. If you will provide a written account of your expenses to Mr. Salvat when you submit your bill, I'll see that you're reimbursed at once."

"There won't be any bill," Gideon said. "This is what we came here to do."

"Only you wouldn't let us," John pointed out, ever helpful.

Bertaud's blue eyes flashed, but only for a moment. "No," he said with something like a sigh. "So I did not." He clasped his hands behind him in a gesture that was already becoming familiar. "Gentlemen, I owe you a great apology."

"Oh, hell," John said good-naturedly, "forget it, you were doing your job."

"Not very well," Bertaud said. "The truth is, Nick Druett is a very old friend . . . a trusted friend. After you first came to see me, I spoke to him, in confidence. He assured me, without qualification, that there was nothing to your claims." He compressed his lips. "And I, I accepted this. Well, I was wrong."

Very formally, he offered his hand to each of them in turn. "I assure you, you will find me more cooperative in the future."

*   *   *

Once Bertaud had left them, Gideon sat down at a counter that ran along the wall, his back to the body, and began to write in a pad he had found there.

"Ah, he's not such a bad guy," John said. "What'd you have against him anyway?"

Gideon continued to write.

John was leaning against the wall, thinking, his arms folded. "Hey," he said suddenly, "did I tell you Bertaud and Nick were tight, or did I tell you?"

"You sure did," Gideon said.

"Sometimes, amazing as it may seem to you, I'm actually right."

"You sure are."

"And you're actually wrong."

"I'll admit it to you," Gideon said, "but don't ever let Julie find out. Or my students."

"So what are you writing?" John asked.

"A list of what we need. If you drop around to the market and pick it up, I'll start getting things ready here. I'm going to get off all the tissue I can by hand."

"Sure." John took the list. "'Three pairs rubber gloves . . .'" he read aloud, nodding, "'. . . bleach . . .'" But, as Gideon thought it might, the next entry stood him up straight. "'Biz?'" he cried. "'Liquid-Plumr?'" He stared at Gideon. "'. . . ADOLPH'S MEAT TENDERIZER?' No, come on, Doc, you gotta be kidding me!"

"No, I'm not kidding you. Get plenty of each."

"You're telling me you use . . . you use meat tenderizer to . . . to . . ."

"Why not? That's what it's for, if you look at it the right way. It's the papain in it. And look, if you can't get Adolph's and Biz and Liquid-Plumr, just get whatever they use here instead, as long as the drain cleaner has sodium hydroxide and sodium hypochloride in it, and the—here, I'll write it down for you."

He jotted a few notes at the bottom of the list and gave it back to John. "But try for the Biz first. I like the way it macerates a partially defleshed body."

"Gee, did you ever think of doing endorsements? There's money to be made there, Doc." He held an imaginary container up beside his face. "Have a partially defleshed body that needs macerating? Well, take it from me, the Skeleton Detective—"

"Just get the stuff, will you?" Gideon said, laughing. He unsnapped his dissecting kit. "Oh, and I'll need something to scrub the bones down as we go. A small scrub brush works fine—soft as you can get. Pick up a couple, will you? A couple of toothbrushes too."

John nodded, pocketed the list, and made for the door. As he was closing it behind him he stuck his head back in.

"What brand toothbrush? Personally, *I* recommend Py-co-pay."

"Py-co-pay," said Gideon, "will do just fine."

True to Bertaud's promise, Mr. Boucher, the administrative director of the hospital, proved eager and able to help. At 5 P.M., when the laundry workers left for the day, a covered gurney was wheeled by two orderlies from the morgue to the hospital laundry. There, a huge, lidded, cast-iron vat, in which sheets had been boiled in the days before the hospital had gotten its new gas-powered washers, had been placed at Gideon's disposal, as had the two orderlies. By 5:30 the skeleton, now largely disarticulated, and with the smaller bones in several net bags, was soaking in meat tenderizer and water, its first of four warm baths. At 7:30 the vat was drained and the bones placed on the rimmed, metal-topped gurney, where Gideon gently scrubbed and teased away some more of the soft tissue and carefully snipped apart stubborn joints with scalpel and scissors.

In his mind he had already divided the work to be done on the skeleton into two mutually exclusive phases: first, the preparation of the bones for examination, which was tonight's job, a charnel-house business of bone-scraping, defleshing, simmering, and disjointing; and second, the examination itself, which would be tomorrow's. Phase one was dull, hard, nasty work, phase two was physically easy, mentally challenging, and engrossing; phase one was dirty, phase two was clean; phase one was unpleasant from start to finish, phase two was—well, pleasant might not be the right word, but satisfying in its own absorbing way, a return to order and meaning after the dissolution of the night before.

Over the years he had learned to get through the nasty phase without entirely focusing his attention, without being altogether "there." He rubbed, scrubbed, and teased as needed, but everything was kept at a mental distance, as if seen through a veil. Observation and interpretation of the skeletal features were suspended until the examination itself. After all, it wasn't as if whatever it was wouldn't hold. Thus, it took something extraordinary to make him sit up and take notice.

Like the screw in the middle of Brian's skull, for example.

✳   ✳   ✳

Even then, it was John who spotted it.

"What the hell is that?" he said suddenly.

Gideon surfaced with a start. He had been scrubbing away at the proximal end of a femur, having almost forgotten that John was there, watching over his shoulder with an understandable mixture of fascination and repugnance.

"What's what?" Gideon said grumpily. He'd liked it where he was, in his gauzy semitrance.

"That." John pointed. "There's a screw in his head."

There certainly was, an ordinary-looking metal screw two inches above the nasal bones, its slotted head visible among the rags and tags of muscle and fascia still stuck to the front of the cranium. Gideon quickly cleared the overlying tissue away. (The frontalis muscle, with nothing much to do other than raising the eyebrows and wrinkling the forehead, was one of the thinnest in the body, and one of the few with no tough bony attachments to hack through.) What he found underneath was a substantial collection of hardware implanted in the skull: more screws, four thin strips of surgical steel, and ten or twelve snips of wiring, all of it having been used to hold a two-by-four-inch rectangular piece of frontal bone in place in the middle of the forehead. The reinserted segment of bone had been through a lot. There was a healed linear fracture running from top to bottom on its left side, a healed, smaller, diagonal fracture in the lower right corner, signs of chipping and splintering at several places around the margins. But the surgery had been beautifully performed, and with the exception of one small, round concavity in the upper right corner, the bones had long ago knitted together with no visible complications.

"I'll be damned," Gideon said.

"What is it, Doc? What happened to him?"

"Well, I'm not positive. He's been operated on, that's clear. This big chunk of frontal bone was removed and then replaced—see the little depression in this corner? That's a burr hole; they had to drill that to make a place for the saw to get in. And these metal strips are compression plates to hold the edges of the bone together. And these wires—"

"Yeah, I see, but—I mean, I don't understand. Why would they take a piece out of his skull and then put it back? Did he have a brain operation?"

"No, I don't think so. For brain surgery you generally don't need to remove a huge chunk of bone like this, and even if you did, it'd be done neatly. You wouldn't have all this scarring, and you certainly wouldn't have these fractures. There's been some pretty serious retooling of the bone done here, John."

"Meaning what, plastic surgery?"

"Not the usual kind, no. This is heavy-duty stuff—reconstructive surgery—putting things back together after some kind of horrendous accident; automobile crash, most likely. It's the kind of thing that happens when you hit a windshield frame that's just stopped and you're still going sixty miles an hour. From the looks of it, Brian was lucky to get out of it alive. The whole front of his head must have been—" He shivered. "You mean you didn't know anything about this?"

"It's news to me. How long ago did it happen, can you tell?"

"Long time. Five years, ten years, more."

"Before I knew him," John mused.

"But there must have been some pretty bad scarring, John."

"Of his face, you mean? Not that I ever noticed."

"Well, did he look . . . a little odd? When you have this much repair involved, especially of the bone itself, it's pretty hard to put things back together quite the way—"

"No, nothing, Doc. He was a good-looking guy. Believe me, he looked like anybody else. Better."

"Yes, but there *had* to be—" And suddenly he ran out of steam. He leaned back on the stool he was sitting on and stretched, then sagged, his shoulders drooping. "Man, it's been a long, hard day," he said.

"Tell me about it."

"Look, why don't we save this for tomorrow, when we're fresh? For now, let me just concentrate on getting the bones ready."

"Suits me," said John.

And back into the vat they went, this time to soak in a twenty percent solution of DesTop, the French counterpart of Liquid-Plumr, for another hour, after which, almost free of adherent tissue now except for the fibrous stuff around the joints, they were removed for yet another scrub-down and then returned to the vat, this time in a watery solution of an enzyme-loaded French detergent called Ariel kept at a temperature just below a simmer.

"One more scrubbing, maybe," Gideon said, unutterably weary of scraping and hacking at the greasy, stubborn remnants of what had once been ligaments and tendons—the very machinery of human motion—"and then they'll go back into the detergent for the rest of the night. Bleach in the morning, and that'll be it, I hope."

At eleven, tired, bored, and depressed, John called a taxi, went back to the hotel, and fell into bed.

At 1:30 A.M., tired, bored, and miserably grungy, Gideon left precise instructions with the orderlies, drove to the hotel, showered under scalding water so hard and for so long that he went through an entire bar of coconut-scented soap, and fell into bed.

*   *   *

In the morning, by prior agreement, the two met in the dining room at 7 A.M., when it opened. They were surprised to find their usual table taken, and three or four others as well, with large, jolly, Spanish-speaking people, all of whom seemed to know one another. The Chileans, it appeared, really did patronize the place. Apparently they had arrived by way of the midnight Lan-Chile flight from Santiago, and true to Dean's word, they were a lively, laughing bunch. Children merrily chased mynah birds, adults merrily flipped croissants at one another.

Parks himself, his long face flushed with goodwill, moseyed laughing from table to table, glad-handing his guests, clapping tank-topped shoulders, and chattering away in drawling, Texas-style Spanish.

"What do you know," Gideon mused, "he really does have other customers."

They found an unoccupied table on the slate terrace, a long way from the buffet tables, but out in the fresh morning breeze and within hearing of the gentle, purling waves of the lagoon. Neither of them had eaten dinner the previous night, and they made their way through their heaped trays for some minutes before getting down to serious conversation.

"Find anything else after I left?" John asked around a mouthful of scrambled eggs and hard roll.

Gideon shook his head as he finished his own eggs and bacon. "No, the bones were still soaking in the detergent when I left. By now, the orderlies should have given them a final bath in the bleach, dried them, and delivered them back to the autopsy room."

"The bleach disinfects them?"

"Yes, but it's not that so much; it just cleans them up, gets rid of the grease, makes them pleasanter to work with."

John chewed and thoughtfully watched the waves for a while. "So Brian is now just a pile of bleached bones," he said.

"So will we all be, eventually."

John smiled crookedly. "Yeah, but not literally." He sipped his coffee. "So what happens now, Doc?"

"Now we go back to the hospital, we set the bones out on a table, and we see what there is to find. It's going to be pretty slow, so if you'd rather do something else for a few hours, feel free."

"Well, as a matter of fact, I was thinking of going over to Nick's place. Bertaud stopped in to see him last night to tell him what was going on, that they were starting a full-scale investigation and everything, and Nick called me this morning."

"Mad?"

"Nick? No, I wouldn't say mad. He sounded kind of—I don't know, mixed up. But the thing is, he wants to talk to me about it. And I sure want to talk to him."

"Watch out you don't tread on Bertaud's toes, John."

"Who, me? Anyway, he's on our side now, remember?"

"That's right, I forgot. Look, when you talk to Nick, ask him if he knows how Brian got his face smashed up, will you?"

"Why, is it important?"

"I don't know. I just—"

A callused hand clapped him on the shoulder. "Mornin', gents," Dean Parks said. "Listen, if you don't have anything planned, I hope I can talk you into some of the day's activities. These good folks'd just love to have you along."

"Actually—" Gideon said.

"Snorkeling at ten, beach picnic at twelve, glass-bottomed boats at one—"

"Thanks, Dean, but—" John said.

"—and then we take the *Leaky Tiki*—that's our genuine giant Polynesian outrigger motor canoe—down to Marae—that's a genuine old-fashioned Tahitian village—where two of these fine, fun-lovin' couples'll be married, Tahitian style, body tattoos and everything—"

"Body tattoos?" Gideon said. Fun-loving was right.

Parks lowered his voice. "Well, just cockamamies, really. They wash right off, but still, it's something to see. After that, we've got ourselves a beautiful sunset cruise . . . or, say, do you boys have your own entertainment planned?"

"I'm afraid we do," Gideon said.

Parks leered engagingly. "Well, then, don't let me stand in your way. Maybe tomorrow."

"Come on, Doc," John said, draining his coffee. "Let's go get entertained. I'll drop you off at the morgue."

Chapter 22

As expected, the bones were waiting for him on a gurney in the autopsy room. The room, however, was already in use.

"*Ah, bonjour!*" Dr. Viennot called merrily when Gideon entered. He had a cigar in his mouth, smoked down to a stub but unlit at the moment. "I hope you don't mind sharing the facility."

The police physician, rubber-gloved and white-coated, was at one of the two tables, working on a fresh body with the help of a sober, elderly assistant. The body, its lower half covered by a sheet, was that of an obese, middle-aged Tahitian woman. Viennot and the assistant had obviously been at work for a while. The standard Y-shaped incision of the torso had been made, the skin flaps laid back, and the sternum and central portions of the ribs cut away and removed, along with a few overlying bits of lung, to a pan on the counter. The two men, Gideon saw, were checking for air embolism, an unlovely procedure involving the filling of the pericardial sac with water and the capturing of escaping gases. The exhaust fan over the table was humming, but even so, you didn't need your eyes to tell you that there was a newly opened human body in the room with you.

"Oh, good morning, doctor," Gideon said. "I guess I'd better find someplace else."

"Nonsense," Viennot said, his slender, gloved hands wrist-deep in chest cavity. "Glad to have you. You won't bother us a bit."

But that wasn't the issue, not by a long shot. Autopsy rooms made Gideon skittish even when they were corpseless. The tiled walls, the dully gleaming zinc-topped tables, the sinks, the drains, the basins underneath to collect fluids—all were enough to unsteady his stomach and give him the willies. The fact that a perfectly respectable and even moderately distinguished career as an evolutionary theorist had led to his seemingly always popping in and out of these dismal places was one of the continuing mysteries of his existence.

"No, no," Gideon sang out, "that's all right, I wouldn't want to get in the way."

And over Viennot's well-meant protests ("At least have a cup of coffee—it's over there, by the lung.") he escaped, wheeling the gurney out of the room and into the hallway. He was fortunate in finding an unused conference room just one door down, and there he spread a double layer of newspapers, a three-week-old copy of *La Dépêche de Tahiti*, on the wooden table that took up most of the room, and laid out the bones.

The successive baths had done their work as well as could be expected in a single night. The bones were not quite white but a sort of glaucous ivory, darker near the tips and still just a little greasy to the touch. But for all intents and purposes, they were bare, and that was what was important. As always, his first job was to lay them out in anatomical position, or as close to anatomical position as they could get. For a change, he had a complete skeleton to work with, including every last one of the

106 bones of the hand and foot. (In the adult human, more than half the bones in the body are in the hands and feet, to the great annoyance of forensic anthropologists, many of whom—Gideon among them—had a hard time keeping all the tarsals, the carpals, and the phalanges straight, particularly when it came to telling right from left.) To get them all arranged took him almost an hour, but it was work he didn't mind; it was the first step of phase two, the beginning of the hunt. And there was nothing gooey, or squelchy, or otherwise repellent about it, at least not to him. No embolisms, no lungs sitting in pans. Just nice, clean bones. Bleached bones.

When the skeleton was laid out, he changed his mind and went back to the autopsy room to bring back some coffee (Viennot was delighted to see him: "Come look at this, colleague! Did you ever *see* such a thrombus!"). Then he sat on a corner of the table, sipping from the cardboard cup and looking down at the neatly ordered remains of Brian Scott.

That it was Brian he no longer doubted. There was the diastema, for one thing, the blond hair for another, and now, as he could plainly see, healed fractures of the right ulna and radius, which corresponded to the right arm, broken in two places, that Brian had suffered when the jeep went off the road. Spaces between the teeth, blond hair, and healed fractures were hardly distinctive enough to serve as positive identifiers on their own, but put them all together, with everything else, and they added up to Brian—a conclusion that no one else but Gideon had questioned anyway. Besides, if it wasn't Brian, who would it be? And where was Brian? All the same, bowing to habit—and to be on the safe side—he ran through a quick evaluation of race, sex, age, and height, always the forensic anthropologist's starting points.

Everything fit. The skull's narrow, "steepled" nasal bones, the sharply defined nasal lower border or sill, and the tapering, parabolic shape of the palate assured him that he was dealing with a Caucasian. The generally rugged appearance of the bones was enough to tell him it was male, and application of the anthropologist's "rule of thumb" confirmed it—place a thumb in the greater sciatic notch of the pelvis to see if you had room to wiggle it back and forth; if you did, it was a female. But if the fit was snug, which it was in this case, it was a male.

Age was harder, as it always was, for several reasons. First, the odds were longer. With sex you had only two choices; all you had to do was toss a coin and you were going to get it right half the time. But with age the odds were necessarily against you; it took more than a coin toss to get it right half the time, and even then you were dealing with broad ranges—eighteen to twenty-five, twenty-five to thirty, and so on. Second, once the epiphyses—the ends—of all the long bones had fused to the shafts, which began in the teens and ended in the late twenties, the skeleton was next to impossible to age with any confidence for thirty or forty years; there were time-related changes, of course (none of them good), but they didn't occur in any kind of predictable pattern; at least not one that anthropologists could agree on, although there had been some recent progress on the ribs.

The sole notable exception was the pubic symphyses, the matching surfaces of the two halves of the pelvis where they met at the midline of the body just above the genitals. For reasons nobody had ever figured out, the appearance of these surfaces was the adult skeleton's best age indicator, growing steadily more fine-grained, pitted, and sharp-edged over time.

Using a set of comparison drawings he had brought with him, Gideon placed the symphyses squarely in Phase IV of the Suchey-Brooks progression—approximately thirty-five years old, with a standard deviation of nine years. And Brian, he knew, had been thirty-eight. So that fit too.

As did the height. He used the old Trotter and Gleser equations to estimate living stature from the combined lengths of the femur and tibia. The result was seventy-one inches, plus or minus one inch, which was smack on the button, inasmuch as John had told him that Brian was six feet tall, or maybe a little under.

So Brian it was, no doubt about it. That resolved, he settled down to his real job: a bone-by-bone examination for other signs of how death had occurred. The cuts on the metacarpals he had already remarked, of course, and since then he had found in passing a green-stick fracture of the left humerus, at the point at which it narrowed just above the elbow; two crushed lumbar vertebrae; a snapped left clavicle; and a long, jagged crack in the skull, running horizontally along the parietal, from the occipital bone to the frontal. All of them were perfectly consistent with the fall that Brian had presumably taken from the plateau, and none showed any signs of healing, which meant that they had happened at about the time of death; whether before or after there was no way to tell. Either way, they didn't prove murder, nor even suggest it; not taken on their own.

He brought over a gooseneck lamp from a side table and set it up over the right hand for a closer look at the cut marks. They were knife wounds for sure: straight, narrow, and V-shaped, with clean, sharp edges. Other than those four lined-up notches, there were no other marks on the bones of the hand. Or of the other hand, or of the forearms, all likely sites for defense wounds. That implied that Brian had managed just one lunge at the knife to protect himself; death or incapacity had come quickly. The single line of cuts also meant that the weapon had probably been single-edged. Had it been double-edged, there would most likely have been a matching set of cuts on the bones of Brian's fingers, where they had closed around the opposite edge of the blade.

All right then, he was already able to make some reasonable assumptions. One, it had been a quick death. Two, the weapon was apparently not some professional assassin's murderous stiletto but probably some everyday kind of knife—a kitchen knife, a fishing knife—that might be found anyplace. Fine, but that didn't get him anywhere that he could see. He was certain enough that Brian had been murdered, but he was well shy of proof. Attacked, yes, those deep cuts in the palm attested to that, but you didn't die from a cut palm.

He shifted the lamp to the ribs and bent it so that the light was only a few inches from the tabletop, shining laterally across the bones. When you were looking for tiny nicks or clefts, or even thinly shaved bone, it helped to have shadows to highlight any roughness or smoothness that didn't belong there.

Nothing on the fronts of the ribs or the sternum, nothing on the backs. This was unsurprising because Brian's T-shirt had had no telltale knife slits in it. Still, Gideon had thought that a knife might have gone in above the scooped-out neck or below the hem on the bottom. But no such luck (so to speak). Except for that broken left clavicle there was no damage to ribs, sternum, collarbones, or scapulae. That didn't mean that Brian hadn't been stabbed in the chest or back, of course, it only meant that there was no evidence of it. Once Gideon had examined the skeleton of a man whose shirt had knife holes from thirteen deep stab wounds in it. (He knew they were deep because they had found the knife, and the size of the holes matched the width of the blade just under the haft and almost six inches from the point.) But only one of the thirteen thrusts had nicked any bone. There was a lot of room between the ribs.

On to the region of the throat, then. If there was going to be anything to find, here is where it would be.

And it was. On the front surface of the sixth cervical vertebra was a single, V-shaped, clean-edged, horizontal notch, not a puncture wound but a cut, shallower than the ones on the metacarpals and no more than half an inch long, easy to miss if you weren't looking for it or didn't know what you were looking for, but no less lethal for that. It struck him again how innocent-looking the signs of violence on bones could be, how removed they were from pain and struggle. If he'd found a tiny nick like this on a plastic model of a vertebra that he'd just received from a biological supply house, he would have shrugged it off and said no problem, no real damage done.

Ah, but on a living body! To make that seemingly inconsequential little mark a knife blade would have had to cut through two and a half inches of flesh and gristle: the ventral muscles of the throat, the thyroid and cricoid cartilages, the pharynx, the larynx, the vagus nerve, the phrenic nerve, the jugular vein. And of course one or both of the great common carotid arteries.

And with the carotid arteries severed one's life's blood poured out and was gone in a few seconds. No wonder Brian hadn't done much struggling.

So that was that. Brian Scott's throat had been cut.

Gideon went back to the autopsy room for more coffee (luckily, Dr. Viennot was deep in the pelvic cavity and never saw him come in), then returned to the conference room, sat in one of the comfortable swivel chairs with the bones before him, and pondered. Cut throats were nothing extraordinary in this line of work, but they were usually found in either of two sets of circumstances: first, in suicides (which this wasn't, unless Brian had gotten that defense wound fending himself off), and second, in connection with killings of manic violence, where a cut throat was just one of many wounds from stabbing, cutting, hacking, and whatever else you could do with a knife (which this wasn't either).

The thing was, it wasn't easy to cut someone's throat without a struggle. Vulnerable as it was, the front of the throat made a small, difficult, mobile target, was naturally shielded by the chin, and was easy to protect, at least temporarily, with the hands and arms. You didn't just walk up to someone and do it. Thus, when you found someone murdered in this manner, with very little other violence apparent, you concluded that it was more than likely that the victim was either immobilized at the time (which Brian wasn't, or there wouldn't have been any defense wounds at all), or was surprised from behind, or was already unconscious when attacked.

And of those, the best bet was that he was already unconscious. As in sleeping.

At ten he called Bertaud to make a preliminary report. "Colonel," he said when he had finished and Bertaud had politely but coolly complimented him, "I was wondering about his sleeping bag. Did anyone have a look at it?"

"Sleeping bag?" Bertaud repeated. "I don't believe such a thing was found."

"Wasn't his gear at his campsite up above?"

Papers shuffled at Bertaud's end. "Cooking tools, yes, clothing, food . . . I think there was no sleeping bag."

"But—that seems odd, doesn't it?"

"I suppose it does, but there was no reason at the time—" Abruptly he saw where Gideon was heading. "You think the murderer came upon him in his sleep? That the bag was bloodied and therefore disposed of somewhere to hide it?"

Gideon was glad that Bertaud had come up with it on his own. "It's possible, don't you think? God knows there'd have been plenty of blood."

"God knows. I'll have the area more thoroughly searched, Dr. Oliver. You'll have a written report for me later?"

"This afternoon. You're taking this on as a full-scale investigation, then?"

"Personally," said Bertaud at his most resolute. "And if you will ask Mr. Lau to come and see me and tell me again about these American mobsters of his, you can say to him I will pay closer attention this time."

The rest of Gideon's examination produced nothing of significance, but there were two areas that particularly caught his interest. He spent some time over the old repairs to the skull simply because he was so impressed. The original damage had been even more devastating than had been visible the night before, involving not only the forehead but the delicate bony orbits of the eyes and the zygomatic bones alongside them. They too had been wired back together in several places, and the surgeon had done an amazing job of restoration—the sort of miracle operation that orthopedic surgeons modestly and routinely referred to as "bone carpentry." The fact that Brian had come out of it looking normal, had even been a "good-looking guy," according to John, was astounding.

The other thing that he came back to, had already come back to again and again, was a phenomenon that had him intrigued and frankly puzzled. For at least the fifth time he picked up the fibulas and studied them, running his finger over the unusually roughened surfaces near their upper ends. On the face of it, they weren't anything very startling. The fibula was one of the two long bones of the lower leg—the thin one, not the thick, sturdy tibia that formed the shinbone—and the rough, pitted area at its top was merely the attachment site for one of the leg muscles. Nothing extraordinary in that. The exaggerated roughness simply meant that the muscle attached to it had seen heavy use; habitual, strenuous activity put stress on muscles, as everyone knew, and built them up. And where these built-up, heavily used muscles tugged on the bone—as forensic anthropologists and hardly anybody else knew—they too created stress and eventually built up and roughened the bony surfaces.

Given a knowing eye, these stressed and roughened skeletal

surfaces could sometimes be read like a job description. Occupational indicators, they were sometimes called. There were "seamstress's fingers," "waiter's humerus," "shotputter's ulna," "shoemaker's sternocalvicular joint"; even "executive's foot"— the result of years of sitting at a desk in a tipped-back swivel chair with the heels off the floor and the weight pressing on the toes.

But if there was any common name in the trade for an overdeveloped posterior aspect of the *capitulum fibulae*, Gideon had yet to run into it. The problem was, the muscle that attached to it, the soleus, didn't *do* anything in the usual sense. Well, that wasn't quite true. Its function, according to the anatomy books, was to provide some help to the gastrocnemius—the big muscle that formed the calf—in plantar-flexing the foot; that is, in pushing the toes powerfully downward, an essential part of the human gait. But the fact was that the considerably larger gastrocnemius was more than strong enough to do that by itself, and that it already had the help of several other muscles anyway.

So what did the soleus do, why did we have the things at all? The answer seemed to be that they were muscles of balance. They helped keep the ankles, and thus the body as a whole, firm and steady while walking. While standing still, for that matter. An important function, certainly, but not one that generally made great demands on the muscle fibers or the bone they attached to. Yet in Brian's case, not only was the attachment area heavily developed, but the pull of the muscles had been so powerful that the tops of both his fibulas had actually been tugged out of shape, bowing backward in their last couple of inches.

And this was something Gideon had not seen before. Brian Scott, whose bones in general showed that he was no more heavily muscled than the average man, had had the most extraordinarily developed soleus muscles he had ever run across.

Why? How did you even get such things? If Gideon were asked what sort of exercises to do to develop them he wouldn't have known what to answer. Stand on the edge of a two-by-four an hour a day? Walk a tightrope every evening after dinner for an hour or two?

While he stood there pondering, he heard John speaking to Viennot in the autopsy room.

"I'm in here, John," he called. "Next door." He still had one of the fibulas in his hand when John came in with two cups of coffee.

"Fibula," John proclaimed, setting one of the cups down for Gideon. Some years before, he had attended a seminar that Gideon had put on for law enforcement people.

"That's easy enough," Gideon said. "But which one, right or left?"

"Hey, don't push your luck." He looked down at the bones with a meditative air. "So this is Brian." But he was clearly less disturbed by the idea than he'd been the day before. Cleaned skeletons can be fascinating, informative, evocative, puzzling—but they're not horrifying or pitiful, once you're used to them, and when you come down to it, they all look pretty much the same. See one and you've seen them all. It's hard to feel much in the way of emotion for any particular skeleton, or even to connect it in a visceral way with any particular person.

"So how's it going?" John asked.

Gideon pointed out the nicked cervical vertebra. "Cut throat, no question about it."

John looked at it, even ran his finger over the cut. "That's an awful little ding to kill somebody. Is Bertaud going to buy it?"

"It's not the ding, it's what happened on the way to the ding. And yes, Bertaud's already bought it. I talked to him a few minutes ago."

"Good, maybe we'll finally get some action."

"I think so. He wants you to come in and tell him about the Mob connections by the way."

"I already told him once."

"He says he'll listen this time. How'd you do with Nick?"

"Hard to say. I think basically he just wanted to talk about it. I'll tell you one thing, I'm starting to believe him about Thérèse. I think maybe he did call it off because she was so shook up. And now he's worried about the memorial service and how that's going to affect her. He'd like to have Brian back in the ground by then; you know, so it's over and done. I told him I didn't think there was much chance."

"I don't think so either." Gideon sipped the coffee; stale but welcome. "Tell me, what did he say about the facial surgery? Did he know about it?"

"Not a thing. Brian never mentioned it. I'm not sure Nick believes you."

Gideon sank into a chair and eased his shoulders back; he was still a little stiff from leaning over the bones. "Doesn't that strike you as peculiar, John? Here's some kind of absolutely devastating accident—it had to have been a major event in Brian's life—why would he make a secret of it?"

"Well, I don't know that he made a secret of it; maybe he just didn't like to talk about it. If it was that bad, you can't blame him."

"Yes, but he's been part of the family for what, five years? People would have heard about it by now. At least he must have mentioned it to Thérèse, and she'd be bound to talk about it some time or other—unless he made it clear that he didn't want anybody to know. And why would he do that?"

"I don't know. Why?" John sat down opposite him and tilted his chair back against the wall.

"I don't know either. Let me ask you something else." He

showed him the fibulas and explained about the muscle attachment sites. "I've been trying to think of how he developed those. Any idea?"

John slowly shook his head. "Not a clue."

"He didn't do anything on the farm that required a lot of balancing?"

"Not that I can think of. Bouncing around in a jeep over those roads, maybe, trying to keep from falling out?"

"Uh-uh. You'd need to be standing, not sitting." He thought for a few seconds. "Did he have a sailboat?"

"You could get those from sailing?"

"To tell the truth, I don't know. You'd have to do a *lot* of sailing. But it seems logical, doesn't it? With the deck tilting and shifting and all?"

"You're asking me? How would I know? But I never heard about him being any kind of sailor."

"Well, then, my guess is, this is a result of something he *used* to do, before Tahiti; something he did for a long time. What did he do before he came out here?"

"He was a, what do you call it, a teaching assistant, at Bennington. That's where Thérèse met him."

"He was already around thirty, then, wasn't he? What about before that?"

"Who knows? He was a student, I guess."

"Do you know if he—"

"Doc, what's the big deal, anyway? I mean, the bone stuff is interesting, but what does it have to do with anything?"

What it had to do with, Gideon said, was the fact that there seemed to be an awful lot about Brian Scott that wasn't general knowledge. How had he sustained that awful damage to his skull, and what had his life been like during the many months it must have taken to repair it? How had he developed muscles that were the fibular equivalents of a champion weightlifter's huge triceps? In a family as talkative and open as John's, wasn't it remarkable that nobody seemed to know?

"I guess so," John admitted, "but, you know, Brian always was a pretty quiet kind of guy, not like the rest of us, didn't blow his own horn. And it wasn't like he grew up out here with everybody else. There are probably a lot of things about him we don't know."

"That's my point. What else is there? He was murdered, that we know for sure. But why are we so sure that it had anything to do with his life in Tahiti? He'd only been here a few years. Maybe this was something from his past catching up with him."

John stood up and took a few steps around the table with his cup, thinking about it. "Like that old business with his wife back in the States, you mean?"

"Like anything."

John put down his coffee and chewed his lip. "Doc, what do you say we go have a talk with Thérèse? She ought to be able to fill in some of these holes. I've been wanting to talk to her anyway."

"Shouldn't we just mention this to Bertaud and let him—"

John waved this aside. "Am I getting in Bertaud's way? Am I interfering with him? There are just some things I'd like to know for myself. How about going to see her after you finish here?"

"John, I hate to keep being a wet blanket, but that part of it is your affair. The bones I'm willing to deal with, but I barely know Thérèse; I'd be an intruder."

"Well, what the hell am I supposed to do, ask her how he got hyperdeveloped fibular musculature? And then figure out if what she says makes sense?"

After a moment, Gideon laughed. "Tell you what. Let me finish up here—I need to write up a report—and meanwhile you can go over to the *gendarmerie* and tell Bertaud whatever he wants to know. It should take me a couple of hours at most. I can meet you there when I take the report over. Say one o'clock? Then Thérèse, how's that?"

"Lunch first," John said.

"That," said Gideon, "goes without saying."

Chapter 23

"I don't know what you mean," Thérèse said, her upper lip beginning to tremble.

"I mean," John said gently, "we have to clear up these things. Brian was *murdered*, Thérèse. Don't you want us to find out who did it?"

Her lovely eyes brimmed instantly. "I don't see how you can say . . . how you can know that he was . . . from just a few little b . . . a few little b . . ." Tears flowed down silken cheeks. She bowed her head.

John, in obvious discomfort, appealed to Gideon. "It's the truth, isn't it, Doc?"

"It's true, Thérèse," Gideon said, not very comfortable himself. The interview with John's cousin had been painful from the start. Since Brian's death she had been living at her parents' house in Papara, and they had found her there, down at the beach, in a yellow sundress, sitting in a thatch-roofed pergola with a simple word-puzzle book open in front of her. The twins, happily unencumbered by frocks, or by any clothing at all other than little straw hats, played companionably in the sun a few yards away. She had received the two men warmly—there was no mistaking the affection between her and John—but every question about Brian had been met with lowered eyes, hesitant mumbles, shrugs, and sentence fragments.

Did she know how Brian had suffered the injury to his face? "His . . . I didn't . . . I don't . . ." Shrug. Mumble.

Could she account for the extreme development of his leg muscles? "I don't . . . I didn't . . . Do you . . ." Shrug. Mumble.

What were the details of Brian's break-up with his wife in the United States? "Well, his wife was never . . . she lived in . . . they didn't really . . ." Shrug. Mumble. Blush.

John had been remarkably patient, considering that he was John, but Gideon could sense the exasperation quietly building up. "Thérèse, listen. I want to ask you something else, and I want you to answer me honestly. How did you and Brian meet?"

"Well . . . Claudine, don't do that, honey," she called over his shoulder. "You wouldn't like it if Claudette put sand in *your* ear. Oh, I'm sorry, John, what did you say?"

"How did you and Brian meet?"

"But you already know that. He was a teaching assistant at Bennington when I was there. And then a few years later, when he was here on vacation from his job, he remembered me and gave me a call, and we . . . we got together." Shrug. Mumble. But at least she'd managed a string of complete sentences.

"And what was the job he was on vacation from?"

She frowned uneasily at him. "John, why do you sound so . . . so . . ."

"What was the job, Thérèse?"

"I forget, exactly. In Michigan. It was a computer company . . . CompuLine, I think . . ."

"No, Thérèse."

She blinked. "No? What do you mean, no? I don't . . ."

"There is no CompuLine in Michigan."

"Well, I told you, maybe I—"

"There's a Compuworld, but they never had a Brian Scott."

"Well, maybe—"

"And there was no teaching assistant named Brian Scott at Bennington the years you were there."

"Well, technically maybe he was a, a research assistant, or a—"

"And no research assistant, no temporary lecturer, no graduate student, no nothing. No Brian Scott."

Her mouth opened. For a second or two she couldn't speak. She seemed—it was hard for Gideon to come up with a word for her expression—startled, frightened, wary. "No, you're wrong, John—"

"Thérèse, I checked. I made some calls from the *gendarmerie* just a few hours ago."

"You did?" Her face was rigid with apprehension.

You did? Gideon almost echoed. No wonder John had seemed so preoccupied at lunch, a late bite at a roadside pizza restaurant in Punaauia on the way from Papeete. But then Gideon had been preoccupied too, mulling over the obscure functions of *m. soleus,* and he hadn't contributed much to the conversation either.

"But I *did* meet him there!" Thérèse cried, jumping up, "and he *said* he was a teaching assistant, and he was always around the business department, and . . . and . . ." She was crying again, not just a few becoming tears this time, but with her eyes and nose streaming, her face bunched and reddened, and her body shaking. "Why are you doing this? Don't you believe me? I swear I'm telling the truth!"

The girls had run to their mother and clasped her about the legs, weeping along with her. "Bad man," murmured one of them to John.

John was plainly distressed. He put his hands tenderly on Thérèse's quaking shoulders. "Shh, Thérèse, don't cry. Everything's going to work out. Of course we believe you. We're just trying to put everything together. Come on now, shh. Of course we believe you."

* * *

"She's lying," he said to Gideon as they returned to the car. "From the word go," said Gideon.

* * *

Julie picked up the telephone on the first ring. "Hello?"

"Well, hi," Gideon said. As always, his voice softened, mellowed, upon hearing hers. He was sprawled on a rattan chair in his cottage, his feet up on the table, comfortably relaxed and feeling virtuous besides; after dinner with John at a good French restaurant he had actually put in a couple of hours on his symposium notes.

"Well, hi," she said quietly, her voice a little husky as well. Husky and sleepy.

It was 9 P.M. in Tahiti, 11 P.M. in Port Angeles. He imagined her in one of the living room armchairs, black-haired, dark-eyed, pretty, her face scrubbed, her sturdy, bare feet curled under her, wearing the thick terry-cloth robe and flannel pajamas that she got out of the closet when he was away. She was probably sipping a glass of sherry, or perhaps a cup of hot chocolate, and reading before going to bed.

Virgil, probably. Julie, who was somewhat given to sudden efforts at self-improvement, had decided some months before that her classical education was lacking, that she was tired of pretending to be familiar with classics she'd never read, and that it was time to do something about it. Gideon, an old hand at pretending to be familiar with classics he'd never read, had advised against expending the required effort, but Julie had stuck unflinchingly to her guns, slogging through dense, scholarly translations of Homer, Plato, Sophocles, and Aristotle, and recently moving on to the Romans. When he had left she was a third of the way through the *Aeneid* and giving every indication of enjoying it.

Indeed, he heard the thump of a book being closed, the clink of glass.

"You sound wonderful," he said.

"You do too."

"God, I can't believe it's only been—what, three days?" he blurted. "Ah, Julie, you have no idea how much I miss you. Without you around, I'm just not whole. I can't wait to get back . . . hold you . . . kiss you . . . tell you how much I love you . . ."

"My goodness." There was a pause while she took this in. "Say, who is this?"

"This is your husband," he said tolerantly.

"Husband, eh? How do I know you're who you say you are? You could be anybody."

Sometimes she was like this, kittenish and coy. In anyone else it would have made his toes curl, but in Julie it charmed him utterly. As did just about everything else about her.

"I love the way your *pyramidalis nasi* wrinkles your nose when you laugh," he said. "I never get enough of your incredibly sexy popliteal fossae. Your subtrochanteric—"

"It *is* you!" she cried. "I knew it, I was just testing."

"How's everything there?" Gideon asked. "How's Virgil? How're the elk?"

"The elk are fine, they send you their best. Tell me what's been happening there."

"Well, to start with, John damn near got us both arrested."

"*What?* Start at the beginning." He heard her settle herself more comfortably, and then the plumping of a pillow. She had been reading in bed, not in a chair.

He started at the beginning. He told her about Nick's sudden change of mind when they arrived, about the contretemps with Bertaud, about the adventure in the graveyard and the giant gendarme with his climactic *Arrêtez-vous, s'il vous plaît.* By that time she was laughing, and her pretty laughter had him thinking that maybe it had been funny after all, even if it had seemed anything but at the time.

Julie had always been a good listener, and Gideon went on from there to tell her about Nick, and Maggie, and Thérèse, and the rest of the clan, about the family dinner the evening before, about his tour of the farm with Tari. And about Brian's skeleton.

The end of the narrative was greeted by five cheerful little *pips.* She had taken the cordless telephone and gone to the kitchen to heat some more hot chocolate in the microwave. "So he *was* murdered," she said.

"Yup. Care to offer any ideas on the perp?" He asked the question offhandedly but he knew from long experience that Julie had a way of sorting the data that he gave her and coming up with things that had gotten by him, of making out forests where he saw nothing but trees, or not even trees but only twigs and branches.

"A few," she said meditatively. "What about you?"

"Well, I keep coming back to Maggie. Not in any serious way, but there is that business with the shed and then with the jeep. I don't know, it probably doesn't amount to anything, and besides I can't think of any reason for Maggie in particular to want to get rid of Brian—I mean, any more than anyone else did."

"Oh, I can help you there."

She tossed it out so carelessly that it made him laugh. "Can you, now."

"Jealousy," she said. "And resentment."

Maggie was Nick's eldest daughter, she went on; homely, hardworking, ambitious—

"I don't know how ambitious she is," Gideon said. "She seems to like it pretty well where she is."

Be that as it may, Julie told him, certainly she was possessive enough as a daughter to be hugely resentful when the son Nick had always wanted walked in in the form of youthful, handsome Brian Scott and proceeded not only to appropriate her only sister but to pretty much take over the place piece by piece, including a substantial chunk of Nick's fatherly affections. Wasn't that enough of a basis on which to suppose that Maggie might fervently wish him gone? Possibly even enough to kill him herself?

"You know," Gideon said slowly, "that's a point."

"Are you honestly going to tell me it never occurred to you?"

"Um . . . no, it didn't."

He heard her chuckle. "Gideon, you're amazing. You are probably the most intelligent man I know, and yet sometimes—"

"Well, I guess I wasn't thinking along those lines," he said, laughing. "Hey, what do you mean, 'probably'?"

She ignored the question. "I wasn't really thinking along those lines either, as a matter of fact. You know who I *was* thinking about—"

"Let me guess. Thérèse."

"Why Thérèse?"

"Because I made the mistake of saying she was gorgeous, and as a woman you're naturally inclined—"

"Oh, baloney. You happen to be right, it's Thérèse—"

"Ho."

"But it's got nothing to do with how sexy she is. It has to do with the more pertinent fact that Thérèse happens to be the person who made Nick call the exhumation off."

"*That* did not escape my notice," Gideon said, "but she also happens to be the person who wrote a pitiful letter to Pele, goddess of fire, a few weeks ago, begging for protection for Brian."

"In order to make herself look innocent after the fact, maybe?"

"Impossible. She had no idea John's sister would ever see it."

"And how do you know that, exactly? Because she batted those big, beautiful eyes and said so?"

He paused. "Well, I grant you, that's a point too. It *could* have been a ploy."

"Besides, you and John think she's holding things back too. You said so."

"Well, yes, but . . . yes."

But Julie hadn't met Thérèse, he had. As John had once put it, there were some people in the world who did unto others and other people who got done unto. And Thérèse was definitely a done-unto. A clinging vine, a model of low self-esteem, a mother's (or rather father's) darling—but not a murderer, never a murderer. Still, he'd been wrong about that kind of thing before . . .

"Gideon," Julie said in a softer voice, "when will you be back? I miss you too, you know."

"As soon as I can, Julie. Now that Bertaud is taking this seriously I feel as if I ought to stick around a few more days in case I'm needed. Tomorrow morning he wants John and me at Nick's office at eleven. He wants to have a few things out with Nick, and I think we're supposed to be there to keep him honest."

"About what?"

"About the on-again, off-again business with the exhumation, I suppose, but I'm just guessing."

"You *are* having some fun too, I hope? Relaxing a little?"

"Sure, I even took a nap in a hammock the other day. And the whole thing is fun in a way. You know me."

"Do I ever." They were winding down. "Are you getting all the Paradise coffee you want?"

"Plenty."

"Good, then maybe we won't have to buy any at home for a while."

Gideon laughed. Julie, as much of a coffee drinker as he was, generally went for Starbucks or Seattle's Best; all of Nick's coffees, she felt, were overpriced for their quality. It was one of the few differences in their food preferences.

"Well," he said reluctantly, "I guess I'll get back to my notes."

"And I'll get to bed. I was staying up, hoping you'd call."

"I'll call again tomorrow. Any more words of wisdom before I hang up? Anybody else we should be casting a suspicious eye on?"

"Nick," she said without hesitation.

"Because of the way he waffled on the exhumation?"

"That, and because of how hard he was trying to keep everybody from talking about the Superstar thing in front of you and John. He's hiding something too."

"But I told you, he was just being a good host. He's a courtly kind of guy in his own way, and he simply felt it wasn't good taste to talk business in front of dinner guests. That's all."

"And how do you know *that?*"

"I guess I don't, really," he said with a smile. "Okay, Julie, I'll admit, you've given me a few things to think about. I'll talk to John about them in the morning."

"You know what I keep wondering?" she said.

"No, what do you keep wondering?"

"I keep wondering, what the heck would you guys would do without me?"

Chapter 24

The offices of the Paradise Coffee Company were in a larg
Quonset hut of indeterminate age and origin that had been se
up near the drying shed. This musty fossil had originally been
found abandoned in a jungly section of the land that Dean
Parks had purchased to build the Shangri-La. Nick had bough
it from him forty-five years earlier for $100, moved it to hi
plantation, and set it up as headquarters for his short-lived copr
empire. When that had fizzled and he'd switched to coffee h
had seen no reason for new office space. Nelson's never-ending
arguments that a more civilized habitat was good business prac
tice had finally convinced him to lease a handsome suite of of
fices overlooking the loading docks in downtown Papeete, but
Nelson himself was the only one who used it regularly, along
with his staff of four. The Hut, as everyone referred to it, re
mained the locus of most of the hurly-burly of Paradise Cof
fee's day-to-day management.

But when John and Gideon arrived the next morning at

quarter to eleven, there was no hurly-burly in evidence. The clerk who generally sat in the anteroom was out sick, Nelson was at the Papeete office, Maggie was conducting a training session, and Rudy was off somewhere. As a result, they found themselves looking through a string of empty cubicles at Nick Druett, sitting alone in his Spartan office at the far end. Even through four partitions of cheap glass, they could see the scowl on his face.

"Nelson was right, how does that grab you?" was his muttered greeting when they rapped on the glass wall of his cubicle.

"About what?" John asked.

"About Tari." He slammed shut the account book he'd had open on his desk. "The guy has screwed up everything he's gotten his paws on." He banged the book with the flat of his hand. "The only difference I have with Nelson is that I don't believe it's a bunch of innocent mistakes; I think the big bastard's been ripping us off from here to Patagonia." He puffed his cheeks and let out a long, exasperated breath through his mouth. "Or who knows, maybe I'm wrong, maybe the guy's just dumb. Rudy's in there with him right now, trying to get it all sorted out. Hey, sit down, sit down."

Without asking he poured them coffee from a jug on a side table. Blue Devil, Gideon thought appreciatively at his first sip.

"Listen, Gideon, I've already said this to John, but I want to apologize to you too." He was wearing an honest-to-God shirt, with buttons and sleeves (short) and a collar, apparently in honor of Bertaud's impending visit. "For the runaround."

"That's not necessary, Nick."

"Yeah, it is. I'm sorry I gave you such a hard time. You were right—you were both right—and I was wrong. If you hadn't stuck to your guns we *still* wouldn't know what really happened to Brian. So thanks for . . . well, thanks."

"I'm sorry it's been so tough on your daughter," Gideon said awkwardly.

Nick smiled vaguely, joylessly. "Yeah, me too. But believe me, she's happier going through this than if she knew she was letting somebody get away with Brian's murder." He sipped mechanically from his mug. "John, who killed him?" he asked softly.

"Who knew where he was camping?" John replied.

"Are you kidding? Everybody knew. He used the same spot year in, year out. I've got thirty acres on Raiatea. That's where he set up camp—on the plateau." He shook his big head slowly back and forth. "I'll never build there now, that's for sure."

Gideon's mind had been running along a side track of its own. "Nick, just how was Tari ripping you off?"

"Well, he was—" Nick looked at him sharply. "You think there's a connection? To Brian?"

Gideon shrugged. "Could be." *When a lot of funny things are going on together,* Abe Goldstein had pointed out more than once, *they got a funny way of turning out to be related.* The Law of Interconnected Monkey Business, his old professor had called it.

"Well, he was skimming," Nick said. "Not hard to do in a business like this, where there are a million different prices and they change every day. Say we're buying five thousand pounds of green beans from a farm in Java to go into the Weekend Blend or one of the other low-end products—" Gideon winced "—and they're charging us a buck-eighty a pound. Well, Tari just adds a little zero, records the price as ten-eighty a pound instead of one-eighty, and keeps the difference. The people in Java get their money so they don't complain, and the books balance, and we don't know any better. So Tari just walks away with nine times five thousand."

"Fifty thousand bucks," John said.

"Forty-five thousand," said Nick bitterly. "Let's be fair to the guy. And that's only one example. I can give you at least two more and I guarantee there'll be more to come when we really dig into things."

"But how could he get away with it?" asked Gideon. "That's a big difference, one-eighty to ten-eighty. Surely you, or Rudy, or Nelson, or *somebody* would know what's what, would know what the price was supposed to be."

Nick shook his head. "It's not the way we do business. At Paradise when we give somebody responsibility we trust him," he said righteously, then laughed at himself. "Or did until now. Look. For the past two weeks Tari has been spending half his time at the Papeete office, half here. He's had complete access to everything—the books, the accounts—and complete authority to do anything Brian could do. If he needed help, he asked for it, that's all. We trusted him. Thanks to Maggie," he couldn't resist adding in a grumpy aside.

"So how did you find out?" Gideon asked.

"We found out because Nelson never trusted the big, ugly bugger and he was keeping an eye on him, and when he finally got together with Rudy and compared the figures they didn't match."

John suddenly held up his hand. "That was a shot." He had his head tilted to one side, listening. Gideon hadn't heard anything.

"Nah," Nick said, "it's just one of the vans; got a problem with backfiring."

John listened a moment longer, then settled down again. "Probably so."

"Nick," Gideon said, "how do you know it's Tari who's doing it and not somebody else?"

"I know because it never happened before Tari got a chance to get his fat fingers in the pie, that's how I know. The skimming started when he started, not a day before. It's real obvious, Gideon, there can't be any doubt about it." He glanced up over their shoulders. "We're back here, Léopold!"

Colonel Bertaud had arrived promptly on the stroke of eleven, and with him was the large, bearded gendarme who had surprised them at the graveyard. The two men came down the linoleum-floored hallway, Bertaud's small feet pattering twice for every gallumphing step of his giant assistant's. The colonel was in his dapper uniform, the gendarme in his blue shirt and shorts.

"Good morning, Nick," Bertaud said, in the doorway of the cubicle. He nodded civilly to John and Gideon. "Good day gentlemen. Thank you for—"

At that moment the rear door of the hut, only a few feet away, burst open and banged against the wall. In the doorway stood Rudy Druett, as pale as death, swaying back and forth, his thin hair disheveled and straggling.

"I, er, don't feel very well," he said vaguely.

Several pairs of well-meaning hands were thrust out toward him, but Rudy, snapping out of his semitrance, was suddenly wild. "I'm all right, I'm all right!" he shouted, pushing them away. "Don't touch me, I don't need any help, I'm fine, I'm fine. He's dead, I killed him. I can't believe it, Nick, I can't make myself—"

"Rudy," Nick said forcefully. "Stop raving. Sit down." He slid a wooden chair to him. Shakily, Rudy sat. The hysteria subsided, leaving him limp. His face was a sickly, glistening gray. Only the blue-black bags under his eyes had any color. Even his eyes were gray, almost colorless, something John had never noticed before.

"Now collect your thoughts," Nick told him. "Tell us what happened. Slowly. Who's dead?"

"Dead?" Rudy said after a second. He was staring straight ahead, as if watching something the others couldn't see.

"Come on, pull yourself together," Nick said harshly. "Look at me."

Rudy raised his eyes obediently. The feverish glare dimmed a little.

"That's better," Nick said. "Now. Who's dead?"

"Tari."

"Tari!"

Nick's inadvertent shout made Rudy flinch as if he'd been truck. His hand went to his mouth. "Oh my God," he said, "my God . . ."

"May I?" Bertaud interceded smoothly, edging an unresisting Nick out of the way. He pulled up another chair and set it cross from Rudy's. "My name is Colonel Bertaud. And you re . . . ?"

The tranquil, beautifully modulated voice had its effect. Rudy Druett. I—"

"Very good, Mr. Druett. A glass of water? No? All right, hen. Someone is dead, yes?"

Rudy nodded. "Tari, one of the, the workers. I—I shot him. had to, you see . . ."

"And where did this happen?"

"In the cabin."

"In the cabin. And where is the cabin?"

Nick cut in impatiently. "Right there." He pointed through he glass panel of the door at a small stone shack about a hun-red yards up a path that led up the hill. "Tari's been using it r an office."

"I killed him," Rudy said. "I shot him, in the . . . in the . . ."

He had calmed down under the influence of Bertaud's simple, methodical questioning, but his face was still the color of dust. "Here," he said at last, touching the side of his head.

Bertaud glanced at the gendarme and motioned with his chin toward the cabin. "Dumont," he said.

Dumont left, his big, bare thighs bunching as he took the path at a heavy trot.

"Now then," Bertaud said. "Please explain."

Rudy ran a hand through his scant, rumpled hair. "I wish everybody would sit down," he said, abruptly peevish. "You're all looming over me."

Bertaud waved a hand at the others. Nick and Gideon took chairs off to the sides. John sat on a nearby desk.

"Explain," said Bertaud again, with a little more flint in his voice. "Why did you go to the cabin?"

"I asked him to," said Nick.

"Nick, be quiet," Bertaud said without taking his eyes from Rudy. "Go ahead."

After a couple of false starts Rudy began to talk, disjointedly at first but then more steadily. The dead, flat pallor gave way to bright pink patches in his cheeks and at the sides of his throat. He had gone to the cabin, he explained, to have it out with Tari over the discrepancies in the records and to see if, against all odds, Tari could satisfactorily explain them. Tari had been nervous from the moment Rudy had walked in, as if he had sensed that something was up, and his very nervousness, even before they'd begun to talk, had convinced Rudy that there wasn't going to be any satisfactory explanation.

There wasn't. For the first few minutes Tari had fumblingly tried to talk his way out of trouble, but the discrepancies had been there for them both to see. Tari's manner had grown more desperate by the second, and he had finally reared up in his chair, seized Rudy by the front of the shirt, and begun to slam him against the stone wall in the cabin, shouting "You ain't going to tell nobody!" again and again.

"And you did what?" Bertaud asked when Rudy seemed to run down.

"What any sensible person would have done, of course," Rudy said in a brief stab at sounding more like his old self. "I sacrificed honor to prudence and swore to high heaven that I wouldn't tell a soul." But he couldn't keep it up. His eyes closed, he slumped in the chair.

"He looked frightened, not angry, to tell you the truth," he said, "but he was so excited, so *huge*, and he was *hurting* me . . . my feet were actually off the floor . . . you can't imagine . . . my head was banging . . ." His hand wandered absently to the back of his head and when he took it away there was a smear of drying blood on the palm. He stared at it, open-mouthed. Gideon thought he was going to faint.

Bertaud took the hand and pressed it down, out of sight. "Continue, please."

Tari had kept on thumping his head against the wall, Rudy told them, and at some point he must have blacked out because the next thing he knew he was lying crumpled against the base of the wall and Tari, in a frenzy, was rummaging in the top drawer of a cabinet near the door. As Rudy watched in horror, the Tahitian came up with what he was looking for, a long-barreled, old-fashioned revolver . . .

"That old Ruger Single-Six," Nick murmured to himself. "Tari's had it forever."

"I *knew* he was going to kill me," Rudy said with a burst of energy that sat him upright. He looked up fiercely, taking all of them in. "You have to believe that. If it had happened to you, you'd know too. Otherwise I'd never have had the nerve, not in a million years . . ."

He had jumped up and stumbled half-consciously across the

room, he said, and grabbed frantically at the gun with both hands. The instant he touched it, it went off—

"Must have had the hammer cocked," John said.

"Yes, the hammer, that's right!" Rudy exclaimed, as if this were some vital point. "It makes a little click—I heard it. I think that's what woke me up . . ."

"And the bullet struck him?" Bertaud asked.

"Yes . . . well, the funny thing is, I thought *I* was shot at first. It's amazing—I was sure I felt it hit me, I thought I was dying, and Tari was just standing there without moving . . . but in a second he just—he just fell over—backward, like a big tree falling . . ."

A shiver rolled visibly down his body. The energy went out of him once more. He closed his eyes again and didn't open them as he continued. "There's a fireplace with a raised hearth. He hit the back of his head on it. I . . . heard it crack. He didn't move. When I went to look at him I could see—"

Dumont came back, huffing from his run. "Dead as a herring," he said to Bertaud in French. "Gunshot wound in the right temple, blood all over the place, what a mess. I called headquarters. LePeau and his people are on the way."

"Good. See if Dr. Viennot is available too. He'll want to have a look. Then get this one"—*this one* was Rudy—"off to the hospital to have his head looked after, and then have Brusseau take his statement."

"I don't need a hospital," Rudy said in English. "I'm perfectly fine, all I need is a Band-Aid. I was just a little woozy there for a—"

The policeman ignored him. "Should I seal the cabin?" he asked Bertaud.

"No, I'll take care of it. I want to go and see for myself."

Dumont left, hauling a querulous, weakly protesting Rudy with him.

Bertaud opened the back door, then hesitated. "Mr. Lau, Dr. Oliver—if you would care to see the scene . . . ?"

They both answered at once.

"Sure," John said.

"Good God, no!" said Gideon.

Chapter 25

"Sorry, I just don't buy it," Gideon said with a shake of his head. "I just feel there has to be more to it than that."

"Interconnected monkey business?" John said, munching peanuts. John too had heard Abe discourse on the subject.

"That's right. There's too much going on, John. Brian's murder figures in here somewhere."

John scooped up another handful of nuts from a bowl on the bar and popped some into his mouth. "What happened to that other law you're always spouting off about—the one about how you're not supposed to make anything more complicated than it has to be?"

"Occam's razor, the law of parsimony," Gideon said. "Economy of assumptions. Choose the simplest explanation that's consistent with the data."

"Right, makes sense, so why go out of your way to assume there's some mysterious connection to Brian when you don't have to?"

Gideon sipped from his glass of Chablis. "Then what's your explanation?"

"Of what? When Brian got killed Tari figured that was his chance to get away with a little skimming, but he got greedy—or stupid—he got caught with his hand in the till, he panicked—and he wound up dead. What's to explain?"

"Brian's getting murdered, for starters."

John sighed. "As far as we know, that's an unrelated issue, Doc. Let's not make things any harder than they are. You know what my boss says about you?"

"Yes, I know," Gideon said sourly.

John waggled his fingers to call for another Hinano. "Economy of assumptions, I like that. Uh-oh, watch out, here she goes again."

The bartender, one of a pair of Junoesque Tahitians in floral tiaras, bright *pareus*, and bare feet, used a hammer to whack a mounted pair of cymbals at the center of the circular bar.

"BOOM-BOOM!" she bellowed as the reverberations died away.

"That's three times in three minutes," Gideon said, his head ringing. "Maybe we ought to move away from the bar. What do you say to the terrace?"

"Amen," said John, picking up his glass.

After the wild scene in Nick's office they had not managed to get together again until almost five in the afternoon. They had gone to the Shangri-La's bar to talk things out undisturbed, only to find the place jammed. Thursday, it seemed, was half-price-happy-hour-day, and the bar was packed with locals, mostly couples consisting of merry, matronly, spreading Tahitian women and their lean, aging French husbands, lined, taciturn men who smoked their cigarettes down to quarter-inch stubs and concentrated on getting quietly sloshed.

The specialty drink of the day, at only 100 French Pacific francs, was Boom-Booms, every order of which was accompanied by a ceremonial clash of cymbals and the full-throated cry of "Boom-Boom!" Out of curiosity Gideon had asked one of the bartenders what went into one and listened appalled as he was told: light rum, dark rum, brandy, vodka, curaçao, mango juice, papaya juice, passion fruit juice. And a sprinkling of grated chocolate on top.

"Wow, not bad for a buck," John had murmured, but although he had wavered perceptibly for a few moments he had sensibly stuck with beer.

The atmosphere on the terrace was more pleasant by far. An afternoon rain squall, still visible to the west, had swept through a few minutes before, bringing out the perfume of a hundred different kinds of flowers and leaving the slate paving stones shimmering with reflections from the sky.

"All right," Gideon said as they sat themselves at an umbrellaed table, "how do we know that Tari didn't get greedy *before* Brian died? How do we know it wasn't Tari who killed him to get him out of the way? Or maybe Tari was already skimming, and Brian caught on to him, and Tari murdered him to keep him from telling."

"No good," John said. "If Brian found out something like that, how could Tari afford to wait until he went off on his vacation? He would have had to kill him right away, before he had a chance to tell anybody else. The way he tried to do with Rudy."

"That's true," Gideon said. "How is Rudy, by the way?"

"A little shell-shocked, but not too bad. They're keeping him in the hospital overnight to play it safe. I dropped in on him for a while. All he wants to do now is get out of here and go back to Whidbey Island where it's nice and quiet."

"You can't blame him for that."

"No." He moved his bottle of Hinano from place to place

on the table, leaving interlocking rings of moisture. "Listen, there's something else I want to say about Tari. This is a guy I got to know pretty well over the years, and I always thought he was okay. Yeah, I can see him, you know, yielding to temptation and maybe skimming a little off the top, I can see him panicking when he got caught, I can see him flying off the handle, I can even see him losing it altogether and trying to blow Rudy away—but cold-blooded, premeditated murder? Uh-uh, I just don't see him sneaking up on Brian and slitting his throat."

After a few seconds he added: "Let alone being in on all those other goofy 'accidents.' It just wasn't his style, the poor bastard."

"You're probably right." Gideon sipped his wine and watched the gray, slanting threads of the retreating squall roil a patch of ocean, heading for Moorea. "Besides, we know he wasn't in on those accidents. Not the one with the jeep, anyway."

John frowned. "How do we 'know'?"

"Because he wouldn't have been dumb enough to be right there in the jeep with Brian when it went over the side. He almost got killed himself."

"That's a good point, Doc. I forgot all about that."

"Afternoon, gents." It was Dean Parks, convivial host. "Thought I'd let you know the *Leaky Tiki*'s about to embark on the evening sunset cruise. All aboard that's going aboard. Real peaceful-like, why don't you give it a try?"

John and Gideon looked at each other. "Why not?"

*   *   *

Peaceful the *Leaky Tiki* wasn't. Essentially an awninged platform mounted on two large outrigger shells, it included a bar that continued to dispense Boom-Booms (happily, without the cymbals), and although the Frenchmen merely sank into a deeper gloom, their wives got louder and more talkative, and a contingent of soused Chileans chimed in with a jolly medley of South American songs of death, betrayal, and revenge.

Still, Gideon and John found a relatively quiet place at the rear, sitting at the edge of the platform with their legs dangling, their feet not quite touching the water. From there, with their backs to the others, they sat looking out on a scene so gorgeous that it drowned out the hubbub behind them. They were putt-putting slowly through the lagoon in water that varied, depending on its depth, from bright, pure yellow to green, to aquamarine, to vivid, almost purple indigo. When they looked down they could see schools of small striped fish, yellow and purple and red, wheeling in a body through the clear water. And always in the distance, the strange, moonscape-silhouette of Moorea, with the sun abruptly disappearing behind the tallest peaks so that an incredibly colored sunset suddenly flared as if someone had just flung open the door to a colossal blast furnace.

It was only when the spectacular display began to dim a few minutes later that John spoke.

"I've been thinking about Brian."

"Mm." Gideon was still off somewhere behind the mountains of Moorea.

"I made some phone calls about him this afternoon."

"Phone calls," repeated Gideon, watching the last of the colors fade quickly to rose and then to mauve.

"Yeah, come on, wake up, will you? I was trying to do your work for you."

"My work?" Gideon echoed, but he had drifted back to the real world now. He picked up his wine glass to take a sip but found it empty.

"I was trying to see if I could find out about his face and that weird tibia of his."

"Fibula."

"Fibula," John allowed good-humoredly. "So I looked up his doctor to see what he had to say."

"Good idea, I should have done it myself. What did he say?"

"Nothing. There wasn't any doctor. Brian didn't have one, he never went for checkups or anything like that."

"He broke his arm, he must have gone somewhere."

"To the emergency room at the hospital. And that's where he went back to have it looked after." His meaningful look implied that this was somehow significant.

Gideon frowned back at him. "Well, that's interesting, but I don't—"

"So then I tried his dentist—you know, maybe he'd know something about the damage to his face?"

"And?"

"Guess."

It took a moment for Gideon to see where he was heading. "No dentist?"

"No dentist."

"You're telling me that in five years he never once went to a dentist, never once had his teeth checked?"

"Not exactly. He went to this old Frenchman, about ninety, a real old-fashioned dentist who lives way down in Vairao on Tahiti Iti, who treats the natives around there. Officially, he's been retired for thirty years so he's not supposed to, but the authorities look the other way. And that's who Brian used."

"Even so, some of that maxillary damage must have shown up on his dental X rays—"

"What dental X rays? I told you, this guy's old-fashioned. And he only saw Brian three times. He says he never noticed a thing, Brian had real nice teeth, good healthy enamel."

"No doctor, no dentist," Gideon said thoughtfully. He had

his legs drawn up now, his arms around his knees. "Why didn't you mention it before?"

"I didn't think it was worth talking about—I mean, it didn't get me anywhere, did it?" His face was hard to see in the on-coming night, but he seemed to be studying the wake of the boat, now a curving double trail, phosphorescent in the dim-ness. "But I tell you, Doc, the more I think about it, the funnier it gets. It's almost as if . . ."

Almost as if Brian had been purposefully and persistently try-ing to render himself nonexistent as far as any kind of paper trail was concerned. There were no doctor's records, no den-tist's records. There were no employment or income forms be-cause Brian's shares in Paradise were in Thérèse's name. There was no marriage certificate because he and Thérèse had never married. There was no passport or travel documentation be-cause he had never left French Polynesia after taking that "hon-eymoon" trip to Hawaii with Thérèse five years earlier; in all this time Raiatea had been as far as he'd ever gotten from the is-land of Tahiti.

"That's all true," Gideon said slowly. "He even tried not to leave a record when he died. No church service, no ceremony, no public cemetery, just a hole in the ground in a jungle graveyard."

"Yup. And don't forget that nobody at Bennington or at that outfit in Michigan that he was supposed to be working for ever heard of him either. I'm starting to think there's a whole lot we don't know about Brian Scott."

"Do we even know his name was really Brian Scott?" Gideon said.

John shook his head. "At this point I don't know what we know. I'm gonna get on the horn to the States tomorrow and see what I can find out. In the meantime, I know exactly what I need to do right now."

"Which is?"

John got to his feet and brushed himself off. "I need to get me a Boom-Boom on the rocks."

*   *   *

"I agree with you," Julie said into the telephone when Gideon had finished his rendering of the day's events. "Somehow or other this is connected with Brian's murder too."

"Tell that to John."

"But what I don't understand," Julie said, "is why everybody's simply taking this Rudy character at his word."

"You mean," Gideon said, using his shoulder to wedge the telephone against his ear while he poured himself a glass of chocolate milk from the cottage's mini-refrigerator, "that he may not have been telling the whole truth?"

"I mean," she said, "how do you know that his whole story isn't trumped up? How do you know—this is just for example—that *he* wasn't the one who was fooling around with the books or whatever it was, and that Tari didn't find out what *he* was doing, and that Rudy didn't kill him to keep *him* quiet, and then trump up this story about Tari going berserk?"

Gideon swallowed half a glass of milk. He hadn't followed John's example with the Boom-Booms but his three glasses of wine followed by a Japanese dinner heavy with soy sauce had made him thirsty. "Well, I suppose it's possible, but it's a little unlikely."

In the first place, he explained, it was pretty well established that Tari was the one who was doing the fooling around with the finances. Nick and Nelson agreed with Rudy on that. Besides, if Rudy had been inclined that way he was in a position to have started years ago, but there was no indication of any such hanky-panky before Brian's death and Rudy's subsequent promotion. Besides that, according to John, Tari had recently been showing increasing signs of tension and anxiety.

In addition, Rudy's story of what had happened in the cabin had been strictly borne out by the police examination of the scene. There was a smudge of blood and a few hairs—graying like Rudy's, not black like Tari's—on the wall where Tari had been pummeling him. Also some more blood and hair—black like Tari's, not graying like Rudy's—on the edge of the hearth where Tari had hit his head on the way down. And the angle of the bullet hole in his temple—slightly upward, slightly backward—was consistent with Rudy's having grabbed Tari's gun hand and pushed it up, forcing a bent elbow, so that the guy fired up and back into his own head.

"Oh," said Julie. "Well, you didn't tell me all that." He heard her stifle a yawn. "This is certainly a wonderful conversation to be having before going to bed. Almost as calming as the eleven o'clock news."

"Well, you asked me—"

"I know I did. Just for a minute, though, I couldn't help thinking how nice it must be to be able to say 'What did you do today, dear?' to your husband and hear about something pleasant, like pretty flowers or little babies."

"You should have married a botanist, I guess. Or an obstetrician."

"Oh well, live and learn," Julie said. "Maybe next time."

* * *

Generally speaking, Gideon was a good sleeper, not given to nocturnal (or diurnal) worry or obsessive angst. But in his midtwenties he had gone through a long patch of insomnia, lying awake deep into the small hours and fretting about the way his dissertation was going (or not going), or about his father's failing health, or simply about the way the world was going to hell in a handbasket even back then. Then, somewhere, he had read about Napoleon's method for putting himself soundly and restoratively to sleep at night no matter how anxious the circumstances. The great man would picture in his mind a multi-drawered cabinet and then assign each of the matters that were worrying him to a separate drawer. In his mind's eye he would then glance briefly at the contents of each drawer and slam them firmly shut one after the other. When the last drawer was closed he would be asleep, or so he claimed.

The idea had appealed to Gideon and since then, on those few occasions when his mind refused to turn itself off at bedtime he had been constructing cabinets of his own, stuffing whatever was niggling away at him into the drawers and shutting them away for the night. The technique had worked too, although he wasn't as good a cabinetmaker as Napoleon; once in a while one of the drawers would pop open on its own, so to speak, bringing him awake at four or five in the morning in what seemed to be mid-thought, as if his mind had jump-started on its own, with or without his permission. He would lie there in the darkness, galvanized and yet dopey with sleep at the same time, feeling like an unwelcome observer, holding his breath and afraid to move for fear the fragile chain of logic would turn to vapor and disappear if his mind found out he was watching it.

Usually, that was exactly what it did, but every now and then, if things went right, the chain would hold; where there had been nothing but half-formed questions before, he would see at least the outlines of answers; where there had been only confusion and ambiguity, patterns would emerge.

So it was on this night. At 4:38 A.M. by the glowing display on the clock-radio beside his bed, his eyelids flicked open on their own. His mind was already whirring along in high gear.

At 4:51 he jumped out of bed. "Oh, wow," he whispered to himself.

Chapter 26

Two minutes later, having slipped into shorts and polo shirt, he was banging at the door of John's cottage.

"What, what?" came from within, peevish and muffled.

"John, it's me. I need to talk to you."

A groan. "Jesus, Doc, it's the middle of the night."

"It's almost five," Gideon said. It was nice to be waking John for a change, he thought. "Come on, let me in."

"Let yourself in, the damn door's open." A light went on in the cottage. John was sitting up in bed in a worn T-shirt, squinting at the light but managing to glare at Gideon as well. "Almost five," he snarled. "Really? I must have overslept."

"You're not in a very good mood."

"I wonder why."

"You're probably just a little out of sorts from those Boom-Booms."

"God," John said, which Gideon took as assent.

"Listen, I need to ask you something."

John yawned and massaged his face. The stubble sounded like sandpaper. "Okay, okay, all right, sit down. What?"

Gideon pulled up a chair. "What do Klingons look like?"

John stopped rubbing his face and studied Gideon with one of his less readable expressions. "Well, I can certainly see why you couldn't wait till daylight with a question like that," he said mildly. "How come you didn't wake me up hours ago?"

"Seriously, what do they look like?"

"What do you mean, what do they look like?"

"I mean, what do they look like?"

"You know what they look like. What's the matter, you never watched *Star Trek?*"

"No. Well, once. It had something to do with a lot of these cotton balls taking over the universe. I don't remember how it came out."

John shook his head and addressed the opposite wall. "The weird thing is, I believe him."

"What's so weird?" Gideon said, honestly puzzled.

"Look, Doc, you've seen *pictures* of them, haven't you? In magazines, in previews . . . haven't you just *once* accidentally flipped by a rerun or something?"

"Of course I have," Gideon told him impatiently, getting to his feet again, "but I don't know which ones the Klingons are."

"Worf is Klingon." John was practically shouting. "Gowron is a Klingon. Duras is a Klingon, Kahless the Unforgettable—"

"*John!*" Gideon yelled back at him from all of two feet away. "Just tell me what they *look* like, for Christ's sake!"

"Like this, for Christ's sake!" John exploded, holding his hands out from his head to suggest enormous size. "Big, bulgy foreheads—"

"That's what I thought." Gideon slapped his own forehead with the flat of his hand. "Good God, why didn't I see it before? Why didn't *you* see it before? How could we never think to—"

"See *what?*" John cried, baffled. "What are we talking about?"

Gideon fell back into his chair. "John, I may be four hundred feet out in left field, but I don't think so. I think—get set for this now—I think Brian Scott was Klingo Bozzuto."

John stared. "Brian was . . . you're saying . . ."

"That they were the same person: your clean-cut, good-looking, upright Brian, and Klingo Bozzuto, sleazy Mob-accountant-turned-stool-pigeon. Same guy."

"But—no, I told you, they gave Klingo a new ID and got him a job in the Midwest somewhere—Chicago, I think."

"That was a dozen years ago, John. When was the last report you got on him?"

There was a long silence. "I need some coffee," John said, swinging himself out of bed. He was wearing a pair of thread-bare, cutoff sweatpants to go with the T-shirt. "You want some coffee?"

"Do I," Gideon said.

While John made it (his cottage, like Gideon's, was stocked with an electric coffee-maker and, courtesy of Nick, a pound of Blue Devil), Gideon did his best to summarize the stream of early-morning thought of which he himself didn't yet have too firm a grasp. There were actually two separate streams, he explained, or three, really, but all of them had ended up in the same place. The first, the one that his mind was already working on when he woke up, was the fabric of lies and lacunae that Brian had woven around his past and his present: the nonexistent teaching assistantship at Bennington; the job that wasn't there at the company that didn't exist in Michigan; the shadowy vacuum that represented his past life; and the avoidance since he'd come to Tahiti of work permits, salary checks, passport, medical records, dental records, marriage records, and anything else that might be used to document his whereabouts and his very existence.

Put it all together and it added up to someone who wanted as little known about himself as possible, someone who was quite possibly keeping his very identity a secret. And from there it wasn't much of a leap to wondering if, somewhere along the way, he had perhaps taken the extreme step of *changing* his identity.

"And what," asked Gideon, now rolling along in full professorial mode, "is the first thing you do if you're serious about changing your identity?"

But John wasn't in the mood to play student. "Just tell me, okay?" he grumbled, bending over the coffee-maker. "It's too early in the morning for the Socratic method."

"You change your face, is what you do," said Gideon. "Which led me straight into stream number two; that huge operation—that operation that nobody seems to know anything about—on Brian's skull." He got up, walked to where John was, and spoke with quiet conviction. "It wasn't on account of an accident, John—it was a face-change operation. You told me the FBI gave Bozzuto a new identity and put him into a witness protection program after he testified, right? Well, there you are; don't they do plastic surgery on them to change their faces?"

"Sometimes," John allowed, not quite ready to go along yet, "not always. In fact, usually not." He poured two cups of coffee and added sugar and creamer to his own. "Now if *I* don't know whether they changed Bozzuto's looks, I sure don't see how you do."

"Easy," Gideon said. "He *looked* like a Klingon, right?" He made the same bulbous-forehead gesture that John had made earlier. "Now that doesn't happen to be a very common look down here on Planet Earth, so if they were trying to keep his identity a secret they'd pretty much have to change it; they wouldn't have any choice."

John was reflective. "Well, yeah, sure, you're right about that . . ."

"Is there any problem with their ages? How old was Bozzuto?"

"Um, let's see, he was probably, oh, maybe thirty at the time of the trials, so that would make him a little over forty now, and Brian was thirty-eight—so, yeah, the ages could fit, and changing his black hair to blond wouldn't be any problem, but—" He shook his head.

"But what?"

"But I tell you, it's hard to imagine that anybody could change a strange-looking bird like Bozzuto into a good-looking guy like Brian without giving him a brand-new head altogether. I mean, can they really *do* that with plastic surgery?"

"In a case like this, yes. Look, I think I understand what was wrong with Bozzuto, why he looked like that. From what you've said, I believe he had something called fibrous dysplasia of the skull. It's something like von Recklinghausen's disease—"

"English, please."

"You know, the Elephant Man syndrome—only it's a localized version, pretty much restricted to bony exostoses on and around the supraorbital torus."

"Really," John said, "bony exostoses on and around the supraorbital torus."

"Right, and if you get a plastic surgeon who knows what he's doing, it can be fixed. It's a massive operation—you have to take out a chunk of the frontal bone, do some hammer-and-chisel sculpting on it, and then put it back . . . which, if you remember, is exactly what was done to Brian. All that scarring—even the fractures—wasn't the result of an accident, i was done on purpose, by the surgeon himself. You have to do it to make the piece of bone fit back in after you change the shape; sometimes you even have to put it back in upside down to make it fit. And of course you have to do some substantial whittling around the orbits too, to make it all go together."

"Mm," said John.

"And the reason that you never saw any scars on his face was that they weren't accidental wounds; the surgeon could pick his places to make his incisions—hairline, behind the ears, and so on."

"Mm," said John.

"*Ergo,*" Gideon said, "unless we can come up with something better, which I very much doubt, we now have the reason that Brian Scott was so stingy with the details of his life: there *weren't* any details because there wasn't any Brian. There was only Klingo Bozzuto."

This shamelessly theatrical windup was received with measured silence. John carried the coffee to the rattan table and chairs in one corner and set it down for them. Only after they had their first grateful swallows did he say anything. And even then it was accompanied by a shrug.

"Maybe."

"*Maybe!* Where's the 'maybe'?"

"Well, for one thing, weren't you the guy that was explaining to me a couple of days ago that it *wasn't* plastic surgery, that it *couldn't* be plastic surgery, because if it was plastic surgery the bone would never be that beat up?"

"Well, as I recall, I said it was reconstructive surgery, but reconstructive surgery is just another name for a more radical form of pl—"

"And, let's see, correct me if I'm wrong here, but didn't you tell me that it was all the result of this humongous accident? 'Devastating accident,' I believe you said?"

"Well, yes, but that was just a first reaction. I hadn't given it any thought, I wasn't sure of myself, I was just making a guess."

"You could have fooled me," John said. "You even told me what kind of accident: automobile, you said. You even gave me the speed: sixty miles an hour. I was real impressed. You also—"

Gideon finally gave in, laughing. "All right, I may have been a little premature in my conclusions," he allowed.

"That's one way to put it," John said, laughing too. He swallowed down the last of his coffee and poured them both some more. A few rays of pale gray light were filtering through the wooden blinds now, and in the trees the rowdy mynah birds were waking up and staking their daily territorial claims.

"I tell you the truth, Doc," John said, "what you say adds up—but then, what you said about that accident added up too, only now you're telling me it never happened. I'm not saying you're wrong, but—well, think about it; it just doesn't make any sense. I mean, it's crazy. Brian was a nice guy, a *good* guy. Bozzuto was your typical Mob crud."

"Did you actually know him?"

"Well, no, but it stands to—"

"Wait, there's more, John. What kind of work did they get for Bozzuto in Chicago?"

"Huh? How would I know that?"

"Didn't you tell me they got him a job with the railroads?"

"Oh, yeah, with Amtrak, that's right."

"What kind of job, exactly? Do you know?" He asked the question quietly, but he could feel his heart thudding. Klingo Bozzuto's work experience with Amtrak was the crucial factor in the complex and unlikely scenario he had put together, the linchpin that made it all work.

Disappointingly, John shook his head. "What difference does it make?"

Gideon leaned earnestly forward. "Well, let's say they got him a job as a conductor or a steward—"

"Which I doubt. The guy was a CPA."

"Yes, but wouldn't they give him a whole new life that was different from the old one? Besides, he was a crook. I can't imagine they'd sic him on poor, unsuspecting Amtrak in some responsible position where he could mess with the books."

"Well, yeah, that's true. Okay, say they turned him into a conductor. So?"

"So what does a conductor do?"

John hunched his shoulders. "Punches tickets?"

"He punches tickets," Gideon said triumphantly, "while he walks up and down the train!"

John frowned silently at him for a few seconds. "Am I missing something here?"

"John, what muscles would you use if you were walking up and down a moving train all day?"

John made an impatient sound. "How the hell would I—" He stopped. His eyes widened. He put down his cup so suddenly that coffee slopped over the rim. *"Balance!* You'd use your muscles of balance. You'd be standing on a moving, vibrating platform all day long, you'd always be using those muscles that keep you steady—"

"Bingo," Gideon said with quiet satisfaction. "In particular the soleus muscles. And the soleus muscles attach to the fibulas. And if you used them hard enough and often enough, you might even develop a pair of fibulas that looked like Brian's."

"Whew," John said wonderingly, starting to believe it now. "But . . . I mean, how could it be? What was it all about? Why would he . . . You think Thérèse knew? What about Nick? Why would . . . how could . . ." He shook his head again, this time with a little jerk, as if to clear the fuzz away and get himself going. "First things first. Let's make sure it's even possible. Let me call the Bureau and see about getting some up-to-date dope on Bozzuto." He leaned across the table and reached for the telephone. "If it turns out he's alive and well in Chicago, then we've got a small problem with this theory of yours."

"Back to the drawing board," Gideon agreed. "But I don't think it's going to turn out that way." He looked at his watch. "John, it's only seven-fifty in Seattle. Are you going to get anybody in?"

"Absolutely. The Bureau never sleeps." He punched in a set of numbers, then looked up while the connection was being made. "This is going to take a while. You think you could scout around and see if anybody's working in the kitchen yet? Maybe you could bring us back some breakfast."

"Will do," Gideon said, making for the door.

"I don't want anything healthy," John called after him. "I want something good. No fruit."

*   *   *

It took John another pot of coffee, three telephone calls, an hour and fifteen minutes, and three foot-long sugar-encrusted fried crullers to get the information he wanted. Gideon had stayed with him for a while, but after finishing the cheese, rolls and grapefruit juice he'd brought for himself he went back to his own cottage to shave and shower. When he came out of the bathroom John was sitting in the main room waiting for him, looking seedy and bedraggled in the fresh, clear light of a Tahitian morning, but with the happy look on his face of a man who had gotten somewhere.

"Wait'll you hear this," he said.

Gideon waited.

"I finally got hold of the right guy at the U.S. Marshals Service, which took some doing——"

"What do they have to do with this?"

"They run the witness protection program, didn't you know that? Anyway, I finally got hold of the right guy and convinced him that I was on the up-and-up, which wasn't all that easy over the telephone—I had to have a deputy director in Quantico talk to him and vet me—and he told me all kinds of interesting things about our old friend Klingo Bozzuto."

Gideon settled into the chair opposite him. John was going to draw this out for all it was worth. Well, he had earned a little expansiveness. Besides, Gideon was willing to admit that he had it coming; through the years John had done more than his share of sitting politely and even attentively around while Gideon confounded and amazed him with startling feats of forensic prestidigitation. Turnabout was only fair.

"Such as?" he prompted.

"I will start at the beginning," John said, rather portentously for him. He examined a few notes that were scrawled on the face of a Shangri-La postcard that he'd brought with him. "On June 17, 1983, one Bozzuto, Joseph Rodolfo, known to one and all as Klingo, officially ceased to exist. In his place was a completely new man with a brand-new work history, a brand-new personal life, a brand-new Social Security number—and a brand-new name. And the name they gave him was . . ." He grinned. "You'll never guess."

Gideon's chest had taken up its thumping again. "Brian Scott," he said.

John waited a couple of seconds before answering. "Nope," he said. "Vernon W. Culpepper."

Chapter 27

John's typical laugh was a sunny, explosive, childlike peal, but when he was really amused, *really* tickled, what came out instead was a bursting, choking hee-hee-hee that could grate on Gideon from the first hee and then go on seemingly forever.

"Hee-hee-hee," he said now, his eyes pinched shut, "hee-hee-hee, hee-hee-hee-hee-hee, hee-hee-hee—"

"The humor here escapes me," Gideon said crossly when it appeared that an end was not in sight.

"Hee-hee-hee," John gurgled. "That's because you couldn't see your face. Hee-hee . . . oh, God . . . I'm sorry, Doc, I couldn't help it, you were so—so—" And in he started again.

"I gather," Gideon said stuffily, "that this is a small joke on your part?"

John held him off with raised hand, wiped his eyes, and let go a huge terminal sigh. "Oh, boy. No, it's not a joke. That's what they named him: Vernon Westmark Culpepper."

Gideon stared at him. "But—"

"In 1983 they named him Vernon W. Culpepper. For seven years Vernon W. Culpepper kept a low profile in Chicago, reported regularly to work, and generally stayed out of trouble and followed the witness protection rules. On February 11, 1990, he traveled to Quebec, Canada, which was within the rules, but he didn't come back. The Marshals Service eventually figured either he got tired of the restrictions and took off for good—they do that a lot of times—or that he got careless and that Nutso and the boys finally caught up with him."

"Nineteen-ninety . . ." mused Gideon.

"Nineteen-ninety. And four months later, in June of 1990, presto, here comes this guy named Brian Scott—with a whole lot of holes in his life story—who turns up out of nowhere at Nick's dinner table in Tahiti and never leaves again; never leaves Tahiti, I mean. Meanwhile, nobody ever hears from Vernon W. Culpepper again."

"So Brian *could* be Culpepper; could be Bozzuto, that is."

"I think we can be a little more definite than that. I found out what Bozzuto's job with Amtrak was. Care to guess?"

"No," Gideon said. "I would definitely not care to guess."

John laughed—the more familiar chuckle this time. "I'm really sorry about that, Doc. I couldn't help myself. But this time there aren't any surprises. Klingo—Vernon—was hired by Amtrak as a customer services inspector. Not a conductor, but almost as good. He traveled the trains checking on food services, linens, staff behavior, stuff like that. Typically he'd spend eighty percent of his time—that's about eighteen days a month—on moving trains."

"For seven years, you said?"

John nodded. "Six hours a day. Would that be enough to develop those monster fibulas?"

Gideon relaxed and sank back against his chair. "It'd be enough," he said.

"Then that settles it," John said with a clenched-fist victory gesture.

"I think so," said Gideon. "What with the timing, and Culpepper's disappearance, and those Superman fibulas, and everything else, the odds of being wrong have to be next to nothing."

Spontaneously, John reached across the low table to shake Gideon's hand. "Congratulations, Doc. That's really a neat piece of work."

Gideon shook hands with pleasure. He thought it was a pretty neat piece of work himself, and he was pleased for John's sake too. Although his friend hadn't said anything to suggest it, he knew that John was tremendously relieved to conclude that Brian Scott had once been Klingo Bozzuto. Because if he was Klingo, then the Mob would have been hunting him all this time; he'd probably had a price on his head. And if that was the case, then the chances were enormous that it was the professional bad guys that were behind his death after all.

And that meant that John could stop worrying about Maggie, or Thérèse, or Nelson, or anyone else in his family being a murderer. True, they'd apparently been suckered by an ex-mobster who'd probably tucked their names away under 'future marks' during the trial, but that was merely cause for a few self-recriminations; it wasn't going to tear the family apart.

"Congratulations to us both," Gideon said with a smile.

The telephone chirped. Gideon picked it up. "Hello?"

"Ah, Dr. Oliver, good morning to you." The voice was French-accented; a jovial rasp, vaguely familiar. "I didn't wake you?"

"No, not at all."

"Excellent. This is Viennot."

"Um . . . Viennot?" The name was vaguely familiar too.

"The physician," the voice on the other end said, and then

when Gideon didn't respond: "The police surgeon? We met
t—"

"Oh, yes, of course. Good morning, Dr. Viennot. What can I
do for you?"

"I am calling from the hospital, professor. I have been working on the body of the large gentleman who was shot yesterday—"

Viennot got off to an early start, then. It wasn't much after
even even now.

"—and it suddenly occurred to me that if you are not otherwise occupied you might enjoy participating in the autopsy?"

Not by a long shot, he wouldn't. "Thank you, doctor," he
said politely, "but I don't think—"

"Are you certain? The man is an extraordinary specimen in
many ways."

Gideon doubted this not at all, but it didn't make him any
more eager to watch Viennot open him up. Professional courte-
sies were pleasant things, but this one—which was offered him
from time to time—was one he was generally happy to do without. "I appreciate it very much, sir, but I think I'd better
say no."

"I wish you'd reconsider. I ask as a colleague in need of coun-
sel. There are some things here that puzzle me."

"Well, I'd be glad to help if I could, but I'm afraid I'm no
pathologist. My—"

"Skeletal things," Viennot said with the happy, singsong inflection of a man who had just turned up four of a kind.

Which he had. Gideon's interest was instantly sparked. "Oh?
Like what?"

"I'm sure it would be better if you saw for yourself, colleague," Viennot said smoothly. "I may expect you, say, in an
hour?"

"In an hour," Gideon said. "I'll see you then."

"You going into town?" John asked when Gideon had hung
up.

"Uh-huh. To the morgue."

"Let me get dressed and I'll ride in with you. Nelson wants
to talk to me about something and I told him I'd come by the
Papeete office. And I can swing by the police station first and
let Bertaud know about all this new stuff. Want to come with
me? Should be exciting when he hears."

"I can't. I promised to sit in on Tari's autopsy."

"Hey, lucky you," John said, heading for the door.

✳   ✳   ✳

Quickened interest notwithstanding, Gideon's spirits were
flagging as he took the stairway down to the basement of the
Centre Hospitalier Territorial. He had witnessed the efficient
and enthusiastic Dr. Viennot in action before and he was not
looking forward to seeing the progress he had been making on
Tari's corpulent remains.

He needn't have worried. While he was still in the corridor
Viennot called out to him, not from the autopsy room, but
from the little conference room next door, where Gideon had
worked on the bones two days earlier.

"In here, sir!"

The physician, an intense, ruddy, clear-eyed man in his for-
ties, sat at the table smoking one of his crooked black cigars.

In front of him, on a few layers of brown butcher paper, was
a gleaming object about the size, shape, and color of a soccer
ball cut in half: It was the sawed-off top of a human skull, but
the Stryker saw had been applied lower than was usual in autopsies, sawing through the bone just above the orbits, running
backward and slightly downward through the squamosal and
lambdoid sutures, across the triangular apex of the occipital

bone, and back around the other side. The result was that everything above the eyes was included; in effect, the entire braincase, scrupulously cleansed of soft tissue.

Gideon's initial glance told him it was a male, and a big male at that. There was a neat, round hole—a bullet's entrance hole—in the sphenoidal angle of the right parietal, just behind the coronal suture—in other words, through the temple. Toward the rear of this large, platelike bone and a little higher, where the curvature of the skull was most marked, was a small depressed fracture—that is, a cracked, irregular, sunken island of bone, about an inch long and half an inch wide, with more cracks radiating out from it over the adjacent bone; precisely the kind of wound to be expected if a person were to fall backward and strike his head on a hard, straight, sharp-edged object—the corner of a raised fireplace hearth, for example.

"Tari?" Gideon asked unnecessarily.

Viennot nodded. "Indeed. I thought I would bring the segment here for you, inasmuch as you preferred not to be in the autopsy room."

Gideon's looked at him, surprised. "When did I say—"

"Some things, one doesn't have to say." He laughed. "Of course, if you would prefer that we go to the—"

"This'll do fine, thanks. Now, what in particular did you want me to look at?"

"This. What do you make of it?"

He turned the skullcap so that Gideon could see the other side, the left side. At the top rear corner of the parietal, an inch left of the sagittal suture—on a living head it would have been just behind the crown and a little to the left of center—there was a more unusual wound; another island of bone, much like the one on the right side in that it was cracked and irregular, with rough, crumbled margins. But this one was more nearly round and several times larger, about the size of a silver dollar. And most striking, unlike the other it was *raised*, not sunken; a sort of depressed fracture in reverse, indicating that the bone had been thrust out from inside and not the other way around.

"An elevated fracture," Gideon said, running his fingers around the margin. With a little pressure applied from the inside he could easily have popped the chunk of bone altogether out. "It's the bullet's exit wound—in this case, an incomplete exit wound."

Viennot was pleased. "Yes?"

"The bullet didn't make it all the way out. You should find it still inside him."

"As we did." Viennot produced a misshapen slug. "Wedged between the dura mater and the cranial vault, a few centimeters anterior to the exit fracture."

He handed it to Gideon, who politely examined it and put it back on the table.

"Now then," Viennot said. His cigar had gone out. He paused while he got it lit with a wooden match from a pocket pack. "You understand, we do not see many lethal gunshot wounds here in our pacific little community, and this"—he gestured with the cigar—"this 'incomplete exit wound' is new to my experience. To what would you ascribe the cause of such a wound?"

It was a question Gideon had heard before, from other physicians lucky enough to lack a big-city medical examiner's day-in day-out familiarity with death by firearms. "Well, it's not really all that infrequent. The bullet sometimes just doesn't have sufficient impetus to make it all the way out of the skull, so—"

"Of course, of course," Viennot interrupted, "but consider here we have a case of a point-blank shooting—this was confirmed by the existence of powder marks around the entrance wound in the scalp—with a powerful weapon, and ammunition

nat Colonel Bertaud assures us was in good working order de-
pite its age. The projectile, once fired, cleanly pierces a thin
late of bone—the right parietal—and subsequently passes
hrough the soft mass of the brain for a total of one hundred
nd forty-two millimeters before arriving at the opposite side of
ne skull, yes? Neither a very great distance nor a very arduous
ath for a bullet, you will agree. Why then should it lack suffi-
ent energy to fully penetrate the parietal bone on the other
de?"

"Well, sometimes it can tumble on the way in, especially if
's an old weapon or old ammunition. Or it can be deflected by
ne bone, so that it glances off the surfaces and ricochets around
iside the skull before—"

"My dear man," Viennot said, laughing, "I may no longer be
racticing in Lyons, but give me some credit. The brain has
een partially dissected. The path of the bullet is perfectly
raight, perfectly true."

"Then the most likely reason is that that side of Tari's head
as against some solid object or surface when the gun was
red—"

Viennot's lively eyes lit up. "Ha, exactly as I surmised. I
nought as much!"

"—and that it was hard enough and firm enough to keep the
ug from completely shattering the bone and exploding out."

Viennot raised a finger as if he himself had made a telling
oint. "Ah," he said quietly and cocked an eyebrow, "but ex-
ctly what was it, this object or surface?"

"Oh, well, you know, it could easily have been . . ." He
opped. "Son of a gun," he murmured. "I see what you mean."
lere he'd been airily treating Viennot to a chowderhead version
f Forensic Anthro 101, and Viennot had been three steps
head of him the whole time. It was only now, thanks to Vien-
ot's persistence, that it struck Gideon that there was a serious

inconsistency in Rudy's version of events. Rudy had said that he had grabbed Tari's arm while Tari had been rummaging in drawer for the gun, and that the gun had gone off instantly.

So how could Tari's head have been leaning against anything

"Rudy was pretty excited," Gideon said, thinking out loud "He'd been stunned a moment before. He might have wrestle Tari against the wall without knowing it. The whole thing wa over in a second. In the shock of the moment it would hav been easy to forget exactly what happened."

Viennot shook his head. "I think not. Once shot in this man ner, the man would have dropped like a stone—as he did, strik ing his head upon the hearth. His feet, in such circumstance would naturally have remained in approximately the locatio that they'd been in when he was shot. But in this case, they wer over a meter from the nearest wall."

"Ah," said Gideon appreciatively. Now he was the one ge ting the chowderhead forensics course. Turnabout time again and richly deserved. "Then that settles it," he said slowl "Rudy didn't quite tell it the way it was, did he?"

"Indeed not," Viennot said, twirling his cigar for emphasi "And I think we can hypothesize with some confidence as t what his reason was, don't you, colleague? . . . Colleague?"

Gideon had taken the skull into his hands while Viennot wa speaking and had turned it around to take his first careful loo at the other side, the right side, the one with both the round en trance wound and the depressed fracture suffered when Ta struck his head on the hearth in falling. He traced his finge over the network of cracks between them. Well, well . . .

"Colleague?"

"Hm?" Gideon surfaced. "Oh, I'm sorry. You were say ing . . . ?"

"That we might hypothesize with some confidence as t what actually happened."

"I don't think there'd be any point in that, sir."

The physician's mobile features contracted into a scowl. "No point?"

"In hypothesizing." Gideon replaced the skull on the butcher paper. "I *know* what actually happened," he said with perhaps a little more panache than was strictly required; it was a common failing with him at such moments.

It takes a ham to appreciate a ham, and, as Gideon thought he might be, Viennot was delighted. After an astounded silence during which the cigar stub hung pasted to his lower lip he barked with laughter. "You *know!*" he cried happily. "*How* do *you* know?" He chomped down on the cigar and leaned expectantly forward, elbows on the table, his nose no more than a foot from the bone. Like every true man of science he was at his happiest when about to be instructed.

"I know," Gideon said, "because cracks don't cross cracks."

Chapter 28

Cracks don't cross cracks.

Once a year Gideon taught part of a week-long forensic seminar that the Smithsonian put on for law enforcement personnel from across the country. And one of the first tests of scientific observation that his students were faced with came in the form of a hard-boiled egg that had been briskly tapped in three places with the underside of a tablespoon, so that at the site of each stroke was a small indentation in the shell (not at all unlike a depressed fracture), with a network of hairline cracks radiating from it.

"Pretend," Gideon would say, handing it over for their inspection, "that this is a human skull fractured in three places by blows from a blunt instrument. What I want you to tell me is which is the first blow that was struck, which is the second, and which is the third?"

Sometimes they would figure it out on their own. More often they would be stymied. "How the hell are we supposed to know that?" some grumpy sergeant who hadn't wanted to be there in the first place could be depended on to mutter.

Which is when Gideon would say: "Cracks don't cross cracks."

Once that was understood, which never took long, it was a simple matter. One of the dents in the shell would have a network of cracks that was unimpeded; the spidery, radiating lines would extend until they simply ran of steam and petered out on their own. That was the site of the first blow. The cracks emanating from another one of the dents would also run to their natural limits—except for those that ran into *already* existing cracks from the first one and were stopped dead by them. That was the second blow. And the cracks from the third dent would stop every time they came to a crack from either of the other two. That, necessarily, was the third blow.

What was true of eggshells was true of skulls. A crack could not leap across open space to the far side of an aperture and continue, no matter how narrow the cleft. And in the skull before them, as he now pointed out to the enchanted Viennot, two of the cracks coming from the bullet hole were clearly cut off by cracks radiating from the depressed fracture. Therefore, the depressed fracture already existed when the bullet entered; the crushing blow to Tari's head had come *before* he was shot, not after.

"*Before* he was shot, yes," echoed Viennot, nodding. "And that means . . ."

That meant that Rudy had not merely been forgetful, or unobservant, or overexcited in reporting what had happened. Rudy, seemingly so helpless and distraught, had been lying through his teeth, coolly and calculatingly.

"This explains the incomplete exit wound on the other side too," Gideon said, reconstructing the scene in his mind (minus the blood and brains). "Tari already had his skull cracked open before he was shot. He must have been lying on the floor unconscious or maybe barely conscious. Rudy bent down, put the gun next to Tari's right temple—"

"Yes, that's right, a point-blank wound."

"—and pulled the trigger. The pressure of the floor kept the bullet from exiting completely from the other side of his head."

He had been staring at the skullcap all the time he spoke, but now he looked up to meet Viennot's eyes. "He murdered him," he said with the dreamy satisfaction of a man who had put in a hell of a good morning's work. Not that it wasn't about time he'd done something useful.

"Colleague," said Viennot, leaning back in his chair, "I salute you."

*   *   *

Colonel Bertaud contained his admiration more successfully than Dr. Viennot had ("You're certainly full of surprises this morning."), but he quickly grasped the significance of the new information that Gideon had brought him, which was all that Gideon was really interested in.

"Thibault, call the hospital," he said into his telephone in rapid French. "Find out what room Mr. Rudolph Druett is in. And bring my car around."

"I do see one difficulty, however," he told Gideon in that silky voice. "Not insurmountable but a difficulty all the same." He turned his swivel chair so that he could look out on the avenue Bruat. It was a little after 9 A.M. Papeete's rush-hour traffic, such as it was, was settling down. Only a few motor scooters and bicycles were on the street. "How do you propose that we should account," he asked thoughtfully, "for Tari's having struck his head on the hearth in the first place? Tari was a giant yes? Rudy is a slight man, no more than half his weight. Is it conceivable that he could knock him down or throw him to the floor?"

"I don't think he did. My guess is Tari never did hit his head on the hearth; that the wound was caused by something else."

The colonel swiveled back to face Gideon. "But we have his blood, his hair, on the hearth. Our laboratory confirms it."

"Here's what I think happened, Colonel: I think Rudy clubbed Tari with something—maybe with a poker from the fireplace. Maybe it was premeditated, or maybe there was an argument, I don't know. Something. Anyway, Rudy hit him over the head from behind, then shot him to make sure he was dead, *then* smeared his head against the hearth—and banged his own head against the wall a little too—to back up his story about Tari's trying to kill him and how the whole thing was an accident, and so on."

He glanced at the skullcap on Bertaud's desk (Gideon had carried it from the hospital in a paper sack). "If you think about the placement of the fracture—high up, back, and on the right side—you'll see it's just where you'd expect it to be if Tari had been crept up on from behind by a right-handed assailant."

"Ah, is that so?"

"Definitely." Then after a moment: "Well, it's also where you'd expect it to be if Tari had hit his head on the hearth in falling, so it's hardly proof of anything, but at least it fits. But you know," he added as the thought occurred to him, "if I could have a look at that hearth and the poker and anything else along those lines, I just might be able to match one of them to the fracture in the skull. If nothing else, I ought to be able to rule some things out. Do you—"

Bertaud's telephone buzzed. Bertaud picked it up, listened with the faintest *tck* of irritation, and replaced it in its cradle.

"He's not there," he said to Gideon. "He was released this morning."

Chapter 29

Clearly, Nelson Lau was on pins and needles. "I suppose you're wondering why I asked you to come and see me," he said, twiddling with his ballpoint pen.

"Kind of," John said.

"I trust it wasn't any trouble." He turned the pen with his fingers, round and round, tapping it on the desk at each half-rotation.

"Nope."

"It's just that I thought it would be better to talk here at the Papeete office, rather than back at the Hut. It's more private." Round and round went the pen. *Tap, tap, tap, tap, tap, tap.* "Don't you agree?" *Tap.*

"Nelson," John said, "how about just telling me what you want to tell me? Also, if you don't stop fooling with that pen I'm gonna rip your arm off."

"Oh. Yes. Well." He laid the pen down. Now his upper lip began to pulse with tiny puffs of air. The finicky little mustache twitched along with it. John tried looking out the window. Nelson's office had an expansive view of the busy quays and docks of Papeete Harbor.

"Let me give you some figures," Nelson said, twitching away. "Mostly through our American operation we sell about six hundred thousand pounds of roasted beans a year in the form of our several coffees. Now, inasmuch as it takes a hundred pounds of green beans to make sixty pounds roasted, that means that we have either to harvest or to buy a total of a million pounds of green beans a year. Are you following me so far?"

"I think I'm managing to hang in there," John said.

"Now then," Nelson continued uneasily, "we can harvest only about two hundred thousand pounds a year here, from which it follows that we have to buy an additional eight hundred thousand pounds a year from other growers around the world. Now, of those eight hundred thousand—"

"Nelson, this is really interesting, but how about getting to the point? I've got a lot on my plate today."

"The point is—" said Nelson with heat, but then seemed to lose impetus. He sagged in his high-backed leather chair and crossly mumbled something.

John turned from the window. "What?"

"I said—I said I need your advice."

John forgot all about Nelson's mustache. He stared at him, amazed. "You *what?*" He hadn't meant to say it out loud, but these were words he had never in his life expected to hear from his older brother. No wonder the poor guy was looking so uncomfortable.

"As an FBI agent. You know about these things."

"What things, Nelson? What are you talking about?"

Nelson started fiddling with his pen again. *Tap, tap, tap.* "The thing is, I had it backward. We all had it backward. Tari wasn't stealing from us at all. Tari was *right.*" *Tap, tap—*

John took the pen out of Nelson's hand and placed it firmly in the pen-and-pencil caddy on the desk. "About what?"

"About our paying too much—ten times too much—in some cases *twenty* times too much—for some of the beans we buy from other suppliers."

"Is that right?" John murmured. Wheels began to turn. "Are you sure?"

Of course he was sure, Nelson said. He had spent the last two days poring over the books, and he was certain of his facts. Of the 800,000 pounds of beans purchased annually, 300,000 pounds came from two growers—about 100,000 from Java Green Mountain in Indonesia, and about 200,000 from the Colombian firm of Calvo Hermanos. And in virtually every order from these two suppliers, Paradise had been paying at least ten times the market value. Beans that should have cost $1.50 a pound had been ordered—and paid for—at $15 a pound. Beans that were bringing $2 on the international market had been entered on Paradise's books at $20. Paradise had been buying virtually the cheapest *arabica* beans available and paying the world's highest prices.

What's more, this had been going on for almost five years. The result was that they had been overpaying these two suppliers by about—Nelson had to swallow before he could get it out—$6 million a year.

"Six—!" John looked at him. "You're saying that in the last five years Paradise has overpaid something like thirty million bucks for its beans?"

"Exactly," Nelson said wretchedly.

"Whew," John said. "I think I'm starting to see why you have to charge thirty-eight bucks for a pound of coffee."

"It's not funny, John." He sat there behind his handsome teak-and-leather desk, wringing his hands and looking miserable. "What's Nick going to say when I tell him?"

"Nelson," John said gently, "how could this happen? Why did it take Tari to find out about it? Why didn't you see it before?"

Nelson reared back defensively. "It wasn't my job. Brian was supposed to stay on top of coffee prices, not me."

Ah. Brian. Things were beginning to add up. "But you're the comptroller."

"We don't work that way, John. We're a family, we don't go around checking on each other. The books balance and we make a profit; it never occurred to me to review the invoices themselves. Coffee prices are unbelievably complex. They change every day, sometimes more than once a day. You have to know the industry. And as you know, I'm no coffee expert— I've always been the first to admit that."

Not in John's hearing, he hadn't. "Look, Nel, tell me this: *How* do you make a profit? If you're paying ten times what you should for your beans, then you must—"

"Charge ten times what we should for our coffee. Yes, I suppose that's what you could say we've been doing. But not from any intent to overprice, you must understand that. Our prices necessarily reflect the value we put into the product in the way of labor, equipment, and costs. And the product is simply—"

" 'The World's Most Expensive Coffee,' " John said.

Nelson frowned at him, as if deciding just how much offense he ought to take. Then he blinked and hesitated.

" 'Bar None,' " he said.

For a second, they continued to look at each other, then burst into gales of laughter.

"Oh, dear . . ." Nelson said when he could speak. "Oh, dear . . . what are we laughing at anyway?"

"Probably all those yuppie types sitting around in all those latte bars scarfing the stuff down and talking about how buttery it is, how chocolaty, how, how . . ."

"Piquant," Nelson said, beginning to shake again.

"And all the while," laughed John, "they're drinking the cheapest crap in the world, only they can't tell the difference."

"And obviously," said Nelson, "neither could *we!*"

And off they went again. This was certainly a new Nelson. It was the first time since they'd been children that they'd laughed together this way, and it felt good. Good God, if it kept up, he was liable to wind up actually liking the guy.

"Do you know what?" Nelson said when they quieted down. "You haven't called me Nel in thirty years. No one has."

John couldn't think of anything to say. "Yeah, well." This was followed by a somewhat awkward pause.

"In any event," said Nelson, "the reason I wanted to talk to you was to ask if this has the earmarks of something . . . something illegal. I don't mean on the part of Java Green Mountain and Calvo Hermanos, I mean on our part—that is, on the part of . . . of someone at Paradise."

"Yeah, it does," John said. "It sounds like money-laundering."

Nelson winced. "That's what I was afraid you'd say." He began to reach for the ballpoint pen again but at a guttural rumble from John he pulled his hand back and laid it in his lap. "But look, I'm not clear on what this money-laundering business is about. I thought I was, but I'm not. It has to do with drugs, doesn't it?"

"Usually, yeah."

"But where would drugs enter into this? We pay ten times as much as we should for green beans and we sell the finished product for ten times what it's worth. The growers do very well indeed, the consumers pay through the nose, and we make an innocent, modest profit. It's hardly a model of keen business practice, but where do drugs come into it? Where does money-laundering come into it?"

"It's pretty complicated, Nelson. I'd rather—"

"I think I can manage to hang in there," Nelson said. Definitely a new Nelson.

All right, then, John said. The Colombian drug cartels had a long-established system of working with their American dealers. The American dealers—importers, they were called in the trade—didn't pay for the dope up front, they maintained open "accounts" with their Colombian sources and settled only after the stuff had been sold on the streets.

"Sound business practice," said Nelson with something close to approval. "Receipts first, then payments. It's a question of cash flow. Any sensible businessman would prefer to handle it that way."

But these "businessmen" had a problem unique to international drug-trafficking, John explained. Most of the money that was collected was in great armloads of small- and medium-denomination bills—truckloads, really, amounting to many millions of dollars. The question was: How did you get it out of the country and into Colombia? And the problem was that you couldn't carry more than $10,000 out of the United States unless you declared it with Customs, something these guys were not eager to do. And you couldn't put all that cash in a bank checking account and draw a check on it either, because banks had to report deposits of $10,000 or more.

One way of getting around this involved smurfing, which—

"Ah . . . smurfing?" Nelson said.

Smurfing, said John. Multiple bank transactions of seven, or eight, or nine thousand dollars—anything under ten. A van holding maybe fifteen runners shows up in the financial district of a big city in the morning just as the banks open. The runners pile out, head for the banks, and buy cashier's checks (which can be made out to any name you want, and which usually don't require identification). Then they run off to the next bank with another load of cash, and the next, and the next. A single runner can convert $150,000 in a day. And the following day they're in another city doing it all over again.

"But why is it called smurfing?" Nelson wanted to know.

"Because of the way they all scoot off from the delivery van like a bunch of little Smurfs. You know."

Nelson didn't know. "In any case, I fail to see what this has to do with us," he said irritably.

Patience, John counseled. Once the cash was smurfed into checks it would be "layered," that is, electronically transferred from Account A in Bank 1 to Account B in Bank 2, splitting it up and recombining it until its origins were lost somewhere in cyberspace. Once you had a dozen banks and twenty accounts involved, the money was virtually untraceable. At that point, it could safely find its way into the accounts of an international importer such as Paradise Coffee.

And from there it was an easy matter to move it out of the country in the form of inflated payments for purchased goods. You paid $10 for $1 worth of goods and sold the finished product for ten times what it was worth. You made out, the books balanced—and $9 had been laundered and was on its way back to Colombia. It was done in the gem trade, it was done in the metals trade . . . and, so it seemed, it was done in the coffee trade.

"Are you telling me," Nelson asked slowly, "that in the past five years, we've been responsible for supplying thirty million dollars to . . . to drug lords in Colombia?"

"I'm ready to bet on it," John said. "That Colombian coffee grower, Calvo Hermanos—they wouldn't happen to be in Medellín, would they?"

Nelson's face was all the answer that was needed.

"And the other one, the one in Java, they're probably backed by some of the Colombian drug biggies. It's an old story, Nelson."

"It's horrible," Nelson said. He looked grim, almost sick. *"Why?"*

John understood what he meant. "For money, probably. The dealers typically pay legit firms ten percent for this kind of service. So somebody here was collecting . . . oh, around . . ."

"Six hundred thousand dollars a year," Nelson said.

"Right, but that's only part of it. Think it through; the inflated payments to the suppliers are made with drug money, not company funds, right? But—"

"But," Nelson said, speaking slowly as he took it in, "the inflated *returns* from our sales should go right into our own coffers—only they don't, do they? They've never shown up in our financial records. That means . . . that means . . ."

"That we're talking about somebody raking off a lot more—a whole lot more—than six hundred thou a year."

Nelson groaned and pressed his hand to his forehead. "I feel as if I'm in a nightmare. John, how *could* he? After all Nick's done for him. Oh, I've never thought he was quite as perfect as everyone else did, but never would I have expected this from him. Not in a million years."

It was time to let Nelson in on recent developments. "Nelson, Brian wasn't quite what we thought. There's a lot about him that you and I didn't know."

Nelson's mouth hung open for a minute. "Brian? What does Brian have to do with it?"

John was startled in his turn. "What?"

"I'm talking about *Rudy*. Rudy's the one who actually buys

the coffee. You know that, John. Rudy's the one who signs the purchase orders in the first place, and then signs off on the invoices—not Brian. Rudy's our buyer."

"*Rudy . . .*" John sat back in his chair and digested this latest screwy twist, or maybe it wasn't so screwy. "What do you know?" he said half to himself. "Now that really throws a new light on things."

"What's this about Brian?" Nelson said. "What didn't we know about him?"

"A lot," said John. "I'll tell you later. Right now I want to go over to the hospital and have a few words with Rudy."

"But he's not in the hospital, he's right here, down on the docks." Nelson turned in his chair and pointed out the window. "See the gray-and-white ship, the one with the block and tackle?"

"The rusty one?"

"Yes, the rusty one."

The ship was the *Beaune*, Nelson said, an interisland schooner; that is, a small freighter with a regular local route. Every few months two or three thousand pounds of Paradise beans were put aboard to go to resorts and small roasteries on Bora Bora, Rarotonga, and Pago Pago. As it happened, the beans were being loaded this morning and Rudy was on board overseeing things.

"Well, then, that's where I'm going," John said, standing up. Nelson got up as well. "I believe I'll go with you."

"No, I think it'd be better if I talked to him by myself."

"Pah." Nelson breezed imperiously by him and through the door. "Don't be ridiculous, John. Of course I'm going with you. You don't know how to handle Rudy. It takes a delicate touch."

Say hello to the old Nelson again. For a moment the hair on the back of John's neck automatically bristled, but only for a moment. Then he laughed and followed Nelson out.

"Okay, big brother, show me how to handle Rudy."

Chapter 30

Papeete's commercial harbor was out of another time, a lively, old-fashioned South Seas port from the days before there were huge, anonymous container ships and robotlike, hundred-foot-high cranes. Here, most of the quays were lined with battered, midsized interisland schooners that were being chain-loaded by their Tahitian crews one dented drum or one case of milk or canned goods at a time, for shipment to the outer islands. Lots of bustle, noise, cursing, and laughter.

The *Beaune* was no exception. It was docked between two equally seaworn, equally work-scarred freighters, and you couldn't look at it without thinking of Joseph Conrad, and the old China Sea trade, and grizzled, bleary-eyed, seen-it-all sea captains in dingy whites. When John and Nelson got there, a line of four perspiring Tahitians was swinging the cargo onto the foredeck, where two more men used a block-and-tackle arrangement to get it down into the hold. There were cases of Hinano beer, of Twisties Cheese-Flavoured Snacks, of Biscuits

Mckay ("*C'est OK!*"), of canned beef stew, of soap flakes, of frozen fish croquettes.

"Your coffee's already stowed," one of the men told Nelson. He shrugged his chin at the string of big plastic sacks of ice cubes that was being hefted along the line. "For the captain's drinks," he said, laughing.

"I don't doubt it," Nelson said primly.

They found Rudy on the enclosed bridge with Captain Thorwald, a big-boned, middle-aged Dane whose whites were by no means dingy, but who otherwise made a satisfactory old sea dog, what with his graying Captain Ahab beard and hard, bronzed, windburnt face. The captain bent over a drafting table to scrawl his signature across the bottom of a form, gave Nelson a brusque hello, and went off to speak to the harbormaster, leaving them to the modest comforts of the bridge.

John and Nelson stood just inside the door. "Hello, Rudy," John said.

Rudy seemed to sense something in the air. He looked from one to the other, waiting for them to say something more.

"Rudy," John began, "we've been—"

Nelson cut in, shrill and excited. "Where did all that money go, Rudy? What was it for?"

John almost laughed aloud. Good old Nelson and his delicate touch.

But it brought results. Although Rudy at first swelled himself up to protest, he changed his mind and decided to give it up before the first word was out. He looked stolidly, almost wistfully, at them for a moment—*how could you ever hope to understand?* he seemed to be thinking—then turned sadly away from them and walked to an open window, leaning on a built-in cupboard and staring out across the harbor toward the two sleek, gray missile cruisers tied up at the French naval base at Fare Ute.

"It's a long story," he said.

Here it comes, John thought. He's cooking it up right now. I can practically see the gears turning. *It was all Brian's fault,* he's going to say. *It was all Tari's fault.* Anybody who was dead and couldn't speak for himself.

But John wasn't even close. When Rudy turned back to face them he spoke only two words and they had nothing to do with Brian or Tari.

"Don't move," he said.

He was standing about eight feet from them, no longer even remotely wistful, and in his right hand was an object shaped something like a snub-nosed revolver, like a .38-caliber Police Special, in fact, but made of gaudy orange-and-black plastic. John would have taken it for a clumsy Halloween toy except for the strip of black plastic that jutted down from the base of the grip and held a row of three red cylinders that looked convincingly like twelve-gauge shotgun shells. From where he stood John was uncomfortably able to look straight up the stubby barrel and see that a fourth shell was already chambered. With his thumb Rudy slowly cocked the hammer.

"Now what the hell is that supposed to be?" John said.

"It's a flare pistol," Rudy said. "At least I think it is."

"You can't hurt anybody with a flare pistol," John said, wishing he believed it. "They have to meet safety specs."

"Do they? Well, we can find out easily enough. Who wants to be the guinea pig?"

"You killed Tari, didn't you?" Nelson demanded. "He found out what you were doing."

John looked at him with something like pride. Nelson had more than his share of faults, but lack of gumption wasn't one of them.

Rudy moved the pistol slightly, so that it was directed more at Nelson than at John. That gave Nelson his chance to look up the barrel and now he quailed visibly, for which John couldn't blame him.

Scared or not, Nelson didn't back down. "You . . . you wouldn't kill us," he said, not quite bringing off the intended sneer.

"Wouldn't I now?" Rudy said. "Let me you assure you, Nelson, that underneath this feeble exterior lies a tremendous absence of moral character."

It was the sort of wry crack he might have tossed off at a cupping session, and delivered in much the same tone of voice. He's not panicky, John thought. He's in control, he knows what he wants.

"What do you want, Rudy?" he said.

"I want out," Rudy said. "Nelson, come here."

"No!" said Nelson, white and trembling.

The gun swung around to him again. Rudy extended his arm, took dead aim at his nose. "Nelson, come *here!*"

Nelson moved a reluctant step forward and stopped. "Why?"

"Because you and I are leaving. And John will just stay there like a good little fellow and not say peep while we climb into the van and get on our way. Otherwise . . . well."

Nelson licked his lips but stood his place. "How do I know you won't kill me anyway?" He was barely able to get it out.

The question, a pretty sensible one from John's point of view, seemed to irritate Rudy. "Oh, for God's sake, Nelson—"

"Rudy, what's the point?" John said. "You know you can't get off the island."

"Of course I can get off the island."

And of course he could. There were a thousand places along the shore from which boats could leave and find their way to just about anywhere in the Pacific.

"John," Rudy said, "you'd better tell him to come here. You know I mean business."

"Go ahead, Nelson," John said.

"Backward," said Rudy.

Nelson shuffled backward toward him. His frightened glance met John's once, then dropped miserably to the floor. Rudy put a hand on his shoulder to halt him and moved up closer behind him and a little to the side, the pistol digging into Nelson's hip.

"Now, John," Rudy said, "we'll be leaving. Move away from the door. Sideways. Lie down over by the wheel, on your face. And stay there, John. I warn you."

"No, I don't think so, Rudy."

Rudy's face twitched. So did the hand with the gun. That shook him up, John thought. Great, now both of us are shook up.

"John—"

"Forget it, Rudy. I'm not moving, you're not leaving," he said in his calmest, most resolute voice, hoping Rudy couldn't hear the whomping in his chest. He didn't want Rudy panicking, he just wanted him to decide that he had no chance, that his only recourse was to give up. "Now put that damn thing down and we can talk this over."

"I'll kill him, John," Rudy said and dug the flare pistol into Nelson's side. Nelson stiffened.

"And then what?" John said. "Where does it get you?" He lips were dry but he kept himself from licking them. "You kill im and what do you do about me? There's only one cartridge n that chamber. I'll be on you before you can load another."

"You know, you're absolutely right," Rudy said. "Maybe I'd e better off killing you instead." He was getting very edgy now. His glance kept darting through the windows at the activity oing on on the deck below. Who knew when someone might ecide to come up to the bridge?

"Same problem," John said. "If you kill me, what do you do about Nelson?"

Rudy was still able to dredge up a dry laugh. "Nelson I think I can cope with." He moved the gun a little away from Nelson's hip so it was leveled at John's belt. "I'm really sorry, John." His eyelids squeezed together twice, a queer, nervous tic. Nelson stood frozen, staring straight at John. His eyes looked like bull's-eye saucers.

Christ, John thought, I played him wrong, he's actually going to do it . . . "Rudy," he said quickly, "think for a minute, will you? If you shoot that thing off you'll have everybody on the ship up here in two seconds. What good is that going to do you? I'm telling you, you don't have any way out. Don't make it any worse for yourself than it already is . . ."

But Rudy wasn't listening and John knew it; he was steeling himself to pull the trigger. The barrel came up a little higher to point at John's throat. John's mind was buzzing. He saw only one thing he could do, one thing he could try, and it didn't have much going for it; duck unexpectedly and spring for Rudy's legs. Rudy would have only one chance, and if the shot went over his head or merely winged him, maybe he could . . .

Rudy pressed his lips together. Here it comes, John thought, even as he flung himself down. The squat orange barrel followed him. He was too late, too slow, he was going to take the shot in the face—

Nelson's arm jerked. His hand clamped on Rudy's wrist.

"Damn you, Nelson—" Rudy said testily.

And all hell broke loose. Smoke, flame, noise—banging, whizzing, spitting—and an incredible, hissing, crackling eruption of red-hot sparks, spurts, and streamers that went off in every direction at once.

John stayed low on the floor, on his stomach, while burning

chunks of the flare went ricocheting around the room for what seemed an impossibly long time. At one point something fell onto the back of his head and he hurriedly thrust it away before he realized that it was only the flare's unopened parachute.

"Nelson!" he called when he dared to raise his head. The explosions seemed to be over, but bits of flare were still sizzling here and there, visible only as red glows in the billows of acrid smoke that now filled the room. "Are you okay? Where—" He broke off, coughing.

He was answered by a hacking cough off to his right, and he scrambled toward it on elbows and knees, swept out his arm, caught hold of the collar of Nelson's jacket, and dragged him with the same movement out into the fresh air of the gangway, where they sat with their backs against the wall of the bridge, choking and blinded by tears.

"You all right?" John said when he was able to.

Nelson still couldn't speak. He nodded.

"Rudy's still inside," John said, pushing himself up and wiping his eyes with the back of his hand. He realized for the first time that his knuckles were singed. His cheek too. "I have to—"

"Help," someone shouted wetly. "I don't—" There was a break for coughs and gurgles. "I don't swim very well."

John went to the rail. There was Rudy in the water fifteen feet below, sputtering and flopping around in a pathetic attempt at a dog paddle. Apparently he had fallen or jumped through one of the open windows when the flare went off.

"Oh, lordy," John said, preparing to go over the side but not liking it. Hawaiian or not, he wasn't much of a swimmer either.

But before he could move, one of the Tahitians dove casually into the sea, rising directly under Rudy and hauling him up the ladder in a fireman's carry, then dumping him on the deck.

Rudy lay flat on his face, panting and jelly-limbed, hanging on to the metal deck rivets with his fingertips as if he were afraid of rolling off.

"Keep him there," John called. "Be right down. I'm with the FBI."

The crewman laughed. "Don't worry, this guy ain't going nowhere."

John sank briefly down beside Nelson again. "Nelson, you saved my life. I can't believe it."

Nelson, still hacking away into his handkerchief, shrugged.

"You could have been killed yourself," John said. "He could easily have pumped that thing into you. I just want you to know that I—I mean, that was really brave of you; that took guts. Not many people—"

"Oh, shush." Nelson waved him into silence with the handkerchief and finally got his coughing under control.

"I mean, really," Nelson said peevishly. "You're my brother, aren't you?"

Chapter 31

"*. . . highs in the upper thirties, with more of the same—low clouds and drizzle, occasionally turning to sleet—continuing right on through the week. But cheer up, folks; by Friday chances look good for the occasional afternoon sunbreak . . .*"

"What's funny?" Julie asked.

"Nothing," Gideon said, "I was just thinking it's nice to be home."

He reached contentedly across the seat to squeeze her knee and switched the car radio to KING-FM. The Pachelbel Canon in D Major came on, and they listened in cozy, heated comfort to the calm, stately, inexorable chord progressions as Julie swung the car around the forested curves of Highway 101. Downslope on their right, visible through the firs, was Sequim Bay, gray and rain-pelted. On their left, the foothills of the Olympics rose, disappearing into the mist about two hundred feet up. The windshield wipers, making their slow sweep every second or so, kept steady time with the music.

Gideon had arrived in Seattle two hours earlier. He and John had stayed in Tahiti for another day after Rudy's arrest, leaving depositions with Bertaud (they would both have to return for the trial) and having a last sad, hilarious dinner with Nick and what was left of the clan. Then, leaving John to spend another few days with his family, he had boarded the 12:15 A.M. flight to Los Angeles and caught an 8:50 A.M. hop to SeaTac, where Julie had been waiting for him. They decided to go the longer, more scenic way, and she had taken the wheel for the drive across the Tacoma Narrows Bridge and on to the Olympic Peninsula and Port Angeles. For most of it he had been filling her in on the latest developments from the South Seas.

Rudy, he told her, had so far refused to make a statement on the advice of his *avocat*, but Gideon, John, and Bertaud had pieced together a first, rough set of events that seemed to fit the facts. They believed that the money-laundering operation had been Brian's—that is, Bozzuto's—idea; perhaps he'd had it in his mind from the very time he arrived. Bozzuto, after all, had the racketeering contacts and the firsthand experience with slippery bookkeeping. As if to confirm this, the tricky business with the prices had begun only a few months after he had come to the farm. Besides that, Nelson had now turned up some accounting and telephone records that seemed to show Brian's hand in several of the phony transactions. But Brian wouldn't have able to do it alone. In the first place, coffee-bean purchases weren't made from the farm but from Whidbey Island; Rudy's turf. In the second, Klingo Bozzuto, even with a new face and a new name, wouldn't have been crazy about going anywhere near his old, betrayed gangland associates.

So Rudy was approached, and whether from resentment of Nick (so much more successful than his own father, *so* magnanimous, *so* open-handed), or from simple greed, or for some other reason, he cut himself in. For five years they used Paradise Coffee as a money-laundering conduit. And then something happened to sour the relationship. Bertaud believed that Rudy simply decided to cut Brian out and keep all the profit for himself, and the most satisfactory way to do that was to murder him. John believed that Brian, changed for the better by his relationships with Nick and Thérèse, and by parenthood, had finally seen the light and wanted to go straight, and that Rudy had killed him to keep him from putting an end to the arrangement, and perhaps even confessing to Nick. Gideon kept his opinion to himself, but he thought that Bertaud was closer to the mark.

Whatever the cause, they were fairly sure that it was Rudy who had killed him during that lonely camping trip to Raiatea. Proving it was going to be impossible, they agreed, but Bertaud had assured them that Tari's murder alone, what with Gideon's findings, would be enough to lock Rudy up for a long time to come. Gideon had set the final seal on things when he'd examined Tari's hut and determined what the murder weapon was: not the fireplace poker that he'd anticipated, but a *gancho*—a sturdy, five-foot pole with a crook in it that was used to pull the spindly top branches of the coffee trees down within easy reach. Tari had kept one leaning against a corner in the hut, and although Rudy had wiped it clean of hair, blood, and fingerprints, Gideon had been able to show that the shape of the heavy end of it perfectly matched the depressed fracture in Tari's skull.

Julie and Gideon had been quiet while the canon was being played, but when it was done she leaned forward to turn the volume down. "There are still some things that I don't understand."

"You and me both," Gideon said.

"What about Thérèse, for example? Did she honestly not know what Brian was doing? Are you going to tell me she's really as pure and innocent as all that?"

"Well, yes and no. We had dinner with the family at Nick's house last night, and it was pretty interesting; a lot of things came out. And the answer to your question is, yes, she did know all about Brian's past. That's why she was so desperate to have the exhumation canceled, you see. She was scared to death that somehow or other his real identity would come out and his old gangland enemies would find out about it and come after her and the twins for revenge."

"Well, I guess that makes sense."

"But as for knowing that he'd been involved in anything shady since he came to Tahiti, that was a total surprise to her. She thought he was completely reformed."

Julie threw him a sidewise glance. "And you believe that?"

"I do, yes."

"Well, I don't. How did she really meet him, anyhow? The Bennington story was just so much claptrap, wasn't it?"

"There you're right. It all came out at dinner. Old Klinger had seen her at that first trial years ago and was thoroughly smitten. Never forgot her. Six or seven years later, with a new name and a new face, he called her from the States, claimed he was a reporter—which he wasn't—and said she probably didn't remember him, but they'd met briefly while he was covering the trial in Seattle—which they hadn't—and he was coming out on vacation to Tahiti in a couple of weeks, and could they get together? She said sure, on most Friday nights she went to the movies in Papeete with her friends, and if he wanted to, they could meet for a drink first. And that was that. They fell in love. Later, he did tell her who he really was."

"And how did Nick react to hearing all that? Did he get mad?"

"Mad—no, I don't think so. Shocked would be more like it. I think he had a hard time coming to grips with the idea that his sweet little baby had actually been going around meeting strang

nen in bars. Céline didn't have any problem with it, though. I
hink Thérèse went up in her estimation."

Julie laughed. "Céline sounds like a character."

"One of many."

Like the knowledgeable locals they were, they turned onto
he Old Olympic Highway at Sequim to avoid the downtown
oottleneck, then back onto 101, over the crest with its sweeping
riew of the Elwha Valley and towering Klahane Ridge (ob-
cured at the moment by murk and rain, but they knew what it
ooked like and enjoyed it anyway), and down the long grade
nto a gloomy Port Angeles. Up Race Street, past the rain-
larkened buildings of the university . . .

"But what about those accidents?" Julie asked suddenly.

"What accidents?"

"*The* accidents. All those things that were going wrong. The
oulper, the drying machine, the shed, the jeep—"

"Oh, I forgot to tell you. That was Maggie, all right, but she
wasn't trying to hurt Brian—"

"Well, she sure wasn't trying to improve his health."

"No, what she was trying to do was discredit his ideas. The
eeps, the drying shed, the pulper, the computers, the furnaces,
verything—they were all new ideas that came from Brian, and
he was simply doing her best to foul them up so they looked
ike flops. She never meant for him to be in the shed when it
ollapsed, or in the jeep when it flipped."

"Uh-huh. How do you know all this?"

"Well, I put a bug in John's ear about Maggie a few days ago,
nd after he stewed about it a while he went and talked to her. I
uess he just kept at it until she broke down and let it all out.
he just couldn't stand seeing this stranger come in and drive a
vedge between her and her family—especially Nick and
Thérèse. At least that's the way it looked to her. She also hon-
stly thought his ideas were all wet."

"Has John told Nick about it?"

"No, and I don't think he's going to. He figures it's best for everybody to just leave it alone."

"I think he's right."

"I do too."

"At any rate," she said as the garage door creaked up and the car pulled in, dripping rainwater onto the concrete floor, "you have to admit I had Maggie pretty well pegged. Without ever seeing her, too."

"You sure did. Right on the button."

"I also told you I didn't trust Rudy either, didn't I?"

"Yes, but you also told me you didn't trust Nick or Thérèse."

"Well, that's true but don't forget, if you'd paid any attention to me, you'd have figured out that there was money laundering going on a long time ago. I practically told you as much."

With his hand on the door, he paused. "I would? You did?"

"Certainly," she said. "Haven't I been pointing out for years that their coffee is impossibly overpriced?"

He laughed. "I guess you have at that."

Once inside the house he set down his bags and pulled her close, and for a few long seconds they stood that way, their eyes shut, clasped tightly together with Julie's forehead against Gideon's cheek. He inhaled the sweet, fresh, familiar scent of her hair.

Indeed, it was nice to be home.

"Mm," he said as they swayed slowly back and forth, arms wrapped around each other, "you mean I get to do this anytime I want?"

"It's in the contract," she murmured. "*Ouch.* When was the last time you shaved?"

"Yesterday. Why don't I grab a shave now? A shower too;
I'm feeling a little grungy."

"You don't feel grungy, you feel wonderful," she said with a
final squeeze, then pulled her head back and rubbed the side of
her face. "But the shave I'd appreciate."

The telephone answering machine in the bedroom upstairs
showed that there was a message. He pressed the playback button and listened while he got out of his clothes. John's voice
came on:

*How're you doing, Doc? Welcome home. Listen, you have to hear
this. Nick finally decided to sell out to this Superstar outfit, okay? I
mean, he's had it now with coffee, he wants out; you can understand. So
he tells Nelson to get in touch with them and let them know. Well,
twenty minutes later, who shows up at the house with this grin a mile
wide but Dean Parks? The guy that owns the Shangri-La, remember?
Guess what: Superstar Resorts International IS Dean Parks. The guy's
a multimillionaire, would you believe it?*

Not easily, thought Gideon. Besides, wasn't Superstar head-
quartered in Omaha?

*That Omaha stuff was all smoke and mirrors, you see. Old
Dino's the number-one shareholder. It turns out that all he ever
wanted all along was to have the biggest, best resort in Polynesia, better
than anything Nick had—and he wanted to do it on Nick's property.
Because why? Because, believe it or not, Dean's the guy Nick won that
ten thousand dollars from in World War II—I told you that
story—and then used it to buy the old copra plantation when he first
got to Tahiti.*

*Now here's the beauty part: here's Dean, looking like he just swal-
lowed the canary. I mean, here it's been eating away at him all these*

years—in a friendly way, of course—that it's his ten thousand bucks that got Nick the plantation in the first place and started him off, and now, finally, he's got his own back. So he crows about it for a while and says to Nick: "What do you think of that? After fifty years we're finally even."

And Nick looks at him in all seriousness and says: "YOU'RE the guy I won that money off of? I always thought it was Wolensky."

See you next week. Say hi to Julie for me.

Gideon was still laughing when Julie called from downstairs "Hey, up there, get going, will you? I don't hear the shower."

"On my way," Gideon called back. "Be down in ten minutes."

"I'll put up a pot of coffee and some goodies."

"Fine, sounds good."

But a moment later, he opened the bathroom door and put his head out.

"On second thought," he called, "I think I'd just as soon have tea. All things considered."